The
Outside
Child

Also by Tiffany L. Warren

Don't Tell a Soul

The Replacement Wife

The Favorite Son

The Pastor's Husband

Her Secret Life

The Outside Child

The Outside Child

TIFFANY L. WARREN

KENSINGTON PUBLISHING CORP.
www.kensingtonbooks.com

DAFINA BOOKS are published by

Kensington Publishing Corp.
119 West 40th Street
New York, NY 10018

All Kensington titles, imprints, and distributed lines are available at special quantity discounts for bulk purchases for sales promotion, premiums, fund-raising, and educational or institutional use.

Special book excerpts or customized printings can also be created to fit specific needs. For details, write or phone the office of the Kensington Sales Manager: Kensington Publishing Corp., 119 West 40th Street, New York, NY 10018. Attn. Sales Department. Phone: 1-800-221-2647.

Dafina and the Dafina logo Reg. U.S. Pat. & TM Off.

ISBN-13: 978-1-4967-0875-5
ISBN-10: 1-4967-0875-X
First Kensington Trade Paperback Printing: September 2018

eISBN-13: 978-1-4967-0877-9
eISBN-10: 1-4967-0877-6
First Kensington Electronic Edition: September 2018

10 9 8 7 6 5 4 3 2 1

Printed in the United States of America

Acknowledgments

Thank God this book is finished. I have a process to these things: an outline, then a rough draft, and then edits. I work full-time and raise my family, so there's a rigorous schedule that goes into getting seventy-five thousand words on the page.

This year was tough. Hurricanes Harvey, Irma, Maria, and Nate interrupted my life and my schedule.

But I am done! Thank God!

My thanks to my husband and children. Creamy chicken noodles and black beans and rice for days on end. Leftovers and all that. Saturdays spent watching me holed up in my writing cave (which is just my bed with the TV playing in the background). They're here for it, and have been, since I started this journey almost fifteen years ago.

Thank you to my team at Kensington, especially my editor, Tara Gavin, who has the patience of Job. My agent, Sara Camilli, never lets me rest, either ☺, and I thank her for that.

Thank you to my readers. Thank you to my author tribe. You know who you are! And for my besties who stay on the wall, and deal with my crazy, let's go to the beach. I need some Miami in my life right now.

I am done.

Thank God!

Now pass the Moscato.

Prologue

"'Til death do us part."

I hate the sound of this phrase. Of course, I say it with a smile on my face, because it's at the end of my wedding vows. But why would I want to think about death on the very best day of my life? Why would anyone?

All I want to focus on is Brayden's smile, his flawless ebony skin, and the love in his eyes. All I want to think about is Jamaica, where we first laid eyes on each other, and the beach where he took me on our first date. The same beach we are going to stroll down as husband and wife, on our honeymoon.

"By the power vested in me, by God and the city of Dallas, Texas, I now pronounce you husband and wife. You may now kiss your bride."

Brayden had warned me that he wasn't going to give me a chaste wedding kiss, so his mischievous grin doesn't surprise me one bit. He scoops me into his strong arms as if I'm weightless.

His soft, full lips part as he gently pulls my face to his. His mouth engulfs mine; his tongue traces a familiar path. Brayden's kisses are everything. I struggle not to embarrass myself by moaning.

Can we skip the reception part and go straight to the consummating part?

"I present to you Mr. and Mrs. Brayden Carpenter."

How about Mr. Brayden Carpenter and Mrs. Chenille Abrams-Carpenter? My name doesn't just disappear into his, nor do I disappear into him. At least I don't plan to.

Hand in hand, my new husband and I face the cheering crowd of three hundred friends, family, and Brayden's teammates on the Dallas Knights. I think my face might crack from smiling so hard.

"How does it feel to be an NFL wife?" Brayden whispers in my ear.

"It feels great being your wife. The NFL can kiss my ass," I whisper back.

Brayden throws his head back and howls, probably because he knows I'm serious. I didn't set out to be a football wife, and I don't plan to do any of the typical football wife things. No, I'm not going to sit at all the games wearing his jersey and screaming at hecklers. I'm not going to start a YouTube cooking show, and I damn sure am not going to star in a reality show.

I have a career of my own: makeup artist to the stars. Well, the Atlanta stars, anyway. I built my business from the ground up, from doing fake lashes for my friends in our Clark Atlanta University dorm, to commanding an entire team on movie sets and backstage at concerts.

I don't need the National Football League.

Brayden and I dance all the way down the long center aisle of the church, to "September" by Earth, Wind & Fire. I chuckle to myself as we pass Brayden's mother, Marilyn, whose perfectly lipsticked little mouth is turned downward into a frown. She wanted us to dance out on a Kirk Franklin song. I vetoed that, just like I vetoed her menu of filet mignon and salmon, and her suggestion that we only have three bridesmaids and three groomsmen.

My man, my wedding and my choice.

Luckily, Brayden isn't the mama's boy his mother would like

him to be. He cares more about how I feel than how she feels, and that is exactly how it's supposed to be. I wouldn't have it any different.

My parents beam with pride as we dance past their row. My dad gives Brayden a fist bump and my mom blows us both kisses. My parents are extremely excited to have an NFL son-in-law. Actually, any son-in-law is just fine for them. They were convinced that I would never get married and give them grandchildren. The family whispered behind my back at family reunions that I was probably a lesbian, because everyone in Atlanta flies the rainbow flag.

When we get to the back of the church, I stealthily slide out of the heels my wedding stylist forced me to wear, and into the bedazzled flats that were waiting for me. I will wear the heels in the wedding photos, but then I'm done.

I wish I could pull all the pins out of my hair and let it fall free. My big and heavy mane doesn't like to be restrained. Kara, my maid of honor and my assistant, had done my hair in this intricate updo designed to show off my neck and the diamonds that adorn it. My hair is snatched so tightly that my already almond-shaped eyes are even more slanted.

The wedding coordinator makes announcements to our guests as the entire bridal party is swept away in two limo trucks. We're going to do photographs at the country club before everyone else arrives.

This entire day is exhausting.

"You good, babe?" Brayden asks as he grabs a bottle of water from the limo refrigerator and hands it to me.

I nod. "Is there any wine, though?"

Kara shakes her head, and about three thousand curls all bounce simultaneously.

"Why are you shaking your head?" I ask.

"No wine. You need to stay hydrated. That tight corseted dress and this heat . . ."

I give her three slow blinks and then look at Brayden. "Why is this killjoy in our limo? Can we call security and have her removed?"

Brayden kisses my forehead and hands me the water. "She's right. Water now, and you can have some wine later."

I stick my tongue out at Kara, and she winks at me. I guzzle the water down—guess I was thirstier than I thought.

"Where's my phone?" I ask Kara.

"It's put away in your bag, where you won't be able to get to it until after your first night of wedded bliss," Kara says. "At the groom's request."

I feel my upper lip curl with irritation. I didn't get where I am by ignoring calls for an entire day. That's not how I run my business.

"I can look at it now. We're in the car. I will put it away when we get to the reception venue."

"No work today," Brayden says.

"I could be missing out on money."

"You're not. I'm monitoring our email accounts. Everyone knows to text me if they can't get you. Plus, who's trying to do business with you today? Your wedding is all over the entertainment blogs. They know you're not available," Kara says.

They must not understand how naked I feel without my phone in my hand.

"If you miss out on any jobs, I'll pay you for lost wages," Brayden says. His best friend and best man, Jarrod, gives him a fist bump, and they all laugh—even the limo driver.

"You don't have to worry about money anymore," Jarrod says. His large rolls jiggle underneath his tux jacket with his laughter. "You can let another makeup artist eat now."

"Oh, I am going to continue working. That's without question."

"You're gonna have to get her knocked up real quick," Jarrod says. "Then maybe she'll sit down and be a wife."

I close my eyes, inhale and then exhale. First of all, Jarrod doesn't even have a wife, because he prefers being a man whore. So how does he know what a wife is supposed to do? Second of all, I know Brayden better get his boy before I do.

I feel Brayden's strong hand squeeze my bouncing knee.

He's trying to calm me down, and I appreciate him for that. I don't feel like cursing anyone out on my wedding day.

"Man, I didn't marry her so we can have a bunch of babies. I married this woman because her hustle matches my hustle. Her grind matches my grind. We will never be broke, even if I leave the NFL today. My baby is a boss."

Brayden kisses my cheek and squeezes my hand, but I still give Jarrod a glare that signifies my highest level of pisstivity. But Jarrod grins at me like he knows something that I don't know.

"Kara, make sure you respond to every booking request that comes through over the next seventy-two hours. The bloggers are giving us a tremendous amount of press."

And they are giving us that press because I sent press releases that made sure to mention Beat by Chenille and directed readers to my web portfolio. We're spending eighty thousand dollars on this wedding—might as well make it an investment.

"Already on it, Nille. Don't worry. I won't drop the ball," Kara says.

I believe her. She works as hard as I do. She's the best partner I could ever have.

I flip my thousand-dollar hairweave and ease into Brayden's one-armed embrace, satisfied that my business will survive a few days of my absence.

Finally, I return Jarrod's grin. He doesn't know anything about me, about us, and about this happily ever after. He's a whore with whore ways who chases booty and then tosses it in the trash. What would he know about saying "I do" or being married to a boss?

Chapter 1

Two years ago

My nerves are shot.

I should be ecstatic, thrilled, overwhelmed, and every other adjective to describe a makeup artist on their first big celebrity gig. It's in Jamaica, for crying out loud. That alone should make my spirits soar.

But all I can think about is my brand-new ex-boyfriend, Cody. He was supposed to be here with me. We were going to make love in our suite during my downtime. We were going to lie on the beach and plan our future. We were going to have the time of our lives.

But he couldn't keep his penis out of other women's vaginas.

Every time I close my eyes I think of what I found on his phone. I wish I hadn't looked, because everything had changed after that. Two weeks ago, everyone had looked to us as their relationship goal. Now, we are irretrievably broken.

I remember the events of that night. We had gone out to dinner to celebrate his birthday, had great sex, and were resting in his huge bed.

I'd picked up his phone, intending to text myself the cute selfie we'd taken at dinner. His phone had been unlocked, because he always kept it unlocked. We'd trusted each other.

I'd clicked on his photo, and found the selfie, but I mistakenly clicked on the video that was next to the selfie. It played, and my jaw dropped.

It was Cody and some random girl. He was taking her from behind as she cried, "Happy dirty thirty, Daddy."

I hadn't even roused him from his sleep to argue. I'd gotten dressed and snuck out of the bed and his condo. I'd sent him a text later, congratulating him on his birthday conquest. He'd called me insecure and petty.

So instead of holding hands with my man and looking out at the clouds, I'm on this first-class flight with my best friend and assistant, Kara.

"I can't believe we're about to land in Montego Bay," Kara says as she peers out the airplane window.

"I know. I've never been out of the country."

"If I had a boo, it would be perfect. Maybe I'll pull one of these ballers with this thong bikini."

Kara will pull someone this weekend, even if it's a temporary fling. Late last year, she'd hopped another flight to the Dominican Republic and had all the fat sucked out of her size-fourteen stomach and pumped right into her booty. She'd already had big breasts, so now she looked just like the letter S, with a teeny, tiny waist.

The flight attendant announces that we're about to land, so I make sure my seat belt is fastened, my tray table stowed, and my seat is in the upright position. Kara does none of the above.

The landing goes smoothly, and we emerge from the plane into the Montego Bay airport. I have to say, I was expecting more from an international airport. It's small like a regional airport in the States, and it's sweltering hot, like the air conditioning is broken.

Kara fans herself and cusses as we stand in the long line for customs. I can't even get worked up about the wait. I think after crying for two weeks, I've emptied myself of emotions.

We walk toward the hotel shuttle van that has been reserved for the concert attendees. I see people pulling tickets out of their wallets and bags—everyone except me and Kara.

"Were we supposed to have a ticket?" I ask.

Kara made all of the arrangements for this trip, with my credit card, of course. I haven't seen any of the confirmations, because Kara has booked travel for me before.

"I wasn't provided any tickets."

"Oh, okay."

I walk over to the pile of bags next to the shuttle van, to make sure mine and Kara's luggage is there. It is.

"Are we supposed to have tickets for this shuttle?" I ask the bag porter.

"Huh?"

"Tickets. Do we need tickets?"

The porter's eyes widen. "Oh, you think I work here?"

His American accent immediately makes me know that I've made a mistake.

"I'm so sorry. It's just that . . . you have the same kind of outfit as . . ."

Kara walks up with a huge smile on her face. "You're already meeting celebrities, I see, and we haven't even gotten to the resort yet."

My stomach drops with embarrassment. Who in the world is this guy? I feel like an idiot that I don't know and Kara obviously does.

"Brayden Carpenter," the porter lookalike says as he extends his hand to me. I return his firm handshake, but I still have no idea who he is.

"She's not into sports," Kara says. "He plays for the Dallas Knights. NFL. I'm Kara."

"Oh!" I say. "I'm sorry. I didn't mean to mistake you for a bag porter. It's just that I see everyone with a ticket, and . . ."

"She's just nervous," Kara says.

"Not a problem," Brayden says. "Are you guys going to the Tropical Get Down?"

"Yes, of course," Kara says.

"Well, maybe I'll see you there," Brayden replies.

"I'll be working," I say.

Why did I say that? I'm one hundred percent sure he's just

being nice and doesn't care whether he sees us or not, but I had to tell him that I'm working.

He smiles. "Are you an artist? You sing?"

"Oh, no, nothing like that. Chenille Abrams. I am a makeup artist."

"I heard that. Get your money, then."

Brayden gives us a nod and then walks toward the limo bus that's probably taking him to the resort. As soon as he's out of earshot, Kara bursts into laughter.

"Girl, I can't believe you just called one of the hottest players in the NFL a bag porter."

"It's not my fault! He looks Jamaican. He's tall, muscular, and dark. He had on the same outfit."

"Um . . . no, he didn't. His polo was Tom Ford and his shorts were Ralph Lauren."

"Whatever. Did you find out about our tickets?"

"Something went wrong with our shuttle reservation, but they agreed to take us over to the resort anyway."

"How kind of the driver."

"It might've had something to do with the fact that I said I'd go dancing with him before we leave."

I shake my head. "Girl, why did you lie like that?"

"It wasn't a lie. He's hot, and I bet he is packing heat, chile. That's what they say about these Jamaican men."

"What kind of heat? The burning, you-gotta-take-antibiotics kind?"

Kara rolls her eyes and drags me over to the van where the other passengers (who have tickets) are boarding.

"I still can't believe you didn't recognize Brayden Carpenter."

I shrug. "It doesn't matter. You're the one here to meet a baller. I'm here to network for Beat by Chenille."

"Of course you are, but that doesn't mean you can't have some fun, too."

Lord knows I need some fun after what happened with Cody. But the last thing I need is an NFL player. They're even bigger cheaters than the average man. If Cody is videotaping himself with women, who knows what shenanigans a man like Brayden would get into.

No, as fine and as chocolate and as muscular as he is, Brayden Carpenter isn't for me. Maybe Kara and her brand-new, bodacious hips can score him instead.

Chapter 2

Brayden scanned the crowd in the lobby of Paradise Blue, the five star, all-inclusive resort that was hosting the Tropical Get Down. He was not as impressed as the hordes of attendees seemed to be, probably because having played for five years in the NFL, he'd been to some of the world's most exclusive resorts.

He was, however, impressed by the quality of the women in attendance.

Women of every shade of chocolate, caramel, and vanilla filled the lobby in varying stages of undress. Some wore tiny shorts and crop tops. Others had been to their rooms already and had changed into swimsuits that looked like dental floss. All of them seemed on the prowl—ready to land and possibly trap a baller.

"I am definitely having a threesome this weekend," Jarrod, Brayden's best friend and teammate, announced. "Too many fine women here for me to pick just one."

"Definitely? Don't you have to convince them first?"

Jarrod laughed. "They won't need much convincing. That's why they came. Every woman here wants to hook up with a man like me. They've been looking at the blogs, checking to see who was coming. You probably on at least fifty hit lists, bruh."

Well, he definitely wasn't on Chenille Abrams's hit list. She'd thought he was a bag porter. Hadn't even recognized him.

Brayden finally spotted Chenille and her friend, Kara. They were standing at the front desk, probably checking in.

Brayden had noticed Chenille's beauty at the airport. Smooth, ebony skin like Lupita Nyong'o, with curves like Beyoncé. Not the artificially enhanced curves that a lot of the women present had, but curves created with jerk chicken, neck bones, and jollof rice, and refined with a healthy amount of physical activity. She was solid, and smooth and sexy. She wore her hair in thick braids that cascaded down her back and stopped right above the curve of her behind.

He had to get to know her better. They were in paradise, so it was the perfect time.

Brayden jumped up from his seat, and Jarrod jumped up, too.

"What we 'bout to do? Going to the pool bar?" Jarrod asked.

"No. I want to try and hang out with her, over at the desk."

"The girl who thought you were the help?"

"Yeah."

Jarrod laughed. "There are easier pickings. It might take all week to convince her to holla, and then she might not be down."

Brayden knew exactly what Jarrod meant by being "down." He agreed that Chenille didn't strike him as the type that Jarrod was looking for, but Brayden wasn't interested in just having a fun week. Not with a woman like her. She was a goddess.

Brayden imagined Chenille wearing his jersey and nothing else, in the bedroom, at his home. She was the type he'd bring home and never let her go.

He made his way over to the front desk, hoping to chat with her and maybe walk her up to her room. But as he got close to her, Brayden could see that all was not well. She didn't even seem to notice him walking up to her.

"I need you to check your computer again," Chenille said.

"Ma'am, we don't have a reservation under your name, or under your friend's name."

"Check it again," Chenille said.

Kara looked like she was about to pull out a round-the-way-sista beat-down on the woman if she didn't make some magic happen with that computer.

"Look here," Kara said. "I made the reservation my damn self, so I know it's there. I gave you the confirmation number."

"That confirmation number doesn't match anything we have in our system."

"You think I just made it up?" Kara asked. "I know what you better do. You better press some more buttons and find us a room."

"Can we just have whatever you have available?" Chenille said.

"I'm sorry, ma'am, we are booked solid for the entire week. I can check one of our sister properties for you."

"Yes, please."

Sister property? Brayden didn't want her staying at a sister property. He wanted her right here, all week long. He wouldn't be able to make his moves if she was at a sister property.

Brayden cleared his throat, and both Chenille and Kara looked in his direction. Kara's face lit up with a smile, but Chenille looked right back at the front desk clerk.

"Ma'am, we have a room at our property in Lucea."

"How far is that from here?" Chenille asked.

"It's about forty-five minutes, and we can have one of our drivers take you over there."

Chenille groaned. "I am doing makeup for three of the artists performing. I can't be forty-five minutes away."

"Unfortunately, every resort and hotel in Montego Bay is booked because of this concert. I don't know what to tell you."

The front desk clerk placed her hands on her keyboard, not typing, but with an air of finality.

Brayden knew that this was his chance to step up and be the black knight in shining armor.

"I have a room. You can stay in my room," Brayden said.

"You're inviting us to stay in your room with you? Really?" Kara asked. She laughed out loud.

Chenille wasn't laughing. She was frowning.

"No, not with me. I mean you can have my room. I can bunk with my boy Jarrod. We both have suites. We don't need that much room."

Chenille's jaw dropped, and then finally she smiled.

"You would do that for us? Even though I thought you were a bag porter?"

Brayden shrugged. "There's nothing wrong with that job. I didn't mind at all."

"Would you like me to put Ms. Abrams's credit card information down for incidentals?" the desk clerk asked.

"No, leave everything in my name. It's on me."

"The room and tax as well?"

All three ladies—the clerk, Kara, and Chenille—stared at him in disbelief. Maybe they'd never met a rich gentleman before. He'd like to make their acquaintance.

"Yes, the room charges, taxes, and resort fees. And please make them new keys. I don't want you ladies to worry about me walking in on you."

Chenille gripped Brayden's arm and squeezed. "I don't know how to thank you."

"Yes, she does," Kara said.

Even with tears of thanks in her eyes, Chenille glared at her friend. Brayden cracked up laughing.

"I don't know what she's talking about," Brayden said. "No thanks are required. I'm just doing a good deed."

"To cover up for your dirty deeds?" Kara asked.

"No. Because, I hate to see my beautiful sisters in distress. Chenille said she's here to make her money. I like that."

"You want her to make her coin. That's all right," Kara said.

"You're on the fifth floor, in one of our luxury penthouse suites," the desk clerk said. "The elevators are on the right. A bellman will deliver your bags in a few minutes."

Chenille turned to face Brayden again. "A penthouse suite?"

"I feel like somebody ought to give you some booty, just on general principle," Kara said. "Go on, Nille, throw that ass in a circle."

Brayden wouldn't mind Chenille rewarding his chivalry, but he didn't want it that way. He hated for a woman to feel obligated to have sex with him.

"No, not that, but I'd love for us to have dinner one night while we're here," Brayden said.

Chenille smiled again. Brayden would do and say anything to keep seeing that smile. The full lips, the deep dimple in her left cheek. It was perfection.

"Mr. Carpenter, where should the bellman deliver your bags?" the clerk asked. "Do you need someone to pack them?"

"I haven't unpacked yet. It's the set of black luggage, and it can be delivered to Jarrod Green's suite."

"Thank you so much," Chenille said. "I would love to have dinner with you."

"It's a date, then."

Now, Brayden had to figure out how to keep Jarrod's head from exploding when he found out he had to share his sex den. It wasn't going to be pretty, but Brayden thought Jarrod just might congratulate him when he shared what he did to land the finest girl he'd ever laid eyes on.

Chapter 3

"You did what?"

Brayden knew that Jarrod was going to react badly to him giving Chenille and Kara his room. Since Jarrod was planning for his room to be a mini–Playboy mansion, he probably didn't want to have a roommate.

"Keep your voice down! Someone might hear you."

"You gave those two chicks your room. So now you want to crash in my room?"

"I just had my bags sent up."

"You knew I was going to say yes."

"I knew you wouldn't say no."

"Why didn't you just get them another room?"

"Sold out."

Jarrod flagged down the girl serving drinks and took a tall glass of rum punch. He guzzled it down and took another. Brayden shook his head. His boy was completely overreacting.

"I promise I'll stay out of your way," Brayden said. "I'll barely even be in there. Only to sleep."

Jarrod shook his head and frowned. "That's not good enough, bruh. When most people are sleeping is when I have the majority of my activities planned."

"How many girls can you possibly hook up with?"

"How many nights are there?"

"Your little friend is gonna shrivel up and fall off."

Jarrod scoffed. "Like my grandmama would say, I don't receive that."

"You've got a huge suite, man. Take your activities and hoes into the bedroom, and I'll crash out on the couch."

Jarrod sighed. "You better be glad you're my boy, because other than that, you'd be sleeping on the beach."

"Thanks, man. I'm sure Chenille and Kara would thank you, too."

"One of them *is* going to thank me. Which one you drooling over, so I can get the other one?"

"I'm not drooling."

"You are. You gave up a penthouse suite, and offered to pay for all of it, for two chicks you met at the damn airport. You're the type of dude they're talking about on wheretheballers.com."

"What the heck is that?"

"A website that gives groupies tips, tools, and techniques on how to separate ballers from their cash. There is a whole post about this concert."

"Really?"

"Oh, yes. They tell them what clubs to go to, how to score VIP, and how to trick a baller into giving up his sperm."

"Get the hell outta here."

"I wish I was lying, man. It's rough out here. That's why I got a vasectomy."

"What if you want a kid one day?"

"I've got millions of my little swimmers frozen for the occasion. I'm not getting any random groupies pregnant."

"Wow."

"That's how it is, unfortunately."

Brayden was nothing like Jarrod. He didn't want to tap every groupie in sight. He didn't want to tap any groupies at all. That's not how his mama had raised him.

"I just want to find one woman with the three B's," Brayden said.

"Breasts, booty and . . . what's the third B?"

"I want her to have brains and beauty, and I want her to be a boss."

"Uh-uh. Not me. I don't want a woman that's a boss. You can keep an alpha woman."

"Why? I think they're sexy."

"Nope. They're trouble. Anytime a woman doesn't need you it's an issue."

"Not to me."

The fact that Chenille was at the concert to work, and not just to play and land a baller, was the sexiest thing about her in Brayden's opinion.

"I just don't want you getting all twisted when I bring the ladies up here to play."

"What you want to do? Hang a sock on the door?"

"Nah, that's too obvious. I want to leave the hoes some dignity. I'm gonna put the football outside the door."

"The hoes? Man . . ."

"Look, I'm not like you, bruh. I'm not a gentleman. I don't claim to be. I'm a straight-up dog."

Jarrod set his glass on the table and did an impromptu fraternity step. His tongue wagged from side to side as he stomped and barked. Several of the women at the bar stopped what they were doing to watch Jarrod, and Brayden observed their reactions to the show.

Some appeared intrigued, and even threw Jarrod bedroom gazes. One girl, who seemed too young for this kind of activity, maybe a college freshman, bit her lip and said, "Here, here, puppy."

Brayden hated this kind of attention, and never wanted it, but Jarrod wanted all of the women looking at him. He posted videos of himself on social media, gazing at the camera with his green eyes. He got millions of likes, but Brayden wanted more than that.

Brayden wanted what his parents had. They'd been together forever—married for fifty years. Even when his father had strayed, his mother prayed and prayed until he came back home to his family. That, to Brayden, was real love.

"You have an audience," Brayden said as Jarrod sat back down.

"I know. It's all part of the game."

"That's your mating call?"

Jarrod nodded and grinned. "You can call it that. Like that honey over at the bar. She's staring me down."

Brayden looked where Jarrod was looking. The honey *was* staring him down. She took a sip of her wine and then slowly licked her lips.

"Watch what she does next," Jarrod said.

The honey slowly turned to face the bar, giving a full view of her perfectly round, perfectly squeezable behind in tiny black shorts. The shorts were so tiny that half of each butt cheek peeked from beneath.

"Damn!" Brayden said. "So you gonna holla at her?"

Jarrod shook his head. "Not yet. She's not ready yet. She still thinks she's in charge. She thinks she's pulling me."

"I mean. Look at her."

"Nah. She's got to be panting over me."

Brayden closed his eyes and shook his head. "Panting over you? Isn't that what you do? You're the dog, right?"

"Game has changed. I'm the prize. She ain't ready until she understands that."

"Well, damn. I ain't even got nothing to say to that. I'm 'bout to go and see if Chenille and Kara got settled."

"You know, I was actually surprised that you went all out for her. I mean, she's okay, but she ain't the baddest chick out here."

"She's the one who caught my eye."

"I mean, she's okay. Just kind of regular. You could've found her at any Starbucks in Dallas. Probably making your coffee."

Brayden couldn't believe what he was hearing. Chenille was anything but regular. He didn't know what her lady parts looked like yet, and he could bet a year of his NFL salary that they weren't on display on Instagram. Unfortunately, Chenille was irregular in this crowd. She was a damn unicorn. And different was exactly what Brayden wanted.

Chapter 4

I have never been in a hotel suite like this. This suite looks like an entire apartment, shoot, a condo. There's a huge king-size bed with a jetted tub in the same room. Champagne and chocolate-covered strawberries chill on a cart in the sitting area. The view is crazy. The patio door opens right up to the beach.

How could Brayden give this up? I don't know that I would've. Not for a couple of strangers. I take a bite out of one of the strawberries.

"My goodness! Kara, taste one of these."

Kara rushes over from her suitcase and plucks a strawberry off the tray. She closes her eyes when she bites.

"There's alcohol in this strawberry; rum, I think," she says. "It is so good."

We eat them one after another until there's only one left on the tray. Just plain old greedy.

"Girl, he must really be digging you," Kara says.

She walks back to her suitcase and spreads five tiny swimsuits out on the bed.

"It's that dress clinging to your pop-out booty, and all that co-conut oil that you have shining up your chocolate skin," she says.

"There's plenty of beautiful women here. I'm nowhere near the hottest one walking around. I think he honestly felt sorry for us, and was being nice."

I hope Kara doesn't think I'm being modest or anything. I'm dead serious. There are so many surgically enhanced body parts at this resort that I almost feel inadequate. I never thought I would ever consider plastic surgery until I walked into this resort. And Brayden could have his pick. He is fine, muscular, and rich. When I grabbed his arm, I wanted to feel his embrace. That's how strong his arms felt.

I also know that I'm attractive, though. I get my fair share of attention from men. Lately, I've been getting hit on by a lot of white men. It's like all of a sudden, they woke up and decided that if their women could swirl, then so could they. And they love my chocolate self. Like, if they're gonna cross over, they want the darkest berry they can find.

I'm not mad at them, because I am very juicy and very sweet.

I've gone out on a few dates with some of them, too. Some were creepy and weird, some were regular, and some were an awesome time. Just like when I date black guys.

But Brayden is a whole other level of delicious. It's like God reached into my fantasies, sculpted Brayden out of black-man clay, breathed swag into his lungs and said, "Let there be foine."

"How will you repay his kindness?" Kara asks.

"He asked for a date. I'm gonna give him one."

"You ought to give him some booty, too, girl. For all of this, he deserves it."

I don't respond to this, because I don't agree. I don't trade in sexual favors. I know that's the in thing to do; I also know that's what Kara would do, but I can't let a man think that he can purchase a night with me. This cookie is not for sale.

"Who is my first client?" I ask. "Or do you know?"

"Wow, really? Of course, I know. I have your whole itinerary."

"Because you had the room situation taken care of, too, and we just stood at the front desk looking like idiots."

"I don't know what happened with that."

This isn't the first time Kara has screwed something up that was supposed to be handled, but this is absolutely the most embarrassing time. This time I want to fire her, but how do you fire your best ride-or-die friend? Kara is the friend who would help me murder an abusive boyfriend, hide the body, and lie on the witness stand. She's *that* friend.

So, when she volunteered to be my personal assistant, how could I say no? It's just that she's horrible at the job. I think she can get better, but she has to take constructive criticism without getting her feelings hurt all the time.

I watch Kara go into her backpack and pull out a clipboard. She walks over and thrusts it in my face.

"Your itinerary, boss."

I take the clipboard and glance over the information. It is a list of names and the nights they perform. I hand the list back to her.

"What time do I need to show up? Where? Are there any special requests of each client?"

Kara stares at me, blinking. "How am I supposed to find all of that out?"

"You can start by going over to the concert area, letting them know we've arrived, and asking for additional instructions."

She rolls her eyes and glances over at her bathing suits.

"We're not here on vacation," I say. "We're here to work. We can go to the beach when we have downtime. Right now, you're on the clock."

Kara looks like she wants to say something back, but then appears to change her mind. She tucks the clipboard under her arm and starts toward the door. Then she stops and turns to me.

"I am sorry about the room. I had the confirmation number. I honestly don't know what went wrong."

"I forgive you, Kara."

"Promise you aren't angry?"

The remorseful tone in her voice evaporates any irritation

that I might've had at Kara's lack of organizational skills. I have to learn to be more patient. She can learn to do this job better, but I'll never, ever find a more loyal friend.

"How can I be mad, girl? We got upgraded."

She smiles as I give her a high-five. "Yes, we did."

There's a little bounce in her step as she crosses the room now, like she knows that fun is on the way. She's got the easy part, really. She's only got the organizing. I'm the one who'll have to pull out every trick in the bag to make some of these average-looking artists look like glamour queens.

Kara opens the door, and Brayden is standing there with his fist raised, like he was just about to knock.

"Hey Mr. Brayden," Kara says. "I was just leaving, but Chenille was planning to relax a bit until it's time for the first show."

I chuckle. There is no time for me to relax, but I appreciate her trying to hook me up.

"I'm gonna let you get your rest," Brayden says. "I just wanted to make sure everything was okay, and that y'all had gotten settled in."

Kara scurries out of the room, pushes Brayden over the threshold, and slams the door behind her. We share an awkward moment, because neither of us says anything. He shifts his weight from one leg to the other, and I bite my lip.

"So, where are you from?" Brayden asks, finally breaking the silence.

I'm glad he said something. I might not be aggressive when it comes to dating, but I don't want a shy boy. Yuck. There's nothing more unattractive to me than a man who doesn't know how to be assertive and get what he wants.

"Atlanta."

"Born and raised?" he asks.

"Yep. A Lithonia-born Georgia peach."

"Yes, you are."

I laugh out loud. Now, he's getting somewhere. A little boldness, a little innuendo. Okay, I see you Mr. Chocolate. I also see his chest muscles ripple when he laughs. The tank top he's wearing can hardly contain it all. He looks good enough to touch.

And I'm sure I'm not the only one who's noticed.

"What about you? Where are you from?" I ask.

"Texas born, Texas bred, and when I die, I'll be Texas dead."

Now I really burst out laughing. Every Texan I've ever met has been crazy about Texas. I've never dated one, though.

Am I already thinking of dating him? Let me pull myself together. This is too good to be true. The only reason he gave up this room is because he intends on being laid up in here with me the whole week. He ain't slick. He's just invited me to his love nest, so he can have easy access, and my dumb self and my dumber assistant have set up shop.

"You must've been planning to entertain in this gigantic room. You even had snacks at the ready."

"I agree. They *were* at the ready. It looks like you and your homegirl smashed, though."

"We did. Those strawberries were good."

"I'm glad you enjoyed them."

"What if I tell you I'm not having sex with you? Am I going to need to pack my bags and figure out somewhere else to stay?"

His eyes widen with genuine shock. He looks offended.

"I didn't give you this room so that I could sleep with you. I wanted to help. You looked so distraught, and I knew I could stay with my friend."

"So, this wasn't some elaborate plot to get my booty?"

"I could've gotten it without giving up my suite."

I almost hit him with rapid-fire word bombs of the very profane and hood kind, until I see he's on the verge of laughter again.

"You think that's funny?" I ask.

"It is. You looked like you were about to swing on me."

"I would never put my hands on anyone. I was about to get my things and bounce, though."

"No need. I was joking. I'm gonna go and let you get your rest. I don't want you saying you're tired when it's time for our date."

"When is this date supposed to be taking place?"

"I'm not sure. It'll be before the week is out, but I need to think about it first. How can I top giving up my baller suite in an act of chivalry?"

"That is going to be very hard to top."

If he does anything more spectacular than this, he probably will get the booty. It'll probably offer itself up as tribute.

"Challenge accepted," Brayden says. Then he does a deep bow like a Japanese sumo wrestler before a match.

He crosses the room and removes all the space between us. My breath is caught in my throat with anticipation.

"I have a question," Brayden whispers.

"Okay."

"If all of this *had* been an elaborate plot to get the booty, would I have gotten it?"

"What?"

Then he laughs, "I'm kidding."

"Oh!"

"I'll see you later, Chenille. Did I tell you I love your name?"

I shake my head.

"Well, I do. Get some rest. I'll holla later."

My breathing doesn't normalize until he leaves the suite. I walk over to the bed and sit down on the edge, so I can gather my thoughts.

Brayden is nicer than I thought he'd be. A lot nicer. Not like any athlete I've ever met or been around. They're mostly arrogant, like to display their money, and they never talk to girls my shade of brown. I honestly didn't expect to be distracted by men, at all, this weekend.

I go to these "celebrity" outings all the time in Atlanta. Girls who look like me get to have fun, but we don't get the ring. Not from the celebrity guys, anyway. We pull plenty of African tycoons and princes. Well, they call themselves tycoons and princes, but I don't know who's verifying any of this.

Anyway, I was good with coming here to work, because all I expected was work. I didn't expect an NFL player to be interested in me. Not here with so many blow-in-the-wind-haired

Latina and mixed chicks present. I was just being real with myself.

Now I feel like I should've planned better. Maybe I shoulda rocked a weave instead of these braids. Maybe I should've brought some sexier swimsuits.

Maybe I should've scheduled myself some downtime.

Know what? I'm not even gonna worry about it at all. I didn't come here to find a man, I came here to brand my business. So if something happens, great. If it doesn't, I'm going to enjoy this great suite in paradise . . . and make this money.

Chapter 5

I am having the worst day ever. Well, maybe not ever, but the worst day this week. This is supposed to be paradise, shoot!

Everyone told me that this new R & B artist, Taneeka, was a handful. Just yesterday, she fired the makeup artist that she brought with her from Atlanta. A makeup artist I know and respect, and who has a hell of a lot more experience than I do.

So, when the concert organizer begged me to slide Taneeka into my schedule, I was apprehensive. I let Kara, who is a big fan of Taneeka, talk me into it.

I need to make myself a note and put a reminder on my calendar to never, ever, let Kara talk me into anything. Again. Ever.

"I'm not glowing enough," Taneeka says when I hand her the mirror for the fifth time.

Yes, the fifth time. This is the fifth look I've given her. The first four were perfect. The first was bold and colorful—fun. The second one was a glittery and frosted look. She looked positively stunning. The third look was all earth tones and grit— she was serving bronzed goddess. The fourth look was natural and fresh, like a teen next door. This final one, the one that isn't glowing enough, captures old school Hollywood glam, with big red lips and a smoky eye.

I turn her chair and add more shimmer on the balls of her cheeks and down her nose. Then I shove the mirror in her hand again.

"Do I sense an attitude?" Taneeka asks.

"You sense a very tired makeup artist."

"Well, you're being paid, so you need to perk the hell up."

I swallow all of the profane words that bubble up into the back of my throat, because I cannot cuss this little girl out. It'll be all over the blogs in Atlanta, and they'll say that I'm unprofessional. Even though Taneeka is stank as all get-out.

"What do you think? Glowing enough?"

"I guess it'll work. I mean, we really don't have time for you to keep practicing on me."

"Prac . . ." Shoot. Swallowing again. "I'm glad you like it."

"I didn't say I like it. I said it'll work. The only other choice I have is to do my own damn makeup."

A waitress walks up to us with a drink on a tray.

"I didn't order that. What is that?" Taneeka asks.

"Are you Ms. Chenille?" the waitress asks.

"Oh, that's me, but I didn't order a drink."

The waitress smiles. "It's from Mr. Brayden Carpenter."

Now, I can't wipe the smile off my face. Ain't nothing this heffa can say to kill my vibe now.

Taneeka rolls her eyes and snatches off the makeup apron.

"Groupies kill me coming to these things, just trying to get a baller."

"Excuse me?" I ask. "I'm not a groupie, sweetheart."

"Everyone in the industry who isn't an artist is a damn groupie. Every makeup artist, hair stylist, nail tech, choreographer. Every one of y'all. Sucking the artists dry. Like I bet you didn't even go to school for makeup. You just woke up one day and said, 'I'ma be a makeup artist,' 'cause you ain't cute, you can't sing, and whatever else."

Okay, damn the blogs.

"Listen here, you little wannabe Rihanna. You have not arrived. You ain't there yet. You are an opening act at a week-long concert. Ain't nobody here to see yo' ass. And the reason why you don't like what you see when you look in the damn mirror is because of that ugly spirit that shows in your eyes."

Let me just say . . . the way this child's bottom lip starts trembling. Oh, my goodness. She bursts into tears.

"Wait, no, no, no, don't cry. You're going to mess up your makeup."

She is bawling now, and here comes the concert coordinator. Shoot. I'm probably about to get fired from this concert. Damn.

"What's happening?" Raven, the coordinator asks.

"She's so mean." Taneeka wails at the top of her lungs.

"Who's mean? Chenille? I've seen Chenille get cussed out and not break a sweat. She's not mean," Raven says.

Taneeka pouts and throws herself around in the makeup chair. She looks like an oversize toddler.

"Are you going to perform? I do have a backup group if necessary," Raven says.

Raven clearly isn't here for Taneeka's tantrum. When she said "backup group," Taneeka got it together real quick. I have never seen tears dry up so quickly.

I take two very large gulps from the drink Brayden sent me to keep from laughing.

"Um, Chenille, can you fix my makeup?" Taneeka asks.

Oh, so she wants the groupie to fix her face now? Okay, I won't be petty. I'll be the professional that I am and help this child.

After I correct all the streaks and send Taneeka to do her non-singing on the stage, I pack up my equipment. I am finally done for the day. The first time all week that I'm finished before sunset. The main acts are tonight, and they all have their own makeup artists.

Finally, I can rest.

I wish I could enjoy the island, but it seems like I don't get out of here every evening until after dark. I'll have to live vicariously through Kara's tales.

As tired as I am, I can't help but smile when I see Brayden waiting outside the makeup tents. I've been in here for hours, so I wonder how long he's been waiting for me. He returns my smile.

"You're a sight for sore eyes," I say. "You're missing the concert, though."

"I decided to bypass the concert tonight. I'd rather spend my time with you."

I am tired, but suddenly I'm getting my second wind.

"You're too sweet. Is it time for our dinner date?"

"It is."

"But I'm all sweaty and sticky from working all day."

"Do you want me to walk you up to your baller suite, so you can change?"

"Do I have time?"

"I'm on your time. I'm just hoping you have a few moments to spare in between getting your coins."

"I've got a few."

Brayden takes my makeup bag out of my hand and slings it over his shoulder. The crowd roars with applause at something that we can't hear, but we're walking away from the noise and back toward the resort.

"How'd you know when to pick me up?" I ask.

"I got your schedule for the day from Kara. She told me things had gotten hectic on your other days, and to just stay there until you come out."

"And you waited."

"Of course I did. The week is almost over. You owe me a date."

He smells so good. I can't place the scent, but it's incredible. I don't want to do anything that might make him think I'm interested in activities beyond dinner, but I also want to get just a little closer to enjoy his cologne.

We get to the suite, and I open the door. Brayden sets my bag inside the room but remains in the hallway.

"I'll wait for you out here. Don't be long. I've got something nice planned for you."

"You don't have to wait outside. I trust you."

"I'm good out here."

He takes a seat in one of the wicker chairs on the landing, overlooking the ocean. His chivalry is almost overboard.

"What, you think you can't control yourself, knowing I'm in my underwear in the next room?"

Brayden grins. "I can control myself, but it doesn't feel right. You're not a groupie, and I don't want anyone to see me coming out your room and thinking you're one."

Damn. That's more than chivalry. I almost feel like he checked me a little bit. I don't even know what to say in return, so I just nod and walk into my room.

I choose my outfit carefully. A long, flowing sundress that I didn't even think I was gonna get the opportunity to wear here. I wasn't planning on having a date or even fun, but I'm now picking which bracelet to wear on my date with an NFL player. This is unreal.

As much as I love giving everyone else a glam makeup look, I never do that for myself. I take a nude lip gloss out of my purse, shine my lips, and throw some highlighter on my cheekbones. That's it. Shimmer and gloss.

When I emerge from the room, Brayden quickly stands. He smooths out his black linen shirt and holds out his hand to me.

"You look so beautiful," he says.

"Thank you."

"You ready for my surprise?"

I feel like I look stupid with this silly grin on my face, but I can't believe this. I've never had anything romantic happen to me before. I mean, I've had dates. I've had relationships. But they've always been practical, because I'm a practical girl. If I'm attracted to a man, and he's attracted to me, it just makes sense for us to get together.

I don't play games. I barely flirt, and so maybe that's why I've never been wooed. But Brayden seems like this is his typical behavior.

I take his hand and let him lead the way.

I wait for him to start chatting, because that's what people always do when it's quiet. But I'm enjoying the sound of the ocean crashing against the shore. It's such a peaceful sound.

Brayden surprises me by enjoying the quiet, too. He looks out at the water and back at me, but he doesn't say anything. Almost like a spell would be broken if he does.

We stop at a staircase that leads down to the beach.

"We're going down there?" I ask.

"That's where the surprise is," Brayden says.

I hold onto Brayden's arm as he leads me down the winding staircase. The scent of Jamaican spices tickles my nose as we descend and makes my stomach growl. This makes Brayden laugh.

"You hungry, Chenille?"

"I'm starving. I'm so glad I smell something delicious."

"I got you. This should be good."

When we get to the bottom of the stairs, and I see the scene set before me, my jaw drops.

"Brayden . . . oh, my goodness."

In front of me is a candlelit path leading to a table set for two. There are three servers, all wearing smiles on their faces.

"So, you ready to eat?" Brayden asks.

He's clearly enjoying my reaction to his surprise. He can't stop smiling, like he's proud of himself.

"Yes, I'm ready to eat."

Brayden pulls me over to the table and helps me get seated. Immediately, wine is being poured and food is being served. I feel like royalty.

"Did they make this happen because you're a celebrity?" I ask.

Brayden shakes his head. "No. It costs a little extra, but they'll do it for anyone who wants it."

"Well, it's beautiful. Thank you. No one has ever done anything like this for me."

"This is nothing. Wait until I cook for you."

My eyes widen. "You cook?"

"Yes. I make a mean grilled cheese sandwich and a banging pot of Texas chili."

This makes me laugh loud and hard. I just knew he was about to say something like some blackened red snapper or some sort of steak. That would just be perfect to go along with this romantic image he's been giving me since he rescued me from having to sleep on the beach.

"Well, I do cook, actually," I say. "When I have time."

"What's your specialty?"

"I'm from ATL, baby. My specialty is soul food. I fry the heck out of some chicken, make macaroni and cheese that makes you want to smack your mama, and a pound cake that will have you going right to the jewelry store to buy me an engagement ring."

"I can't wait to taste some."

"So, you intend on asking me to cook for you?"

"I hope it'll happen organically. Is that something you would do for your man?"

"You're not my man."

"I'm going to be."

I take a bite of my grilled lobster tail to keep from responding. I mean, I don't know if he's going to be anything outside of this trip to Jamaica. It would be nice to think that he might, but my business is popping right now, and a relationship with an NFL player sounds just like drama, and counterproductive to my money.

"What if I'm not looking for a man?"

Brayden's eyebrows shoot up, like he's not expecting this to be a possibility. I know his confidence may be dashed a little bit, but I don't want to give him unrealistic expectations.

"I'm sorry. I assumed you were single."

"I am."

"But you're not interested in dating?"

"I didn't say that. I don't know if I'm looking or not. You seem nice."

Brayden nods. "I am nice. I'd like us to get to know each other better."

"Even if I don't know how I feel about starting a relationship?"

"Yes. I think when you get to know me you'll change your mind. I think you won't want to lose me."

Again, I'm at a loss for words. He's convinced me that I just might want to pursue this. If only I hadn't just gotten out of the worst relationship ever.

"This is nice, but, I . . . I just broke up with someone. I kinda need a break from being a girlfriend, or from having a boyfriend."

"Someone broke up with you?"

"I broke up with him."

Brayden nods. "Ah. Did he hurt you?"

"He did."

"I have horrible timing, then."

"Unfortunately."

The waiters remove the dinner plates and set several different desserts in front of us. Key lime pie, rum raisin ice cream, and bread pudding. It's all delicious, but the mood is somber now. The romance has faded.

"Have you ever been to an NFL training camp?" Brayden asks.

"No. I don't follow sports, remember?"

"Right. Would you like to attend one?"

"What would I do there?"

"There are times when you can watch some of the training, but mostly we could just hang out in my downtime."

Now I'm lost. I just told him I wasn't looking for a relationship, and that I'd just broken up with a guy, but he's still in hot pursuit.

"I don't understand why you're inviting me to the camp. I'm sure there's another girl who might actually want the experience and enjoy it."

"I don't want another girl to come."

"I'm confused. You're still trying to holla at me?"

He nods. "It'll just take longer. I'm patient."

I sit back in my chair and watch Brayden devour his desserts. I want to believe that he's different than the other men I've dated, but the thing is, you never know until the hurting has already happened. It's always hindsight with me when it comes to men. But . . .

"Okay, I'll come."

I'll go. Only because he seems so different from Cody. Hell, he's different from any guy that's ever tried to get with me. I hope my instincts are right.

Chapter 6

Brayden had checked his phone five times in the last thirty minutes. He was waiting for Chenille's plane to land in Los Angeles for the training camp. He hoped that she wouldn't get cold feet and change her mind.

Since Jamaica, they'd talked a few times on FaceTime and on the phone, and Brayden had learned a lot about Chenille's life. He considered her a friend, and thought she considered him one, too, but he had no idea if he was making any headway on her becoming his woman. And that was the goal.

"Man, what's wrong with you?" Jarrod asked as he downed a wheat germ smoothie.

They were in training camp, so alcohol was off limits, but they went to the hotel bar every night anyway, trading in their cognac for healthy beverages.

"Just waiting to see if Chenille is going to show up."

"You don't know? Did you buy the plane ticket?"

"Yeah, but she's always working. If she gets a good enough gig, she'd probably not come, and then reimburse me for the ticket."

Jarrod closed his eyes and shook his head. "What is your point with this girl, anyway? You didn't get any in Jamaica, or since then. Shit, you can't even get a naughty picture in your inbox."

"You don't know what's in my inbox."

"The makeup artist isn't the type to send you nudes. If she was, you would've tapped that in Jamaica. No, she's—"

"The type of woman you marry."

Jarrod hollered with laughter. "No. She's the type of girl *you* marry. The girl I marry is gonna be a straight-up freak. She's gonna give it to me on the first date, and then bring her friend for us to share on the second date."

Brayden frowned and checked his phone again. No texts, so he checked Chenille's social media posts. Then he smiled. He held the phone up for Jarrod to see it.

Chenille had posted, *Wheels up, finally. Missed my first flight fooling with this Atlanta traffic.*

"So she is coming to see you," Jarrod said. "Too bad you can't get any during training camp."

Their head coach, Bill Wyatt, hated for the players to have any distractions during camp. Alcohol, women, and family were off limits, although most everyone snuck in a girlfriend or groupie. But if a player even so much as yawned during a morning practice, it was on and popping. Coach Wyatt went on a rampage.

"We're just friends right now, though, so it's all good," Brayden said. "I just want to spend some time with her. See her in person again."

"You sound sprung."

"How can I be sprung? We've started a friendship, and that's it. Nothing to be sprung about."

"I've got lots of friends. I didn't fly any of them to training camp like they're my family."

"We've already established that you and I are two totally different people."

Jarrod finished his smoothie and stood up.

"I'm about to go and get some sleep, bro. See you at practice in the morning."

"It's still early."

"Nah, I'm tired. We're getting long in the tooth. Gotta be able to keep up with these rookies."

Brayden agreed. Both he and Jarrod had been in the league since they graduated from college. Those five years had flown by. All of the battering and bruising that their bodies had taken on the field had started to take a toll. They weren't as swift as they'd been in the beginning of their professional careers.

"See you on the field, then, bro."

As much as Brayden needed the same rest Jarrod was getting, there was no way he was going to bed until Chenille was safely tucked into bed.

Brayden's phone lit up with a Messenger notification. He couldn't click the button fast enough when he saw it was from Chenille.

Got the in-flight internet to let you know I'm on the plane. I land in about two hours.

Brayden replied, *Okay. I will meet you at the airport. I'll be driving a white Escalade.*

☺ *ok. I'm about to try and get a little nap. See you soon.*

The two hours it took for Chenille to arrive seemed like the longest two hours of Brayden's life. He had to check himself for a moment, because he couldn't remember ever being this excited to see a woman.

Brayden stood in the baggage claim area trying to look inconspicuous, with his cap pulled low to his eyebrows. But every football fan (and groupie) knew that the Dallas Knights were in town, so keeping a low profile was impossible.

A young woman, probably in her early twenties, walked right up to Brayden. He tried to act like he didn't see her, but she tapped her manicured nail in the center of his chest.

"You're Brayden Carpenter," she purred. "Running back. Dallas Knights."

Brayden smirked. He wasn't impressed at all. Every groupie did her homework. This was typical.

"Hello," he said.

He wasn't overly friendly, but he also wasn't a jerk. He just wasn't interested in this young lady who'd decided to invade his personal space with her fingernails. Plus, her breath smelled of alcohol. She'd probably been tossing them back on her flight.

"So, I bet you know where all the good parties are," the girl said. "Hook a sista up."

Brayden took in her outfit. Surgically enhanced breasts spilling from a baby t-shirt at least two sizes too small for those silicone monsters. She had a tiny waist that couldn't possibly have occurred without a plastic surgeon and a perfectly round bottom crammed into neon green leggings. He'd seen this kind of apparel before. On reality television.

"I'm not here to party. I'm working. Sorry."

"That is unfortunate, because we could have a really great time together."

And there it was. The brazen invitation that always happened. This was the attention his homeboy Jarrod thrived on, but Brayden hated.

"There's my friend," Brayden said, ignoring the proposition. "Have a good evening."

Brayden erased the tartlet from his mind as soon as he saw Chenille. She'd changed her hair. The cornrows were replaced by a curly afro that was pinned up on the sides. The smile and the dimple were the same, though.

Brayden quickly navigated the hordes of people waiting for their luggage to close the space between himself and Chenille. Her eyes lit up as he adjusted his cap and made eye contact with her.

When he reached her, Brayden swept Chenille into his arms and off her feet. He placed a little kiss on her neck as he set her back down on the floor. He paused for a moment to enjoy the scent of her light perfume mixed with whatever products she put in her hair. It was intoxicating.

"Brayden," she said as she wrapped her arms around his neck, stood on her tiptoes and kissed his cheek. "I'm so happy I made it."

"Me too. I just wish I wasn't working."

"I wanna watch you working, though."

Brayden felt the butterflies again, although he'd been trying to ignore them. The nervousness made him feel like he was slipping a bit. He didn't want to fall too fast, or too hard, but he didn't know if he could help it.

The groupie from earlier walked up to Brayden and Chenille. Brayden hoped there wasn't going to be any drama, because girls like this were known for causing scenes just to post on social media.

"Is this your girl?" the groupie asked.

Brayden nodded. "Yes, she is."

Chenille's eyes widened, but she didn't make any comments to dispute his claim. Brayden knew they weren't officially a couple yet, but the groupie didn't need to know that. Plus, he was proud of Chenille and glad to have her on his arm.

"Well, that's sweet," the groupie said. "If y'all want, we can all have fun. Together."

Boldly, the groupie put a small slip of paper in Brayden's front pocket. Then she winked at Chenille.

"You a pretty dark girl," the groupie said. "And you got a fat ass."

Then the groupie walked away, giving them a full view of her probably purchased behind as it jiggled in her leggings.

Chenille laughed out loud.

"Oh, my goodness," she said. "Is this what this week is going to be like?"

"Unfortunately. Welcome to my life."

"She was bold."

"A lot of them are."

Chenille let out a long sigh. This worried Brayden, but he didn't say anything else. He couldn't stop groupies from making advances, but he could show her that he wasn't into any of them.

"There's my suitcase," Chenille said. "The royal blue one."

Brayden grabbed her bag off the conveyor belt. It was heavier than it looked. He rolled it back over to Chenille and took her hand in his free hand. He waited to see if she would flinch or reject him outright. She didn't. She gave a little squeeze, letting him know his touch was welcome.

"Where am I staying?" Chenille asked as Brayden placed her suitcase in his trunk.

He smiled. "You're staying at my condo."

"Your condo?"

"You don't want to stay at my place?"

"It's not that. I was just expecting a hotel, I guess."

Brayden opened the passenger door of the Escalade and helped Chenille climb inside. Before he replied to her concerns, he went around to the driver's side and got in the truck. There were still questions on her face as he strapped on his seat belt. Finally, he decided to calm her nerves.

"You're staying there, but I'm not. The team is staying in suites at the training facility."

Chenille's exhalation was loud in the quiet vehicle. He could sense how relieved she was. It bothered him a bit that she couldn't see his good intentions.

"You can relax around me," Brayden said. "I am never going to disrespect you, or make you do something that makes you uncomfortable. I know how to treat women."

"Thank you. It's just that, I see what you're used to, and I don't know . . . I don't think I can compete with girls like the one in the airport. I'm not just going to offer up my goodies like that."

"Your goodies?"

Now it was Brayden's turn to laugh. Of course, he knew exactly what she meant, but it sounded hilarious in the middle of a very serious declaration from Chenille.

"Boy, you know what I mean."

"I do. I am happy you're not just out here offering up your goodies to just any baller."

"I don't care that you're a baller."

"So, you would've talked to me even if I was just a regular guy?"

Brayden started the car and waited for her response.

"I would've."

Brayden had no way of knowing if that was true, but hearing her say that she would've liked him without his money made him feel good.

Chenille gasped as Brayden pulled up the driveway to his Los Angeles condo. It was impressive from the outside—all white with tropical landscaping. The trees were imported from all over the world, along with tropical flowers in hues of orange, red, and purple. Even at night, it was brightly lit so that everyone who drove by could see how beautiful it was.

"You can use my Ferrari while you're here. It's in the garage," Brayden said. "I want you to feel completely at home."

"I walk around naked at home."

Brayden grinned at Chenille's flirtatious tone. He'd love to see her in all her ebony, naked glory. Maybe wearing a pair of expensive stilettos.

"You're free to walk around however you want, but unfortunately I won't get to enjoy it."

"So, I'm only going to see you at your practices?"

"Well, we can go out to dinner, we just can't . . . we can't do anything else that you may have been expecting to happen, but it's okay if you weren't expecting it to happen. It's okay if you don't want it to happen."

"Why are you talking in code?" Chenille asked. "I got it. You don't want to have sex this week. Is it because of work?"

"Wait, were you offering . . ."

Chenille quickly shook her head. "I wasn't offering, but to be honest, I hadn't ruled it out. I just decided that if things went there, I wouldn't try to stop them from going there."

Damn training camp.

"As soon as training camp is over, I'm going to put a smile on your face that you won't be able to wipe off."

"Sex is banned during training camp, huh? How will your coach know? Y'all that close?"

Brayden howled with laughter. "We're not that close. He somehow just knows. And the punishment he wreaks on the team because of one player's indiscretion is brutal."

"So, it's more about the team, then. You don't want to break the rules, because the team will have to pay."

"Well, yeah. Everyone is abstaining, so it would be wrong . . ."

Brayden stopped talking because the twinkle in Chenille's eyes made him think she was teasing him. Yeah. She was teasing him.

"Let's just go inside," he said. "I have a surprise for you."

"A surprise? It's late."

"I know. I'm going to have to drop you off and head back, but I want you to enjoy the surprise first."

Brayden grabbed Chenille's bags out of the car and led her up the front walkway. She took in the careful landscaping and ornate trail of colorful rocks going up the walk.

"It's sea glass. I found most of it myself on beaches all over the world."

"You brought the beach home with you."

"Yes. Both my houses have a sea glass walkway."

"Your other home is in Dallas?"

Brayden nodded as he opened the door. "Mmm-hmm. South-lake."

Chenille pressed her lips together tightly as she walked through the door. Brayden couldn't read her expression yet, but he wanted to know what she was thinking.

"You don't like Southlake?" Brayden asked.

"It's nice. . . ."

"But?"

"But I think positive male role models shouldn't leave our neighborhoods when they make it. It would be nice for young boys to see you in the community."

"They do see me in the community. I run mini-camps for kids in the off-season."

Brayden watched Chenille's gaze as she took in the chandelier in the foyer and his artwork. He'd hired an interior designer when he bought the condo, but Chenille's assessing eyes made him wish he'd refreshed his décor.

"You have good taste," Chenille said.

"Thank you. I'm glad you approve."

She chuckled. "What's the surprise?"

"Oh, it's in the master suite. Follow me."

Brayden left Chenille's bags in the foyer and took her hand. He liked the way her tiny hand felt in his, and the way she squeezed it. It was a warm squeeze that made Brayden feel chosen.

He opened the door to the master suite, and Chenille squealed with excitement. He had transformed the entire space into a mini-spa. Three massage therapists waited with smiling faces. The scent of roses and jasmine filled the room as the master bath was filled with rose petals and essential oils.

"Welcome home," one of the massage therapists said.

The smile on Chenille's face was reward enough for his hard work in putting this together.

"This feels like . . . a dream," Chenille said.

"A good dream?"

Chenille threw her arms around his neck and pulled him in. She kissed him deeply and passionately, ignoring the giggles of the massage therapists. Having her fingers laced around his neck was the sweetest restraint he'd ever known.

"Thank you," Chenille said when they finally separated.

"You're welcome. Enjoy this tonight, and breakfast in the morning."

"You sure you can't stay."

The husky, whispery tone of her voice almost made Brayden want to risk the wrath of his coach and his teammates.

"I want to, but I'm not going to. When camp is over, though . . ."

Chenille kissed his throat. He shuddered. If he didn't leave in the next thirty seconds, his resolve would evaporate.

"I gotta go, babe. I will see you tomorrow at camp. I've left instructions for you there."

Chenille released him from her grasp and leaned back on her heels. "Okay. I won't try to get you to betray the team."

"Could you tell I'm slipping?"

"Yeah, but I like that you have this kind of discipline. That says a lot about you."

Brayden laughed. "Yes. It says I'm stupid."

Brayden leaned down and kissed Chenille's cheek, even as his throat still sizzled from the kiss she'd left there.

One of the massage therapists led Chenille away, and Brayden bit his lip at the sight of Chenille walking away. An ebony goddess. That's what she was. And he was leaving her here alone in his condo, massaged, relaxed, and oiled. Yeah, he was stupid.

Damn training camp.

Chapter 7

I don't know what I expected at this training camp. Maybe I thought there would only be a few people, because they're not playing real games. I was so wrong. There are thousands of people here. And hundreds of those thousands are groupies.

These girls are everywhere, poured into leggings and tiny t-shirts, wearing dangerously high heels that I wouldn't be able to walk in. It appears to be the uniform, but I didn't get the memo. I'm wearing a blue-and-white shorts romper and flip-flops. At least it's in the team colors.

The ticket Brayden left for me is in the VIP section. It is a groupie-free zone, with mostly children, wives, girlfriends, and players' parents. I feel more comfortable here. I take a seat and watch what I guess are the wives of players hugging and greeting one another. I see lots of white women with caramel babies, and bright-skinned black and Latina women. I'm the only young woman who looks like me—a chocolate-covered queen.

I'm never self-conscious over my shade of brown. I love every bit of me. It just makes me sad that with all that chocolate on the field, I don't see more of it represented in their families. Well, I shouldn't say families. Many of their mamas are brown. It's just that when they chose wives and mothers for the children, their mothers' pretty brown skin wasn't good enough.

It makes me wonder if I should even take Brayden seriously. Is he going to trade me in for a lighter version at some point? What if he brags about me, and his boys on the team mock him? Men want to impress their friends.

Then a woman walks in who looks like Brayden in a wig. She has to be his mom.

"Mrs. Carpenter!"

Yep. I knew it.

One of the white girls that were clustered with the other wives/girlfriends runs up to Brayden's mom and gives her a hug.

"I keep telling you to call me Marilyn!" Brayden's mom says as she gives the girl a warm hug.

"I know," the girl says. "I just can't do it, Marilyn. You're too classy."

Marilyn links arms with the girl as they walk down to the very front row of the friends-and-family section. Is this an ex-girlfriend, current girlfriend, or potential girlfriend? She's got to be one of the above, or Brayden's mom wouldn't be so chummy with her.

I want to get closer so that I can hear their conversation, but I'm afraid. What if Marilyn turns around and asks me who I am? What am I going to say to that? *I'm the girl staying in your son's condo. Yeah, I'm waiting to give him some booty after training camp.*

Plus. And this is a big plus. Why the hell did he not tell me his mother was going to be here? I feel like there should've been preparation for this. He should've given me a heads up.

Maybe he isn't ready to introduce me to his mother. I can't be mad about that. Shoot. I'm not ready to meet his mother.

I stand when everyone runs to the railing at the front of the section of seats. Something important must be happening, because no one stays in their seats; they all run up to the front. I purposely snag a spot far from where Brayden's mother stands.

"What's happening?" I whisper to the little girl standing next to me.

"The players are coming out. They're going to say hi and give autographs."

Oh. So I want to go back to my seat. I can get an autograph from Brayden later. Let him focus on his fans. But, when I turn to my seat, there is no one else in the stands. Sitting down will just draw more attention to me, so I turn around and wave at the field like everyone else.

When Brayden comes out, I feel my heart rate speed up a bit. This is the first time I've ever seen him in his uniform, and he looks good in it. Muscular, toned legs, and a perfect, round, conditioned behind. Physically, Brayden is everything I've wanted in a man. I feel my mouth water at the thought of his kisses.

All the players run toward the rail and grab footballs and pieces of paper from the fans so that they can sign them. The little girl next to me waves a picture of Brayden.

Brayden smiles at the little girl, and then at me. He runs up and signs the little girl's picture. Then he takes my hand and kisses it. I giggle, but the people standing around me make *ooh* and *ah* sounds.

I hope his mother didn't see that.

I glance to my right to see if she *did* indeed see Brayden kiss my hand. She is glaring in my direction, so I'm going to take it that she did see it. And not only is she glaring . . . she's making her way over to me.

Well, shoot. If he's not trying to hide me, I'm not going to hide.

This lady gently shoves the little girl sideways and steps to me. Yes, *steps* to me. Like how a chick steps to another chick when she's trying to steal her man.

"And you are?" she asks.

"I am Chenille. And you are?"

Her eyes widen with surprise. I'm not sure how she expected me to respond, but she surely doesn't look pleased with my question.

"I'm Brayden Carpenter's mother, Marilyn. Are you a friend of my son?"

I wonder how much I should divulge. Since I wasn't briefed by Brayden, I have no idea what this woman might say or do.

"Pleased to meet you. We met in Jamaica at a concert. He's a nice guy."

It's truthful. I did meet him at a concert in Jamaica. He *is* a nice guy.

"Did he invite you here?" she presses.

"He did give me a complimentary ticket. I appreciated it."

"Ah, I see. Well, enjoy the practice."

She gives me a smirk and sashays away. I don't know what the smirk means, and I damn sure don't know what the sashay means. Dammit. I should've said I was his date. I should've said I was staying at his fancy condo.

Or maybe I shouldn't have.

Thank goodness this waiter walks by with a tray of wine. I need a whole bottle, but I settle for two glasses.

I can't even enjoy the rest of the practice worrying about Brayden's mom. I keep glancing over at her to see if she's glaring, and she isn't. She doesn't give me another look for the rest of the practice. It's almost like she's ignoring me. I guess she's decided that I don't matter.

After it's over, the players greet their friends, family, and loved ones out on the field. I don't know if I should go out there. I hesitate as the guests file out of the stands and onto the field. If I escape now, maybe Mama Carpenter won't see me leaving in her son's Ferrari.

But when I get to the exit, Brayden is right there, beaming at me. He extends his hand to help me down the last few steps.

"Did you enjoy the practice? Were you impressed with my skills?"

I chuckle. "Well, I don't know anything about football, but I was definitely impressed with you in that uniform."

Brayden throws his head back and laughs. "I love your bluntness."

"Really? Do I remind you of your mama? She strikes me as extra blunt."

His laughter immediately stops.

"Did she say something to you?" he asks. "Chenille, I apologize if she said anything out of line."

"Oh, she didn't. I was just a little bit caught off guard. Why didn't you tell me she was coming?"

"I didn't know until we came out and said hi to the people in the stands. She surprised me. I mean, she had tickets, but she told me she wasn't coming."

Whew. Okay, I don't have to be mad at Brayden now. He can still get it.

"Here she comes," I say.

"Don't worry. I got this," Brayden says.

Mama Marilyn walks up to me and Brayden with a little friend in tow. The friend is the white girl from the stands. They both smile like they're up to something.

Brayden hugs his mother so tightly he lifts her off her feet. "Mama! You surprised me."

"My plans changed, and I decided to pop in and see my baby. Is there a problem with that?"

"Never."

Marilyn touches the white girl's arm and pulls her close to Brayden. She ignores me like I'm not even here.

"Brayden, this is my friend, Ashley. I've been wanting the two of you to meet."

Brayden smiles and extends his hand. Ashley looks confused that he wants to shake her hand like he's meeting a business associate. I bite my bottom lip to keep from laughing.

"Nice to meet you. Mama, I'd like to introduce you to my friend, although it sounds like you already made her acquaintance. This is Chenille. Chenille, this is my mama, Marilyn. I would've introduced you two beforehand if I'd known you were coming. You could've sat together."

Marilyn narrows her eyes in my direction. "She didn't mention she was your friend. Only that you'd met in Jamaica."

"I thought it would be better for Brayden to facilitate our introduction. I didn't want to go ahead of him."

Marilyn gives a tiny headshake, as if she's shrugging off this entire event. "I'm tired, son, and I know you're staying here with the team. I'll just let myself into the condo."

I bite my lip again and force myself to let Brayden handle his mother.

"Mama, I can get you a hotel room at the Four Seasons if you want. Chenille is staying in the condo, and I'd like her to have her space."

Oh, Marilyn is mad now. She blinks slowly and frowns. Her eyes sweep me from head to toe.

"Mama, I'm sorry . . ."

"No, you didn't know I was coming, and you're a grown man. You have a right to keep your women wherever you want to keep them."

Oh, no, she didn't.

"That was rude, Mama. I don't have *women.* Nor do I keep them anywhere. Chenille is my girlfriend . . ."

Wait. I am?

". . . And I won't allow you to be rude to her."

Marilyn sighs.

"My apologies, dear," she says. "I didn't mean to be rude. I suppose I was just being blunt about my bachelor son."

"No offense taken."

I'm lying through my teeth. I am good and offended. But I'm also intrigued by this girlfriend announcement.

"Do you need me to call for a driver, Mama?" Brayden asks.

"Of course, baby."

Brayden laces the fingers on his left hand through the ones on my right, and pulls me away while he dials a number on his phone. When we're a few feet away from Marilyn, Brayden starts to giggle. It's a playful and youthful giggle, almost like I'm tickling him in his ribs.

"What is so funny?"

"Yours and my mama's faces when I said you were my girlfriend."

"I didn't make a face."

"Chenille. Yes, you did."

His laughter makes me laugh. "What did my face look like?"

"You looked scared. Like you just saw a *Walking Dead* zombie or something."

"I did *not.*"

"And my mama looked like she wanted to go gangsta on both of us."

"That part you got right. Your mama wants to choke you out."

"She's still staring at us. I know her. Don't look back."

Brayden pulls me into an embrace. He looks down at me and smiles mischievously.

"You trying to get a felony on your mother's record?"

Brayden shakes his head, then kisses me on my forehead. "Did I tell you I love your hair like this?"

"You loved my braids."

"I love this, too."

"Which one you like better?"

"Your lips. I like your lips better."

His kiss turns my insides to water. I could just melt on through his arms and seep into the ground.

His hands travel down to the small of my back as he savors every part of my mouth. If I could think, I'd probably be horrified and embarrassed. But I can't think. I can only feel. His kiss makes me feel like I've never been kissed before.

"I have to stop," Brayden says.

"Why?"

He bites his lip and moans. "Damn training camp."

Brayden releases the embrace, but pulls my hand to his mouth and kisses my fingers. His teammates, who have clearly been watching, cheer and whoop.

"They're congratulating you," I say.

"Nah. They're glad I haven't given in to temptation yet."

"You want to, though."

"My mama still looking?" Brayden asks.

I glance over to where Marilyn and Ashley were standing. They're gone.

"Nope. She left."

"Don't worry about her. I will handle my mama. She's gonna fall for you, just like I'm falling for you."

He's not the only one falling . . .

Chapter 8

Brayden's teammates roared with laughter as he rushed out of the final meeting of training camp. He didn't care about their laughter. None of them had an ebony goddess waiting for them in their condo like he did.

Chenille had been luxuriating all week with the pampering Brayden had provided. She had to be just about ready for him to partake.

He showed up at the condo with one thing on his mind: pleasure. Giving it and receiving it in return.

But first, he needed a sandwich. He'd missed breakfast at the hotel, and needed plenty of energy for what he had planned.

"Chenille," he called from the kitchen. "I'm here. I'm not an intruder."

It was the sound of Chenille's feet sliding across the tile floor that made Brayden turn his head. The sight he saw was not a tantalizing woman ready to be devoured. This was . . . this was scary.

Her afro was standing out on her head on one side, and the other side was smashed down onto her head. She didn't make any attempt to fix it. She stopped in front of the counter and sighed.

"What's wrong?" Brayden asked. "Did you have breakfast? Lunch?"

"I'm sick."

Brayden immediately dropped the sandwich fixings on the counter and embraced Chenille. He tried to smooth down her hair, but was unsuccessful. He kissed her on the forehead anyway.

"What kind of sick? Do you need medicine? I can go out and get it."

"I got my period, Brayden. I'm so sorry . . ."

Brayden hugged Chenille again and chuckled. "It's cool. I've waited this long. I can wait until next time."

"I must've miscalculated on the calendar."

"Don't worry about it. Let me take care of you. What makes you feel better?"

"I already took a warm bath. It didn't help. I was going to try taking a nap, but when I laid my head down I got nauseous."

Brayden thought for a minute. "So maybe tea will help. Come sit down in the family room."

Brayden led Chenille into the family room, which was equipped with a big-screen television on the wall and a comfortable brown suede sectional. He got Chenille situated on the long piece of the couch and found a blanket to cover her.

Chenille's eyes were wet with tears that threatened to over-flow, but she accepted the blanket and wrapped herself up in it. Brayden kissed her on the forehead again because she looked so pitiful.

"You're gonna be mad at me," Chenille said. "You didn't fly me here for this."

He shook his head. "Are we going to spend time together today?"

"I guess."

"Then I'm getting exactly what I wanted when I flew you here. I wanted us to spend time together."

Brayden rushed back into the kitchen to start the cup of tea. Of course, he was disappointed. He was beyond ready to go to the next level in their friendship, and he could tell that she was, too.

When the tea was ready, he loaded up a tray with tea, crackers, and cookies and took it back into the family room along with the sandwich he wanted to eat for lunch.

"You want to just watch movies?" Brayden asked. "Your flight doesn't leave until tomorrow, so you can relax today."

"What kind of movies do you like?"

"Sci-fi. The *Aliens* franchise is my favorite."

Chenille closed her eyes as her body shimmered with laughter. "You want to watch alien movies?"

"I always like a good alien movie."

"Since you can't have any booty, I'm gonna let you have these aliens."

Brayden plopped down on the couch and positioned Chenille so that he cradled her upper body in his arms. She breathed in deeply and exhaled.

"You smell good," Chenille said.

"I do? Not on purpose. What do I smell like?"

"You smell like a man. I think it's just your natural scent that I like."

Brayden wanted to sniff his armpits to see if he was ripe. He'd never had a woman comment on his natural scent.

"Attraction is all about chemistry, you know?" Chenille asked.

"What do you mean?"

"I mean, our bodies are having chemical reactions right now in response to each other."

"That sounds incredibly sexy."

Chenille gave a weak laugh and allowed her head to rest on his chest. "Nothing about me feels sexy right now. I'm in pain."

"Let me help take your mind off the pain."

"I thought you wanted to watch your aliens."

"In a little bit. I just wanted to say that I'm so glad you came. You're the first woman that I've invited to camp."

"Really?"

"Yeah. I haven't really had a real girlfriend since I joined the NFL."

Chenille gave him a skeptical look. "What about your mother? I know she's brought plenty of women for you."

"That's a whole other story. She thinks she knows what I want and need. She doesn't."

Chenille pulled her legs underneath her on the couch and closed her eyes. He stroked the top of her head. There was sweat on her brow. Finally, the pain seemed to pass, and Brayden felt her muscles relax.

Brayden massaged and rubbed her arms, hands, and shoulders—any place on her body he could reach. She purred as he lightly kneaded her flesh trying to make her relax.

Soon, Chenille's breathing slowed. Her chest rose and fell slowly. She was asleep.

Brayden stopped massaging and kneading and encircled her body with his arms. Even though she wasn't feeling well, she still smelled like coconut and shea butter. It was her hair. He inhaled deeply and let more chemical reactions happen.

As she slept, Brayden thought more about what Chenille had said. He mostly agreed with her ideas on attraction, but thought she might be wrong about one thing. Attraction wasn't just chemical reactions. His attraction to her was spiritual. She was a soul mate whom he wasn't ever letting go.

Chapter 9

Ineed to go shopping. Brayden invited me to come to the first home game of the season, and I know his mama's gonna be there. I'm going to be sitting next to his mama at the game. And I don't even own a football jersey. I feel like a fraud.

Marilyn already doesn't like me. The last thing I need is to show up to this game unprepared.

Thank goodness, Kara came over for moral support. She picks up a pair of jeans out of my suitcase and shakes her head. "You can't wear these. They're too tight."

"All of my jeans are tight. They make my booty look big."

"You're not trying to look like an Instagram model when you see Brayden's mother again."

"Brayden knows she wasn't feeling me, so I don't know why he didn't get me a seat somewhere other than next to his mother."

Kara laughs. "He wants y'all to get along. The two ladies in his life."

That's true. Training camp proved that. I have to admit that it is incredibly sexy to have a man this determined to be my boyfriend, especially since he hasn't gotten any of my goodies yet.

I was mad as hell when my period came. I had been looking

forward to rubbing up next to those washboard abs. Even when he held me while I cramped, I could feel his abs through his t-shirt.

"What can I wear, then?" I ask.

"A sundress."

"To a football game?"

"Yep. You gonna look real virginal."

"Who said I'm trying to look virginal?"

"Oh. I thought you were reclaiming your virginity, since you haven't given Brayden the booty yet."

She has jokes. And they aren't funny. At all.

"He's not pressuring me for sex, but I was about to give him some. My ovaries are some haters."

"Well, he's a baller. He already knows the booty is inevitable, so he ain't even gotta be pressed like regular guys."

"The booty isn't inevitable, though. Mine isn't."

"Well, not you, but I'm saying, though, how many girls ain't giving it up after a dude like Brayden starts wining and dining?"

"None. Zero. That's why I don't know if I want to give my heart to him."

"Well, tell me the reasons you do want to give your heart . . . and the booty to this man. 'Cause you got about ten pair of matching bra and panty sets in this suitcase."

I laugh out loud. "There is nothing wrong with wearing decent panties."

"Naw, but you act like he's getting it every day, three times a day."

"At this point, I'm not ruling that out."

"Ooh, you nasty."

"He took care of me and massaged me until I fell asleep when I had my cramps."

"Really? Most guys I know act shady as hell when my period comes. I don't hear from them fools for a week. Guess that's side chick time."

Not Brayden. There were hordes of groupies in town checking for him, so he could've dipped in any honeypot he wanted. But he came home to me and stayed there. I just knew I was gonna fall asleep and wake up to find him gone. I woke up still cradled in his arms with my face on his chest.

"I don't even want to think about side chicks. Ugh. I gotta make it through this football game, where the groupies are football experts and his mama is a critic."

"Are you up on football lingo? Do you know how the game works?"

My eyes widen a little. I *think* I know the rules. "They run down the field and make downs until it's a touchdown."

"Do you know what position Brayden plays?"

"Ummmm. . . ."

I know Brayden gave me this information, but it must've gone in one ear and out the other, because I don't remember at all.

Kara shakes her head. "You are not going to impress a football mom like this," she says.

"I know. It's bad, right?"

"The worst. Football moms are basically our mothers on steroids. They know all of their son's stats from peewee football to the big leagues."

I whip out my phone and pull up a browser so I can search for Brayden's stats.

"He went to University of Texas," I say. "Played wide receiver in college."

"What's his position in the NFL?" Kara asks.

I hit the back key to go to a different website.

"This is taking too long," Kara says. "Brayden's mother has already written you off at this point. You're beneath her son."

"Okay. Found it. He's a running back."

"Do you know what a running back does?"

I groan. Why do I need to know all this? I'm not planning to try out for an NFL team myself. I just want to date a player.

Wait.

Do I want to date one? Like really date an NFL player?

"Kara. This isn't important. I promise I'll know what a running back does by the time of the game. But tell me something. Would you date an NFL player?"

"I can't even believe you're asking me that question, heffa. You're living my dream right now."

"And you've thought about what that means? When I went to the training camp, there were hoes everywhere. Some girl offered to have a threesome with us. At. The. Airport. Who does that?"

"Hoes do that. Ignore them."

"Ignore them? They're everywhere. Like roaches."

"Stomp them, then," Kara says with a laugh. "But, seriously, girl. Brayden doesn't seem to be interested in those girls, so you don't have anything to worry about."

"What if I'm like . . . the girl you marry, but the hoes are just women you play with. You know how men say they love you and it doesn't mean anything when they smash the next chick."

"You are a wounded woman," Kara says, sounding like a wise old person.

I am wounded, but I want to try with Brayden.

"Come on. He took care of you when you were on your period. And your cramps are just . . ."

"Horrific."

"I know, right. And you're insufferable."

I suck my teeth. "Well, *he* suffered me."

"And no bodily fluids were exchanged?"

"We've kissed, but you're not . . ."

"I'm not talking about kissing and you know it."

"Well, no. None of those bodily fluids were exchanged."

"Hold onto him, Chenille. You like to run guys off, but hold onto him."

Chapter 10

I changed my mind about the sundress for the game. I'm not worried about Marilyn thinking I'm virginal. I'm wearing tight jeans and Brayden's jersey. I had a gig last night, so I had to fly early this morning, but I made it. I'm here for my boo.

Yes, my boo, and not my man. I'm not quite ready to call him my man yet. I'm almost there, though.

I change clothes at my hotel and head over to the football stadium in the car Brayden sent. The traffic is abysmal, but the driver seems to know all the shortcuts and uses all the lanes that look forbidden to other drivers. I guess the Dallas Knights, and girlfriends of the Dallas Knights, don't sit in traffic.

I bet the Dallas Knights' mamas don't sit in traffic, either.

Why did I have to think about Marilyn? I wonder if I should try to impress her this time with how awesome I am. I'm attractive. I'm fit. I make my own money. I'm not a ho. She should love the hell out of me.

When I get to the players visitors' box at the Knights stadium, I don't feel as confident about Marilyn. I walk into the first class, elite box area that has plush sofas, chairs, and waitresses with trays of wine and mixed drinks. This is nothing like the training camp. This isn't for fans or groupies. Not even new girlfriends. This is for immediate family and significant others.

I am a significant other.

Since I've been grown, I don't think I've ever had a man claim me as his own without me having sex with him. Brayden is giving me wife treatment before I "deserve" it. That's typically what women do—give men too much without getting anything in return. Well, not me, but my friends. They're cooking, cleaning, and screwing a man every way including sideways, without being the significant other.

There are several rows of seats inside the players' box, so I take a drink and sit in an available seat. Marilyn isn't here yet, so I can't purposely choose a seat far away from her. That's my new plan—to not be near her.

Unfortunately, Marilyn has other plans. My nostrils flare as she tiptoes toward my seat in dangerously high heels with a man who I'm assuming is her husband. Escaping now would be rude, although I don't know why she would want to sit by me.

"You're here," Marilyn says. "So, you're not a one and done."

I choose not to allow her to offend me. Breathing slowly yet steadily.

"Hello, Marilyn. Is this your husband? Are you Brayden's father?"

The man seems friendly and has a smile that matches Brayden's. "I am. Joseph Carpenter. Pleased to meet you. You must be Brayden's lady friend, Chenille. He's been bragging on you."

"I wouldn't say bragging," Marilyn says.

"Yes, sir, I'm Chenille," I say, bypassing Marilyn's diss. "He's been bragging about me? What has he told you?"

Marilyn plops down in an available seat and pretends to ignore me and her husband while we chat. I want to laugh, but I don't.

"He says you have your own makeup design company and are making big-time money. I like that," Joseph says. "A woman ought to have her own money."

"Give me a high-five on that, Mr. Carpenter. I'm going to always have my own."

"Please call me Joseph. It'll make me feel young."

Marilyn makes a loud, annoyed-sounding huff as we slap hands. I decide to stop antagonizing her, so I take a seat next to her, and Mr. Carpenter sits down on the other side of her.

"You're not the first young lady Brayden's talked about," Marilyn says.

"I plan on being the last, though."

Mr. Carpenter almost chokes on his beer, as he bursts into laughter. I'm glad he doesn't really choke, because Marilyn looks so disgusted that she probably wouldn't even help him stay alive.

Unlike Joseph, I'm less amused by Marilyn's antics. I'm irritated. Why would she have a problem with me? I'm respectful. I'm not dressed badly. I have my own business. Her son has found a jewel in a pile of rocks.

"Wouldn't you like to see your son settle down with one woman?" I ask.

"How many children do you have?"

Oh, my goodness. I just figured out what this reminds me of. It feels like that one time that I dated a white boy in high school, and he brought me home to his racist parents. His mother asked me this exact same question. She also suggested that I take up a trade, because she'd read that black women have a hard time getting married.

"I don't have any children," I say. "What makes you think I have any?"

"Women who target athletes typically have multiple children by multiple men."

Joseph scowls at his wife. "All right now, Marilyn. That is enough. I apologize, Chenille, on behalf of my wife."

"You don't have to apologize for her. She's not sorry."

"I'm not," Marilyn says.

"That's fine," I continue as I feel an angry heat rise on the back of my neck. "I will say that I didn't target Brayden. He pursued me. I'm afraid I didn't even know who he was when we met."

Marilyn chuckles. "Sure, you didn't."

I drag in a long, uncomfortable breath. This is not going well. I don't want to spend the entire game verbally sparring with Brayden's mama.

Marilyn folds her arms across her chest and grins as if she's won. She hasn't, but I hate the idea that she might think she has.

"You can't run me off, you know. Brayden is the sincerest guy I've met in a long time. Ever. We're going to be together even if you don't like it."

Joseph laughs again, but this time he doesn't choke on his beer. Marilyn gazes at me with eyes that seem to want to burn a hole through my soul. The expression on her face, however, doesn't seem to be anger or surprise.

I think that maybe . . . maybe I've earned the smallest kernel of respect.

Shoot. I'll take it.

Chapter 11

Brayden was dog tired after the Dallas Knights' opening game. He'd caught two long passes and run them in for touchdowns, contributing to their win. But no matter how tired he was, he was going to muster up the energy he needed for his night with Chenille.

"I see you're still bringing sand to the beach," Jarrod said as they gathered their shower supplies.

"What you talkin' 'bout?" Brayden asked.

"You know what. You brought that girl to training camp and now the first home game. You on lock, son?"

Brayden nodded. "Yeah. I am."

"Man, you ain't even sampled enough cake to be on lockdown. There are too many women out here for that nonsense. Don't do it to yourself."

"Everybody ain't like you. Maybe I want to be on lockdown."

"You don't. It's against nature. Men are created to spread our seed to as many willing, child-bearing-age women as we can. I'm just doing what I was born to do."

"Like I said, I am not you."

Jarrod shook his head and limped his way into the shower. Brayden wished his friend would lay off.

Brayden showered and dressed quickly, and although he

usually iced his sore muscles after the game, he decided against it. Chenille had joined his father on the field at the end of the game, and her congratulations kiss made him duck the paparazzi on the way to the locker room lest he be embarrassed on the blogs.

Chenille was waiting for him with the other wives and girlfriends, as he emerged from the locker room in his fitted t-shirt and jeans. Seeing her wearing his jersey sent a surge of desire through his body. She was his, and everybody knew it.

Chenille ran into Brayden's open arms and planted a hundred kisses on his neck as Brayden lifted her off her feet. The chemistry she said they had was evident. Brayden didn't know if he was feeling chemical reactions, but he knew he felt better than he ever had.

Brayden set Chenille down on the ground and then kissed her neck right behind her ear. It smelled sweet, like perfume. The scent intoxicated him.

"I can't wait to make love to you," he whispered in her ear.

Chenille's response was arms wrapped around Brayden's neck and another kiss.

"Let's go, then," she said.

Brayden ushered Chenille to his Escalade, which had been brought to the exit for him. He helped Chenille into the passenger side and then got in the truck himself.

"No driver tonight?" Chenille asked.

"I'm the driver. I'm in charge."

"Okay, then."

"You smell so good," Brayden said. "What is that scent you're wearing?"

"Oh, it's perfume that I made myself. Jasmine and patchouli are the main scents, but there is a little bit of orange also."

"You're freaking incredible."

Chenille gave a full and throaty laugh, one that sounded sexy. The laugh was desire, passion, and confidence combined. It made him want to pull the SUV over on the side of the road.

Brayden had to calm himself down, or they'd never make it to Chenille's hotel room.

"My mom usually comes down on the field after the game. Did you notice if she was okay?"

"She was okay. Just mad about me being at the game, and wearing your jersey. She's not really feeling me."

"Give it time. All she wants is for me to be happy. When she sees how happy you make me, there won't be any problems."

Chenille slipped her hand around Brayden's as it rested on the gear shift. "I make you happy?"

"Yes, you do. My boys have been clowning the hell out of me, because I'm walking around with stars in my eyes. You've got me open."

There was the laugh again, this time a little louder, but no less sexy.

"And all of this is before you get my goodies. What are you going to be like afterwards?"

"Spent."

Chenille laughed hard now, like he'd told the funniest joke ever. Like he was Dave Chappelle, Kevin Hart, and Cedric the Entertainer, but better.

"I'm serious, though," Brayden said.

"I know you are. That makes it even funnier."

"You're okay with this, right? I'm not pushing it too quickly, am I?"

"I want this as badly as you do."

This time Brayden did pull right over onto the I-35 service road. He couldn't last another ten minutes without tasting her.

"Is this the exit?" Chenille asked.

Brayden pulled the car off the road, as if there were an emergency. Well . . . there was. It just wasn't an automobile emergency.

A slow grin teased the corners of Chenille's lips as Brayden put the car in park. He hoped she was reading his mind, because it was hot and steamy in there.

"This isn't the exit . . ."

Without any additional explanation, Brayden took Chenille's face in one hand and gently pulled her toward his waiting lips. She moaned before their lips touched, then moaned louder when they did touch.

"Sorry," Brayden said. "I couldn't make it all the way to the hotel."

"You can pull over anytime to kiss me like that."

"That's good to know. Thank you for the invitation."

Brayden put the car back into drive and pulled onto the freeway. He could hear Chenille's shallow breaths, and it made him even more excited, if that was possible.

"I enjoyed watching you play tonight. I'm so glad I came," Chenille said in a rush of words and breath.

She couldn't be happier than he was.

"You haven't yet," Brayden replied.

"I haven't what?"

"Come . . ."

"What are you talking about?"

Brayden closed his eyes and shook his head. That's what he got for being over-the-top nasty. The joke had gone completely over her head.

"My bad. I just told an unfunny joke."

"I know what you're talking about. I just wanted to see you squirm."

"You're gonna see me . . ."

"Ugh, no!" Chenille said, as she laughed hard enough to bring tears to her eyes. "Get me to the hotel before I change my mind."

Brayden winked at Chenille as he floored the gas pedal. In a short while he was going to taste more than her lips. He was going to taste all of her, and he was more than ready. And then nothing would ever be the same.

Chapter 12

I squint over at the clock on the nightstand next to the hotel room bed. It's only one in the morning. It feels later, like I've slept for twelve hours and then some, but I've only been asleep for an hour. It was a deep and restful slumber, too. I even started dreaming.

But now I'm wide awake.

I stare at Brayden's bare back as he is sprawled across the bed, taking up more than his half. His shoulders look carved out of the smoothest dark chocolate. Right in the small of his back is a little droplet of sweat—no doubt left over from the work he'd just put in.

I want to lick it off, but I restrain myself.

I squeeze my thighs together and close my eyes. I'm still warm and tingly. Brayden's tongue and fingers had sparked a fire, and his thrusts stoked it. I don't think it can be put out, and I'm pretty sure I don't want it to be.

I've never been loved like this before.

Part of me feels guilty and a little . . . dirty. Some of the things we did should probably only happen once a ring has been placed on a finger. Really.

I feel my face get warm thinking about our passionate night. Then I wonder if this is real enough to become forever.

Brayden stirs, as if my staring down at his body has disturbed his slumber. He stretches and then rolls over to face me.

"You're awake," he whispers.

I nod. "Couldn't sleep."

"What? I thought I put you out for the night."

He props himself up on one arm and smiles. That smile is full of promises and suggestions. I trace his lips with my finger, making my own promises in return.

"I had a nice nap."

"Dang, girl. I'm whipped. You're better than me."

"You haven't a care in the world," I say. "That's why you sleep like a baby."

Now he sits all the way up. He licks his bottom lip, but his gaze becomes serious.

"What are you worried about? Is it something I can help with?"

I don't know if I should tell Brayden what's on my mind. He'll probably think I'm nuts. Guys always think that when women get all crazy after having sex for the first time. But what if he's just going to be a story I tell a few years from now? What if he's just going to be the NFL player I used to sleep with? At twenty-nine, I'm getting too old for that. It's time for something solid.

"Sex complicates things," I finally say. "I guess I'm feeling complex right now."

"There is nothing complicated or complex about the way I feel. You're the one."

"How do you *know* I'm the one?"

Cody always said I was *the one*. That was his favorite thing to say to me when I asked him about his cheating. I would find an inbox message, or an email, and ask who the girl was. His reply was always, "Why would I want someone else when I've found the one?"

I never asked Cody what he meant by that. I never questioned it. I took it for granted that *the one* meant one and only. But it didn't. It meant one of many. I don't want to be one of many anymore.

"I know," Brayden says, "because I made a list of what I wanted in a woman two years ago, and then I told God about it."

"You told God about it? What?"

"Yeah, I was in New Year's Eve service with my mother. Pastor told us to write down the thing we really wanted in life. At the time, I had everything but a good woman."

"So, what was on your list?"

Brayden reaches over to the nightstand and picks up his phone. After a bit of scrolling, he shows me a picture of the list.

"The first thing on your list is sexy. You wrote that in church?"

"God knows I like sex. He gave me testosterone."

I lift my eyebrows at this. I am not a frequent churchgoer. I sometimes go with my parents for special occasions, but not very often. I do know that what we're doing, right now, in this hotel room does not line up with the church thing, but anyway . . .

I guess I am everything on his list. I'm sexy, driven, independently successful, kind, and not starstruck. Well, I'm almost independently successful.

"This list could apply to a whole lot of women, Brayden. I know plenty of women who have all of these characteristics."

"Are you trying to hook me up with someone else?"

"No, I'm just saying that I don't know if this narrows it down to me being the one. If there's another one that could fit this list, then, maybe . . . I don't know."

"You'd be surprised. There are a lot of women who have some of those, but not a lot who have them all. You're a unicorn, baby."

That's a first. I've never been called a mythical creature before. And he called me "baby." A mythical creature and a pet name in one sentence.

"Thank you. I think."

Brayden pulls me into his embrace. I snuggle up to his body and inhale his scent commingled with my own. Skin against skin. It makes me feel warm again.

"Why don't you believe me?" Brayden asks as he puts little

kisses on my neck. "Don't put me in the same box as that other dude."

"I'm not."

"You kinda are."

"You're right. I am. Shoot. I can't help it. It's hard to trust again after you've been hurt. You're the one who insisted on dating me."

Brayden laughs. "I did insist on dating you. Because I knew. You're it. When I saw how hard you worked in Jamaica, even when you had a baller trying to chase you down . . . I knew."

"So, if I had let you catch me in Montego Bay, we wouldn't even be here right now?"

Because I totally considered letting him catch me. If it hadn't been for my clients and the need to collect my coins, my booty just might have been in the air. I think he's giving me too much credit.

"I'm not saying that. But you were there for a purpose. You came and did your professional thing. It was impressive. It was the sexiest thing I've ever witnessed. Even sexier than these dimples."

"Thank you."

"How could you not believe me when I say you're the one? I mean it. And we just had the best sex ever."

"The best?"

"It wasn't?"

I chuckle. "It totally was."

"Oh, 'cause I was about to get right out of this bed and carry myself on home."

"I don't know if I was supposed to tell you that, though. Men get the big head when they think they've put it down."

"Not me. I just like positive reinforcement."

I don't know why, but this tickles me as if he'd held a feather under my chin. The giggles tumble out, and I have no way of stopping them.

"That's funny to you?"

"Y-yes!"

Brayden squeezes me tightly and turns my face to his. He kisses me so deeply that the laughter melts away. The warmth that had never subsided revs right back into a flame.

"I want some more positive reinforcement," Brayden says as his hands travel down to the small of my back.

"You do?"

"Yep. Because you haven't told me that *I'm* the one. But you will."

I've got nothing but compliments for him, yet the path to his being my one and only has nothing to do with the warm place between my thighs. He has to get that part right—and does—but there's more to winning my heart and trust than giving me orgasms. He's got to give me mindgasms, heartgasms, and soulgasms, too.

Chapter 13

Brayden sat in the VIP area of the Knight Ryders club, feeling uncomfortable. He was supposed to be hosting a party with Jarrod, but Jarrod was doing the hosting. Brayden was hiding—from groupies.

He hadn't moved from the table once, not even to refresh his drink. At some point the waitress would come back around, because her tip depended on it, but the action was taking place in the middle of the floor where Jarrod and several of his teammates had taken over the dance floor.

As far as Brayden was concerned, he was off the market. And he didn't think Chenille was the type of woman who would be okay seeing her man posted up with groupies in a nightclub. He wasn't going to let the bloggers destroy his new love.

To be fair, not all of the women in the VIP area were groupies. Some of them were the classiest women in Dallas. They'd gotten in because they could afford the price of a ticket and bottle service on their own, without a baller chipping in.

One of these women, Sarah Sanchez, sat down at his table. She was a white girl with a Latin name. Blond hair and silicone for days. Like a corporate Playboy bunny.

Brayden took in a sharp breath. His mother had been trying

to hook him up with Sarah for years. She had even brought her out to training camp a time or two.

"Is someone sitting here?" Sarah asked as she got way too comfortable when she was about to have to move.

"Yes."

She laughed. "Who? Jarrod? I don't think he's coming back for a while. He seems to be quite occupied."

Occupied was one word to describe Jarrod's status. He was sandwiched between two women. One was bent over in front of him, hips gyrating into his crotch. The other was twerking in a way that each butt cheek bounced against Jarrod's thighs and butt as she moved. He had a look of pure ecstasy on his face. Brayden shook his head.

"I wasn't talking about Jarrod. I'm holding the seat for a guest."

"Is it that girl you invited to training camp? The one your mother didn't seem to care for?"

Brayden sipped his now watered down drink and didn't take the bait. Sarah got on his nerves. He'd slept with her once and never wanted to again. She had been trying to get a repeat performance out of him ever since.

"Are we not on speaking terms?" she asked.

Brayden looked around for the waitress. He needed another drink. A stiff one.

"We're not on any terms, Sarah."

She shuddered. "Wow. So cold."

Brayden closed his eyes slowly and squeezed. He knew exactly how this was going to go. It was difficult rejecting certain white women when they were intent on sleeping with a black man. He'd had to deal with this type since he joined the league.

"Not being cold, Sarah. Just waiting for a friend. That's all."

"Is she on CPT?"

Sarah laughed at her own joke, by her damn self, because it wasn't funny. She didn't have a pass to say "colored people time" just because she'd been impaled by an African-American penis on occasion. Especially when she was saying it the way she was saying it, like it was some sort of judgment on the black woman she thought he was waiting for.

"It was good seeing you, Sarah . . ."

"Can't I just rest my feet a little until your friend gets here? It looks like I wore these stilettos for nothing. You're not biting."

Brayden got to his feet. Darth Becky wasn't leaving, so he'd have to make his own escape.

"You can just have this table. Enjoy your night."

Sarah pouted as Brayden cut across the dance floor to the bar. Other partygoers made a path for him. He was a celebrity, an irritated celebrity at that. No one asked him to take a selfie or for an autograph, so his anger must've shown on his face.

"A shot of Maker's Mark, please. On the rocks."

Brayden took the drink and downed it in one swallow. The smooth bourbon warmed his throat and midsection instantly, but it didn't calm him down. He was contractually obligated to do one more hour, but Brayden was close to walking out the door.

"Bruh," Jarrod said as he walked up to the bar and took a seat next to Brayden. "You are missing all the fun."

"Not missing a thing."

"This relationship Brayden is boring as hell. Where's my brother?"

Brayden shook his head. "This is a more mature version of your brother."

"Next thing you know you'll be walking down the aisle."

"Will you be my best man in the wedding?"

Jarrod slapped his hand down on the bar. "Now you're just talking crazy. You just met this girl."

"I know. But she's it. I'm done looking. She's perfect."

"You sure about that? Sarah Sanchez is over there looking at you like a starving man eyes a T-bone steak."

"First of all, Sarah was horrible in bed. So, even if I wasn't in love with Chenille, I wouldn't look her way."

"You just said 'love.' "

"I just said 'best man,' too! You think I'm kidding, don't you?"

"I think you fell into some good poom poom and lost your identity."

Brayden threw his head back and laughed. Maybe it was the drink helping to loosen his mood, or maybe Jarrod was just that funny.

"Yeah, I'll do it," Jarrod said.

"Do what?"

"I'll be the best man when you throw your life away and marry that dimple-having sista."

This made Brayden smile and give his best friend a one-armed man hug and fist bump. This was Jarrod's way of accepting the inevitable, and Brayden was glad he was finally on the Chenille bandwagon.

Brayden had a best man for his wedding. Didn't quite have a bride yet, but a best man was a start.

Chapter 14

I wonder if it was a good idea for Brayden to reacquaint me with his mother during their annual family reunion. When he invited me, it seemed fine, but now that I'm here, at the airport waiting for him to pick me up, I feel some anxiety at the thought of seeing her again.

I've only been introduced to three mothers in my entire lifetime of dating. Does that bode well for my marriage material factor? I mean, only three guys have ever thought I was special enough to bring home to their mothers, and one of them was falling into every open orifice that he came across.

And why in the hell is it so hot in Dallas? Labor Day weekend is usually still warm in the South, but it feels like I got off the plane at the Seventh Level of Hell airport.

My phone buzzes in my hand, and I look down to read Brayden's text.

Be there in two minutes. Can't wait to see you.

I can't wait to see him, either. It's only been a few weeks since I was here for his opening game, but it feels like it's been months.

My stomach drops as Brayden's Escalade approaches. There are multiple heads in the car. As he gets even closer I can see

Marilyn's little head and big hair in the front seat and his father in the back.

Great.

I thought I was going to get to talk to my man for a few minutes before I had to fight off Marilyn's attacks. Guess not.

Brayden stops in front of me and jumps out of the car. He goes to his mom's side and opens the door. She looks at him like he's crazy.

"Son?"

"Mom, I'd like for you to sit in back with Dad if you don't mind. I want Chenille in the front seat with me."

Marilyn's jaw drops, and she glares over in my direction. She doesn't move at first. But when Brayden doesn't seem to be budging, she grabs his hand and steps out of the SUV. She takes her time, though.

I wait patiently, trying unsuccessfully to wipe the grin off my face. I think it's stuck there.

Brayden tucks his little mother in the back seat and then runs over to me. He scoops me up into his arms like he's done every time he's greeted me. He takes my small bag and puts it in the trunk along with everyone else's bags. Of course, he helps me into the SUV as gingerly as he helped his mother out.

"Hello, Mr. and Mrs. Carpenter," I say as I put on my seat belt.

"Hey there, Ms. Chenille. I'm pretty sure I wanted you to call me Joseph. No need to be so formal."

Brayden's dad is so sweet. I don't understand how he survives with that sour lemon that he's married to.

"You ain't gone speak, Marilyn? Brayden's lady said hello."

Marilyn grunts something that sounds like words, but not quite. I'll accept this as a greeting, I suppose.

Brayden hops back in on his side, completely oblivious to his mother's rude behavior. I should've waited to speak until he'd gotten in, so he could see his mother disrespect me. Doesn't matter, though. Joseph heard her act a fool.

"Where exactly is the family reunion? Is it in Dallas?"

"Oh, no," Joseph says from the back seat. "This is my side of the family. We're in Longview. East Texas."

"The country. We're going to the country," Marilyn grumbles.

"Mom gets mad when we go to the Carpenter family reunions," Brayden says.

"No, I get mad when you make me go. You three could've gone without me."

"Well, we won't actually be staying in the country, will we?" I ask, now feeling a little concerned. "We're staying in a hotel, right?"

Marilyn cackles. "He didn't tell you."

"Baby, we're staying at my uncle Ralph's house. He's got six bedrooms."

"And no air conditioning, like this isn't Texas," Marilyn says. "Take me home."

"No air conditioning?"

"There are window units," Brayden says. "And fans. Lots of fans."

Oh, my goodness. What did I get myself into? That crazy cackling Marilyn is doing in the back seat is scaring me.

"Good thing your hair is already nappy," Marilyn says, "because can't nobody keep a hairstyle in Ralph's hot house."

Now this is funny, even though I'm sure Marilyn meant it as a low-key insult.

"I am happily nappy," I say as I fluff my afro.

"And I love it," Brayden says. "I love my baby natural."

"We get it. She's your girlfriend," Marilyn says.

"I'm glad, because I'm keeping her."

He's keeping me?

"Good for you, son," Joseph says. "That's what Carpenter men do. We stake our claim."

Part of me wants to argue about this. Staking a claim sounds like something a caveman might do to capture his woman, right before he bopped her upside the head and dragged her away by her hair. I don't know if I want to be claimed if it includes bopping or dragging.

Then, another part of me likes the idea of a man wanting me for his very own. Brayden's persistence in this is attractive and has worn me down. He's starting to feel like family; like he belongs in my life. Permanently.

Even though I feel like he's one hundred percent my man right now, I hope he doesn't think he's getting some of this cookie while we're underneath his uncle's roof. Hell and no. There will be no union at the family reunion.

Chapter 15

"**B**aby . . . please?"

Brayden tried giving Chenille his most pitiful face as he asked her for the tenth time if she'd let him get a little treat in their bedroom at Uncle Ralph's house. He could tell by her face that she wasn't budging.

"These walls are thin as a piece of paper," Chenille whispered, "and this bed is squeaky and loud. I think they gave us the loudest bed in the house."

She was right. The bed was extremely loud, and the walls were so thin you could hear someone breathing in the next room. But everybody knew that Brayden was a grown man visiting with his grown lady. There was the expectation that something was going down between them. No one minded them sharing the same bedroom, so no one would mind them doing what adults do in the bedroom.

"Everybody knows we're having sex, Chenille."

"Everybody who? How do they know? You told your mama we had sex?"

Brayden laughed. "No, but come on. They know I'm an NFL player. I been getting coochie thrown at me since middle school."

"Coochie? Yuck. I hate that word."

"Okay. What do you want me to say? I've been having lady parts offered to me since I was a boy."

"Better."

"Milady. Will you please let me partake of your lady bits and parts?"

"So you just gonna keep asking like I didn't already answer you on this?"

Brayden sighed and nodded. "You're right. That's rude."

"Now if you want to get us a hotel room . . ."

"Can't do it. Uncle Ralph will be hurt, and my mama will want to go with us."

"Absolutely not."

Brayden watched Chenille unpack her small bag and place the items in drawers. Then she did the same with his bag, hanging his shirts and jeans in the closet. He imagined her doing the same thing in their own home.

Brayden couldn't wait to have a forever with Chenille.

"A friend of mine told me that the Atlanta Sharks are looking for a makeup artist for their cheerleader calendar."

"The NBA team?"

Brayden nodded. "I told them to stop looking, because you are exactly who they need."

"Thank you, babe."

Chenille put the last of his clothing to the side and crossed the room, joining Brayden on the edge of the bed. She kissed his cheek.

"Did you tell me about that recommendation so you could get some?" Chenille asked.

"No. I just hadn't had the chance to tell you yet. I gave them your number and the highest recommendation I could think of."

"I appreciate that. Thank you for telling people about my business."

"I want you to be successful, even if you don't need to be."

Chenille's eyebrows furrowed into a knotted frown. "What do you mean, even if I don't need to be?"

"I just mean that you won't need to work or make money

soon. I'll take care of every bill you have to pay. You won't have to worry about anything."

"So, you think if we're living together or married that I won't need to work?"

"You won't need money."

"I don't just work for money. I love what I do."

"I know."

Brayden watched Chenille ball her fists tightly and then loosen them again. She relaxed and looked into Brayden's eyes.

"You have to understand, Brayden, I'm not one of those women who is sitting around waiting for a man to rescue her. I know you're rich. I don't care about that."

"And I love that about you. I still want to take care of you, though."

"Taking care of me doesn't mean paying my bills. Taking care of me means having my back, supporting me, and not cheating on me."

"That other guy didn't take care of you."

"He did not."

Brayden slipped Chenille's hand in his, lifted it to his mouth, and kissed each of Chenille's fingers. Their eyes met, and Brayden held her gaze for a long moment.

"Baby, I'm always gonna take care of you."

Tears fell from Chenille's eyes, and Brayden kissed them away. He didn't know or understand the pain behind her tears, but Brayden knew that he didn't ever want to be the one to cause her pain.

Chapter 16

Brayden and I sit down at the card table, because it's our turn to play spades against his uncle Ralph and RJ, Ralph's son. I should say it's our turn to spank their butts, because I am a beast in spades. Brayden probably just picked me as his partner because I'm his girlfriend, but he made the best choice.

And these two have been cheating all night. I see what they're doing.

RJ tells Uncle Ralph how many spades he has in his hand by either scratching his head or flicking his nose. If he has six spades, then he scratches six times. If he has two, then he flicks two times. Ralph flares his nostrils when he has at least one of the jokers in the deck.

"You ready, babe?" Brayden asks.

"Sure am."

"No talking over the table," RJ fusses. "Y'all think 'cause y'all a couple you gonna use your secret mind language on us."

Secret mind language. Oh, dear God, he's not very smart.

"We don't have any secret mind language," Brayden says.

"But we still 'bout to whoop y'all," I say.

RJ and Uncle Ralph start making all kinds of noise now. All I can do is laugh, because we really are about to whoop them. Uncle Ralph only scratched his head twice, and Ralph ain't flared nostril the first. I have no hearts and no clubs in my hand. Straight diamonds and spades.

"Your girl a shit talker, I see," RJ says.

"I can back it up, though. Stop yapping and let's get this over with."

Brayden drops his first card. Ace of hearts. I play one of my four diamonds. RJ's and Ralph's eyes widen. They can tell now who's carrying all the trump cards in this game.

I wink at RJ. "What you say now?" I ask.

Brayden's turn again, since his ace walked. He plays the ace of clubs. Again, I play a diamond, and let my partner's high card win.

"Y'all sure y'all don't want to throw this hand in?" I ask. "You're not gonna make those four books you bid. You're not even gonna make one."

Uncle Ralph scoffs. "We don't do that 'round here. We play the hand."

"All right. I was going to let you save your dignity."

Brayden plays a king of clubs and a king of hearts, winning back to back books. The rest of these are mine, of that I'm sure. Brayden starts off their destruction by playing a five of diamonds, opening the door for all my trump cards.

The next nine books are mine. We run a Boston on them, which in spades means we got all the books.

Brayden high-fives me across the table.

We go on to spank every other team that sits down at the table with us. This is our table. We might as well pack this table up and put it in Brayden's Escalade. It's ours. We run this.

Then Marilyn and Joseph sit down. Brayden lifts his eyebrows at me.

I clear my throat.

"I hope you two don't think we're going to let you win," I say.

Marilyn laughs. "*Let* us win? Honey, you just don't know."

It's a long and drawn-out game. Brayden and I take the first two hands and get a sizable lead, but then Marilyn and Joseph set us in the third hand. This means they kept us from getting the number of books that we bid, subtracting major points from our score. Then they win the next two hands in a row. Brayden looks worried, but I think we might get it in the next hand.

The next hand I'm dealt is marginal. Maybe three or four books, but all vulnerable to a trump-heavy hand by either Marilyn or Joseph. Brayden has a horrible poker face, so I can tell that his hand is just okay.

"How many books you want to bid?" I ask.

Brayden shrugs. "What do you have?"

That's a bad sign. He's not confidently declaring what he can pull, so I know it's little to nothing.

"Let's go six," I say.

"We only need five to win," Brayden says.

"True, but they only need seven to win. We need that little extra."

Marilyn cackles. "Good strategy. If only you had the hand to pull it off. I can tell by the contents of my hand what you're *not* holding."

"Just play the hand," I say.

As we play out the hand, it is obvious who's going to make the most points in this game. As long as we can pull out six books, though, we have a chance to win.

Marilyn turns the first five books on her own. There is no way we're going to get eight more books.

Finally, Brayden pulls in a book with the ace of diamonds. We get a couple more points with aces and kings of our own. Then, both Marilyn and Joseph take the hand over, taking turns winning books, until all the cards have been played.

Set again. Shoot.

"You two played an honorable game," Marilyn says. "You were just no match for grown folk."

"We were ready. You and Daddy cheat," Brayden says.

"No, we don't," Joseph objects. "Your mama just knows how to play some cards. You ought to get her to teach your girlfriend."

"Maybe next time," Marilyn says, "Brayden will bring a girl who can be more of a challenge at the card table."

If she'd gotten up, slapped me in the face, and gouged my eyes out, it would've hurt less. Brayden's smile fades as quickly as mine, and he pulls me close to his side.

"She brings a lot to the table. Period. And I won't be bringing another woman here, so get used to my baby."

I smile, but I still feel insecure. Maybe it's because of Marilyn's cackle, like she knows something I don't know.

Chapter 17

Brayden could tell his mother didn't like Chenille. What he couldn't figure out was why she didn't like Chenille.

At the family reunion, Chenille had been classy and witty. She'd dressed modestly and had sparked interesting conversation at the dinner table. Everyone loved her except his mother. Brayden thought his mother should have been thrilled with his choice. He could've chosen a groupie.

So Brayden invited Marilyn to brunch, just the two of them, because she wouldn't be candid in front of his father. She never was.

Brayden was early. He wanted to get his mother's favorite seat at the high-end Tex-Mex brunch buffet. He preferred a soul food brunch, but this was about his mother's feelings, so he was going to butter her up with her favorites.

"Mr. Carpenter, we've reserved your table," the hostess said. "Let me know when your mother arrives."

"I'm here!"

Brayden scrambled to his feet. He hadn't seen his mother walk in. She was wearing white, and with her freshly straightened hair and expertly applied makeup, she looked more like Brayden's date than his mother.

Brayden hugged her and kissed both of her cheeks.

"I am starving," Marilyn said. "I've been fasting for the past few days."

Fasting? Brayden sighed. His mother fasted and prayed when she believed she had an insurmountable problem.

They sat at the table, and a waitress appeared immediately.

"I will have a pineapple juice mimosa," Marilyn said. "And would you mind bringing me a selection of items from the buffet? I am worn out."

The waitress seemed confused and unsure of what she should do next. She wasn't supposed to serve guests from the buffet, but since Brayden was a star player from the Dallas Knights, Marilyn felt the rules didn't apply to her.

The hostess, who was used to seeing Brayden and Marilyn at the restaurant, ran up to the table.

"She wants me to serve her from the buffet," the waitress said.

"Absolutely, Mrs. Carpenter," the hostess said. "Would you like that as well, Mr. Carpenter?"

Brayden opened his mouth to object, but his mother beat him to respond.

"Yes, he would like that. Thank you, dear."

Brayden smiled at the hostess and waitress, hoping that it conveyed his apologies. Their tip was going to be epic.

"Why do you dislike Chenille?"

Marilyn's nostrils flared just a tiny bit, showing her mild irritation at the question.

"Oh, goodness. You're getting right to the point, I see. She was perfectly fine, just not my daughter-in-law."

"What does that mean?"

"It means I don't have any intentions on getting emotionally attached to her. She's not your wife."

"I think she might be my wife. I have never met anyone like her."

"I didn't send you to all those private schools and to the University of Texas for you to marry a 'round-the-way hood chick."

"She's not that."

"A respectable young woman wouldn't show up to our family reunion with those nappy little ropes all over her head."

Brayden stared at his mother in disbelief. He wanted to rewind the conversation and never ask her opinion.

"I love her hair in braids."

"What happened to the kinds of girls you dated in high school?"

Brayden shook his head. The majority of the girls he'd dated in high school had been white or biracial.

"And you just had to find the darkest berry in the bunch," she blurted in an exasperated tone.

"Mama, she is your complexion."

It was true. Chenille's skin color was the same smooth ebony as Marilyn's.

"Listen, I'm not saying anything bad about her. I'm just saying you can do better. Get a woman befitting your status."

"She is befitting my status. Chenille is incredible, and I hate that you can't see that."

"Have you met her family yet?"

"No, not yet."

"I want to make you a small wager, son. Five dollars says that she's the best her family has to offer. She probably made it out of a broken home. I bet she learned to apply makeup by watching her mama get dressed for dates with different men every night."

Brayden scoffed. "You're being ridiculous."

"Five dollars. Wait, you don't have to give me the money. When you find out that what I'm saying is true, I want you to walk away and act like you never knew her."

Brayden remained silent. He didn't care what kind of home Chenille came from. If what his mother said was true, then it made Chenille even more of a miracle. It meant she had the tenacity to overcome any situation.

"I can tell you aren't listening to me, as if I haven't lived a lifetime," Marilyn said. "If you don't hear anything else I say, hear this: whatever you do, don't get that girl pregnant."

"I'm going to marry her and then get her pregnant. Maybe three or four times. I want sons and daughters with her. And they're going to be your grandchildren."

"There's nothing I can do to stop you, but I really wish you would investigate further before giving this woman your entire heart and your last name."

Brayden shook his head sadly. He had already given Chenille his entire heart. He wished his mother would celebrate with him.

"Mama, can you please just be happy for me?"

Marilyn sighed. "I've spent your whole life protecting you. I can't help feeling like this."

"I'm a grown man now. And I've chosen my woman. You don't have to like her, but you'll respect her, or you won't be in my life."

"Meet the family first, son, before you decide to kick me out of your life. Then, talk to me afterwards."

Brayden wasn't afraid of meeting Chenille's family. If anything, meeting them would prove everything that he already knew. The people who raised the love of his life had to be amazing.

Didn't they?

Chapter 18

When Brayden casually mentioned that he wanted to meet my parents, he caught me off guard. I mean, I was going to invite him at some point, maybe even for Thanksgiving or Christmas, but he beat me to it. His request seemed urgent, though, so I couldn't deny it.

I asked my parents to come to my house to meet Brayden, thinking that it might be a more neutral location than their house, in case things don't go well. But I'm tripping. Why wouldn't things go well? They will go well.

Kara is here, helping me clean. The cleaning part isn't for Brayden. It's for my mama. She's always trying to find some dirt when she comes over here, and she always does. It seems my cleaning is never on par with hers. The last thing I want to do is have her embarrass me in front of Brayden about my house-keeping. Because it wouldn't even be on purpose if she did call me out. She can't help it. She just blurts stuff out.

"When is the last time you high dusted?" Kara asks while standing on a chair in front of my bookshelves.

"High dust? Is that different from regular dusting?"

"Yes. It's when you make an effort to get the dust from high places, like the tops of these bookshelves."

She takes a swipe at the shelf and a huge cloud of dust rises into the air. Kara coughs and shakes her head.

"Oh . . . I guess never," I reply. "I had no idea there was that much dust up there. My bad."

Kara wipes the rest of the shelf off and then sits down. There is dust in her hair. I feel horrible about that. I'm sure she just got her hair done.

"Girl, you should've hired a housecleaning service."

"It's not that bad."

"Yes, it is. Brayden is going to think you're disgusting."

"He loves me, and shoot, I run a business. I don't have time to high dust, low dust, or any other dust."

"Do you love him?"

I sit at the dining room table and fold my hands in front of me. I have been afraid to say this out loud, like if I let the words out into the atmosphere something might go wrong. It might be jinxed.

"Well? Do you?" Kara pesters.

"Kara, he's everything."

"What do you mean?"

"I mean all the stuff we sit around and say we want the perfect guy to be. He's all of it."

"So why the hesitation?"

"Because what happens when women fall in love?"

"We get married and live happily the hell after?"

"No . . . we start having children, making casseroles, and decorating for holidays. And then we disappear."

"Maybe you won't. Not with Brayden. He supports you so much."

"He does. And I do love him."

There. It's out. In the atmosphere.

"See. That wasn't so bad. It was a lot easier than cleaning this house."

"Shut up."

"What are you cooking? At least you have that part down. Has he ever had your cooking?"

"I'm doing my buttermilk fried chicken, macaroni and cheese, Brussel sprouts, and candied yams. Baking a couple things, too. Pound cake, and he mentioned that he loves a good peach cobbler."

"When does he get here?"

"In the morning."

Kara bursts into laughter. "Girl, when are you going to have time to cook all that?"

"As soon as we finish cleaning, I'm going to do my baking. Everything else I can do in the morning."

"I was thinking you'd have to pick him up from the airport. He hired a car service, I'm sure."

"No. My daddy is picking him up."

"You're leaving Brayden and your father alone for their first meeting?"

"Yes. What's wrong with that? My daddy is cool."

"Nobody's daddy is cool with the man who's hitting his daughter's spot."

I crack up laughing, but then my laughter fades. I hadn't thought about it like that. I don't think my father is going to say or do anything crazy in front of Brayden.

Wait.

Oh, my goodness. My father is going to absolutely say something crazy in front of Brayden.

Chapter 19

Brayden stood in front of the baggage claim at Atlanta Hartsfield Airport rehearsing his speech to Chenille's father over and over in his mind. It wasn't a coincidence that Mr. Abrams volunteered to pick him up from the airport. It was confirmation that this was the right time to do what he planned to do.

Brayden's mother's words weighed heavily on his heart. He didn't need to meet Chenille's parents to decide about the love of his life, but he wanted his mother to accept the woman he had chosen. Maybe if he complied with this one requirement, Marilyn would stop complaining.

When the glistening white old-school Cadillac pulled up in front of Brayden, he chuckled. He imagined Chenille's father driving a pickup truck or something like that. She was so organic and earthy, he expected her parents to be laid back.

Mr. Abrams got out of the car, and Brayden couldn't do anything but smile. The man was clean. He had his autumn colors on, with his dark mustard shade leather sport coat and cream fitted t-shirt. The jeans were the kind worn by a much younger man, but Mr. Abrams had taken care of himself, and was in great shape, so the fitted jeans looked just fine. The outfit was made complete with his proper brimmed brown hat that matched his shoes.

"Come on there, young man," Mr. Abrams said. "Don't want a ticket. Put your bag in the trunk and get in."

Brayden lifted his eyebrows in surprise. He'd expected a warmer welcome. It's not every day a man's daughter brings home a professional football player. Maybe Mr. Abrams wasn't a football fan.

"Brayden Carpenter, sir. Good to meet you."

Mr. Abrams nodded politely. "Kent Abrams. It's good to finally meet you as well."

The two men got into the car on opposite sides. Brayden wondered if the *finally* was a bad thing. It could mean that Mr. Abrams had been anticipating their meeting. It could also mean that Brayden had taken too long to show his face.

He wasn't sure which was true.

"Mr. Abrams," Brayden asked as they pulled away from the curb, "I'd like to take you for a cup of coffee, before we meet up with your wife and Chenille."

"Coffee, huh?"

"You don't drink coffee?"

"I do. But it's afternoon. I'd much prefer a taste of bourbon."

Brayden laughed. "You're going to get us in trouble with the ladies."

"Nah. One drink won't ruffle them too much. Call me Kent, by the way."

"One drink it is, then," Brayden said with a grin.

Brayden relaxed a little. Kent had put them on a first-name basis. That was a good thing.

"Surprised the hell out of me when Chenille said she was introducing us."

"Really, why?"

"The last guy she brought home didn't end up sticking."

"It wasn't her idea that we meet. It was mine."

Kent gave a laugh that came from his belly. "Might've been

your idea, but Chenille is all grit, son. If she didn't want it, it wouldn't be happening."

"Fair enough. She is all grit."

Kent pulled into the parking lot of a small bar and stopped the car.

"Let's go and get that bourbon," Kent said.

Brayden followed Kent into the bar, noticing their difference in height and width. Kent was not a small man, but he was nowhere near as imposing as Brayden. So much for the idea that women fell in love with their fathers. Looks-wise the men couldn't be more different.

The two men sat at the bar, and Kent removed his hat, revealing a head full of salt-and-pepper curls. He looked much older that way, but still as distinguished.

"Your regular?" the bartender asked Kent.

Kent nodded. "Two. Get one for him, too."

It felt strange not to be recognized. He was known in Atlanta, but not at this hole in the wall bar. There wasn't a place in Dallas Brayden could go without being noticed.

The drinks came quickly: double shots of bourbon in grown-man glasses. Brayden raised his glass.

"Cheers."

Kent nodded and smiled. "I hope we've got something to celebrate."

"Well, now that you say that, there is something I'd like to talk to you about."

Kent drank his bourbon all the way down. Brayden did the same. They set the glasses down on the table and stared at each other.

"Speak your mind," Kent said.

Brayden wondered if it was too soon or if he should just go ahead and say it. He didn't know Kent. Maybe he'd think Brayden was an idiot for doing this. Maybe he'd be insulted that the first thing Brayden wanted to talk about was marrying his daughter.

What if he didn't bless a damn thing? What would the rest of the weekend look like then?

Quickly, Brayden decided.

"I want to ask Chenille to be my wife, sir. I know it's old-fashioned, but I wanted to get your blessing first."

Kent smiled. Then he chuckled. Then his chuckle turned into a full-bodied laugh.

"Sir?"

"I sure appreciate you being a man and asking for my daughter's hand in marriage."

"But . . ."

"She would be mad as hell about this."

Brayden relaxed, exhaled, and joined in the laughter.

"I know she would, but I want your respect, Kent. I didn't think you'd respect me if I didn't ask."

"I'm sure that when I get to know you, I'll have plenty to respect. I trust my baby girl's judgment."

"Yes, sir."

"You planning to do it this weekend?"

"Um, no, sir. I'm still picking out the ring."

"So, it's a secret? You trust me to keep it?"

Brayden nodded. "I don't know if I trust Mrs. Abrams, though."

"Smart man. Let's go see about those women. I'm sure my daughter is panicking about me saying something crazy to you."

"Why would she think that?"

"Because I pegged her last boyfriend from the very start. Said he'd cheat, and didn't mind that he heard me."

"How did you know?"

"He couldn't keep his eyes off my wife's behind. His girlfriend's mother. Didn't even have enough respect to do that."

"She didn't listen to you."

"She did not."

"Maybe she will this time."

Kent shook his head. "This time I'll keep my opinion to myself. It might give you a fighting chance."

Brayden hoped he had more than a chance with Chenille, especially since she already had his heart. He was, however, happy that his mother was wrong so far.

Kent was going to make a great father-in-law.

Chapter 20

My mother loved Brayden from the very start. She's been fussing over him since he and Daddy came from the airport smelling like bourbon. She was easy, though. My father is harder to impress, so I'm watching him more closely.

"You met in Jamaica?" Mama asks. "How romantic. Every woman dreams of meeting a handsome, rich man on a vacation."

I have never dreamed that.

"I was there working, though. I was looking for my paycheck."

Daddy laughs. "My girl."

"She was working, and I was eavesdropping on her conversation with the front desk clerk at the hotel," Brayden says.

"He was a lifesaver," I say. "I owed him a date after he gave me and Kara his hotel suite."

"Well, I don't care what you say, that is romantic," Mama says.

"I suppose."

Brayden clears his throat, I guess sensing my discomfort with this conversation. It's not that I don't want to talk about my man to my parents. It's just that they've only recently seen me brokenhearted, and might not have that image out of their heads yet. The image is only recently removed from the forefront of my mind.

"Any big holiday plans?" Brayden asks. "Or traditions?"

"It's usually just the three of us," Daddy says. "Unless we get on the road and drive to Baton Rouge to meet up with my brother and his family."

Yes, my Louisiana cousins. Mama doesn't really get along with them—they're too bougie—but every now and then we do go there for the holidays. I wonder what Mama will think of Brayden's folks. Marilyn is a step beyond bougie. She acts like a one percenter, but not the mellow generational wealth kind. She acts like the nouveau riche, the ones who are living large now but have government surplus cheese in their history.

Plus, Marilyn doesn't like me. So I think she and my mama aren't going to be fast friends. Or friends at all.

"Would you like to join us in Dallas for Christmas? I wanted to ask Chenille if she'd come, but I haven't had the chance."

I tighten my lips into a line. "You should've asked me. I've got a gig."

I'm not going to mention that it's not an important gig. It's a junior pageant being put on by a local modeling agency. The show is on Christmas morning at an Atlanta megachurch. I can absolutely hand it off to someone else, probably even Kara.

It doesn't matter, though. Brayden should've asked me first before he invited my parents to Dallas.

Brayden looks contrite, but the anger on my face doesn't fade. He needs to stop being such a man's man all the time. It's never necessary and almost always gets on my damn nerves.

"Sorry, babe. Maybe another time, then. Thanksgiving?"

"I'll let you know. Let's talk about it later. I think the food is almost ready. Oven timer on the macaroni and cheese just dinged."

I rush into the kitchen to get the food ready for the table, and Brayden rushes in behind me. I wish he would just give me a moment, but he won't. Whenever I'm angry at him, he hovers until he knows everything is all right.

"I'm sorry, babe," Brayden says. "I thought it would be okay to ask."

I bend over and take the macaroni and cheese out of the oven. It's perfectly bubbly and golden with a few dark brown spots. Exactly how it should look.

"Always check dates with me. My schedule is all over the place. I may or may not be available."

"I don't know what I was thinking," he says. "Do you forgive me?"

"Only if you stop doing that."

"Promise that was the last time."

I can't stay angry at this man. Not with his huge, brown, pleading eyes and his perfectly kissable lips this close to my face.

He bends down and steals a kiss. "That looks and smells amazing."

"Help me finish setting the table then. Bring that pan of chicken and bowl of candied yams to the table."

Brayden and I bring out the remainder of the food: the Brussel sprouts and the biscuits, sweet tea and a bottle of wine.

When we're all seated at the table, Brayden and I facing each other and Mama and Daddy facing each other, I look over at my father.

"Will you bless the food, Daddy?"

"Thank you, Lord, for this lovely meal prepared by my lovely daughter. Bless her home and new relationship. Thank you for this time of fellowship, in Jesus's name."

We all say amen, but I stare at my daddy for a moment. He prayed blessings over me and Brayden. That was nice, but completely unlike him. He never likes my boyfriends. Ever. And he's never been wrong about any of them.

"So, Brayden, Chenille tells me that you're an only child as well," Mama says. "Did you always want siblings?"

"Yes, I always did. My mother wasn't having it, though. She would send me to stay with my cousins in East Texas anytime I got lonely for friends to play with."

"Chenille never wanted brothers and sisters," Daddy says.

"She enjoys having all of our attention to herself, I think."

"Yes, you're right, Daddy. I'm not sharing."

"I hope to have a couple of children one day," Brayden says. "Lots of my teammates are already fathers, and they bring their kids to workouts and training camp. I want my own little mini-mes."

When I don't chime in, Brayden raises his eyebrows in my direction. "You do want children, right?"

"Someday, I suppose. I've got a lot that I want to do first, though."

"Well, you two can talk about that another time," Mama says.

I think she knows me well enough to know that this isn't a conversation I want to have in front of her and Daddy. Brayden has a much more open relationship with his parents than I do. I love them, but I keep my private life private. Outside of an introduction to my boyfriends, I really don't talk to them about this kind of thing.

"The food is delicious," Brayden says, changing the subject to a safer one. "I've never had fried chicken this crispy yet juicy all at the same time. What did you do to it?"

"Buttermilk brine and my cast-iron skillet are the only secrets."

"Well, you could sell this chicken. It's that good."

"You think?"

Brayden's face goes slack, like he wants to gobble his words back into his mouth. He probably doesn't want to give me another business idea. He's having a hard enough time dealing with me as a makeup artist.

"Maybe I could do catering-slash-glam events where women come to get a plate of soul food and leave with perfectly contoured faces," I gush as Brayden looks even sicker. "Thank you, babe. This is a wonderful idea."

"She's just messing with you, man," Daddy says when it looks like Brayden is about to pass out at the table.

Brayden looks so relieved now. Too relieved, if I'm being honest.

"I was just thinking how hard it might be for us to be a couple if you added another dimension to your business," Brayden says. "I only meant to compliment your cooking, because it is incredible. Sorry, I panicked. I didn't get the joke."

"It's okay, babe. My humor is very, very dry sometimes."

"That does bring up an interesting topic, though," my mama says. "What if you two become more permanent? How will you handle your business here in Atlanta, sweetheart? Brayden's job is clearly in Dallas."

"I guess we'll use a lot of airline miles flying back and forth. The core of my business, for now, is here in this city, although I hope to become national."

"Maybe you could start building up clientele in Dallas, too," Brayden says.

Why would I do that when I live in Atlanta? Brayden is dropping bombs left and right in this conversation. First Christmas, and now he wants me to move my business to Dallas? Why is he on hyper relationship drive right now?

"Can I have a word with you outside for a quick second?" I ask.

"We're eating dinner," Brayden says. "Can it wait?"

"No."

Brayden nods and slowly places his napkin on the table. We have to go outside, because my condo is tiny, and there isn't a room in here that wouldn't let my parents hear our conversation.

I close my front door behind us and walk up the driveway to the street. Brayden follows me.

"What's wrong with you?" I ask.

"What do you mean? Nothing."

"You are tripping, Brayden. You come here inviting my parents to Christmas and then asking me to get Dallas clients. We're not there yet in our relationship."

"I'm there."

His two words take all the steam out of my attack. I don't know how to respond now.

"I thought we were here together," Brayden says. "I'm not just trying to have a girlfriend. We're sleeping together. You've met my parents, and my extended family. I told my mother I want to have a forever with you, and she said I need to meet your parents first."

"You're here because your mama said you need to be here?"

"I'm here because I don't want anyone to have anything to say about us. And yes, I mean my mother."

"I haven't thought about moving to Dallas. Like that's not even on my radar."

Brayden inhales sharply and shakes his head. "I never thought this would happen to me."

"This? What's happening? I'm confused."

Brayden paces the driveway with his arms folded across his chest. I'm acutely aware of the possibility that my parents are peeking out my living room blinds to see what's going on.

"Do you think we're moving too fast?" Brayden asks as he stops in front of me.

"I didn't until just a few minutes ago. We were going at a fine pace, and then warp speed. Are we in a rush?"

"I'm not in a rush, but I want marriage and children. I want a family. And I want all of that with you."

I stand staring at Brayden. I'm abundantly clear on what he wants. I'm not so sure he knows anything about what I want.

"And what about me? What do I want?"

Brayden sighs. "Tell me."

"No. *You* tell *me*! You're the one making all the moves and throwing out all the curve balls. You tell me what I want."

"You want to be with me, but you want to remain autonomous. You want your business above everything else."

"Not above everything else, Brayden, but it is very important that I protect my brand. What if you wake up one day and decide you don't want to be with me anymore? I have to be able to sustain myself without your help."

"You don't believe in forever?"

He's right. I don't trust it. I don't trust *this*. I've been here before, in love so thick that I couldn't cut myself out of it. In love so consuming that it stole everything from me. But here I am yet again. Right at the point of letting go.

"I want to believe."

Brayden pulls me into his arms. He plants soft kisses all over my forehead, my nose, and my eyelids.

"Babe. You can have us and your business, just like I can have us and football. You don't have to give anything up to be with me."

"But you're talking about babies."

"One day. When you're ready. Okay?"

"Okay."

"Can I finish my chicken now?"

"Yeah."

He kisses me again, this time on the lips, and then he runs back to my front door. I take my time getting back. I'm letting his words sink in. I can have both. I can have my business and my football player.

Letting go of my irritation now, because I want both. I just have to convince Brayden to press the brakes a little. Maybe it's not time for us to think about babies and moving businesses across the country, but I can give Brayden something. I can give him Christmas.

Chapter 21

Brayden was beyond thrilled that Chenille had switched things around with her gig so that she could accompany her parents to Dallas for Christmas. Now Mr. and Mrs. Abrams were going to meet Mr. and Mrs. Carpenter.

Marilyn had to be prepped for this.

The best way for Brayden to get his mother in a good mood was with shopping. Marilyn loved finally having nice things, and Brayden loved spoiling her. As judgmental and annoying as she could be, Brayden remembered when she'd worked extra shifts to pay for private school and football gear while his father's check paid the household bills.

Brayden picked Marilyn up and took her to her favorite mall in Dallas—NorthPark Center.

"What are you in the mood for today?" Brayden asked as they strolled past the Neiman Marcus store.

"I want to look at the new Louis Vuitton handbags."

"Okay."

When Brayden and Marilyn walked into the Louis Vuitton store, they were greeted with smiles. Marilyn was a frequent visitor and big spender. At least three times a year, Brayden dropped thousands in that store for his mother: Christmas, Mother's Day, and her birthday.

"Would you like to see the new collection, Mrs. Carpenter?" the friendly clerk asked.

"Absolutely, dear."

Brayden ignored the openly flirtatious glances of the store employees. He hadn't always ignored them, but they didn't mean much to him anymore. They weren't Chenille.

Marilyn seemed a bit distracted as she perused the selections the salespeople provided. This wasn't like her at all. Usually, when it came to spending money she was laser focused.

"What do you think, son?"

She draped a small brown-and-burgundy clutch over her shoulder and posed. Brayden smiled, although he had no opinion whatsoever.

"You don't care, do you?" Marilyn chuckled.

"Mama, get whatever you like. It all looks about the same to me."

Marilyn looked at the young woman behind the counter and shook her head. "Men."

"We don't mind, as long as they're buying," the salesperson said.

"Truth," Brayden said. "So leave me out of the selection process."

Brayden absentmindedly checked his phone for any text messages from Chenille. They'd already spoken in the morning, but it seemed like it was too long ago. Brayden hated not getting to see Chenille every day.

Marilyn had her purchases wrapped up and promptly handed Brayden the bag when she was done.

"What's on your mind, son?" Marilyn asked as they walked out of the store.

"Mama, I went to Atlanta, and met Chenille's parents like you suggested."

Her eyes widened. "When did this happen?"

"A couple of months ago. They're great, Mama. Nothing at all like you thought they'd be."

"Well, I'm happy that I'm wrong."

Now Brayden was the one surprised. He'd never heard the words *I'm wrong* come out of his mother's mouth.

"Since you seem determined to be with this girl, I'm glad she's not from a broken ghetto home."

"I would be with her even if she was."

"I know it."

Marilyn fiddled with her shopping bag, clearly flustered, and Brayden enjoyed every moment of it. He was a man, in control of his own life and his own love. Mama was just going to have to get on board Brayden's love train.

"Well, good," Brayden said. "Because they're coming here for Christmas. Staying at my house in Southlake, and we're going to enjoy the holiday together."

Marilyn swooned. Brayden steadied her, although he recognized the theatrics as just what they were.

"You could've given me more warning."

"You didn't need a warning, Mama. They are guests at my home, not yours."

"Is everything in order? Which caterer did you use for dinner? There's so much to do . . ."

Brayden laughed at his mother. He knew she'd want to take over and turn this into a Marilyn function, but that's not how it was going down.

"Well, Mrs. Abrams thought it would be nice if you all cooked together. The women."

"How prehistoric and country. Women are supposed to be in the kitchen while the men do what? Are you going turkey hunting?"

Brayden laughed so hard that his midsection hurt. He doubled over and clutched his stomach.

"When I visited, I found out that Chenille is an awesome cook. She and her mother have a holiday cooking tradition. They're inviting you to join."

"I don't cook, Brayden."

"I'll alert Chenille, so she can only give you the easy stuff."

"No, you won't! You'll do no such thing."

This was going to be hilarious. Brayden almost wanted a camera crew in the kitchen to capture what was sure to be reality-television worthy.

"Okay, okay, I won't say anything. But can you do one thing for me?"

Marilyn cut her eyes at Brayden and scowled. "What now?"

"Will you go over to Tiffany and Company with me, to help me pick out an engagement ring for Chenille?"

Marilyn's jaw dropped, and she nearly dropped her shopping bag. Brayden caught it.

"T-that's happening over the h-holiday?"

Brayden shook his head. "No, not quite. I think she'll be expecting it, and I want to surprise her."

"But you want me to help you pick her ring."

"No one has better taste than you, Mama. And I want her to love it."

Surprisingly, Marilyn smiled. "She will love it."

Brayden hoped his mother's excitement about the ring was a good omen about the holiday weekend. And that it was enough to make her forget about her kitchen duties.

Chapter 22

"**D**o you have everything you need for the holiday feast?" Brayden asks my mama as he shows us around his huge kitchen.

I've been to this house, the Southlake mansion, but we've spent most of our time at Brayden's Dallas condo after the games. This house is gargantuan, and the kitchen is almost overwhelming. My mama is excited, though. You would think she was at an amusement park.

"Baby, you've bought just about every spice they had in the store, didn't you?"

My mama closes the spice cabinet and chuckles. Everything looks brand-new, like no one has ever cooked in here before.

"Has this kitchen been used, babe?" I ask.

"I've hosted a couple of parties here, and the caterers have used it, but then the cleaning crew comes in and makes it look brand-new again."

"What do you eat when you're here?" my mama asks.

"Protein shakes mostly, and I juice."

"Oh, my word."

Brayden doesn't know that he almost took my mother out saying he only has protein shakes and juice. She can't take someone not eating. She's probably going to make sure he eats three or four plates of her food.

Just as my laughter is about to emerge at Brayden's skimpy meals, an even funnier sight walks into the kitchen: Marilyn, in full chef's garb. She's wearing a large white hat with black polka dots and a scarf to match, a black apron that says *I own the kitchen*, and two oven mitts.

"Hello, all. Let's get this cooking show on the road."

"Mama," Brayden says, "let me introduce you to Mrs. Abrams."

Marilyn walks over and extends her oven mitt in my mama's face. "Do call me Marilyn," she says.

"And I'm Charlene," Mama says. "Pleased to meet you."

"Well, what's first? The bird or the pig?" Marilyn asks.

"We're going to do a beef roast and a turkey. No pig. Do you want to have a ham? I'm sure Brayden can find us one," Mama says.

"Oh, no," Marilyn says. "I thought the pork was mandatory for a down-south Christmas dinner."

"We have ham on Thanksgiving and Easter at our house," Mama explains, "and I like to put turkey tails in the greens and green beans."

"Turkey tails? I wasn't aware that turkeys had tails."

Mama helps slide off Marilyn's oven mitts. "Let me show you everything we have in the kitchen," she says.

I grab Brayden and pull him out of the kitchen, struggling to hold in my laughter. We step into the downstairs entertainment room, and I close the door behind us. As soon as the doorknob clicks the giggles pour out.

"Your mother has never done this before, has she?"

"Nah. She's not much of a cook."

"The chef hat, though? Really?"

"She's into the cooking fashion, probably not the cooking too much."

"My mama is nice, Brayden. She won't make her feel bad at all. If it was me in there, by myself, I might be tempted to get revenge."

"Don't be tempted," Brayden says. "She's coming around. She's going to love you pretty soon."

"What changed her mind?"

"I did. She's never seen me this happy."

Brayden wraps his deliciously muscular arms around my midsection. His body presses against mine as he places slow kisses on my neck. There's more heat in here than in the kitchen.

"I can just let them cook, and we can slip away . . ."

Brayden kisses me once more and then releases his embrace. "My mother is looking forward to this, babe. She wants to impress your mother. We can finish this later."

"Promise?"

"Pinky swear."

Brayden opens the door and holds my hand as we walk back into the kitchen. Mama is now wearing a matching hat and apron to Marilyn's outfit.

"Where did you two slip off to?" Marilyn asks, then shakes her head. "Oh, goodness, I don't want to know. Wash your hands, Chenille, dear, and come put on your uniform."

I don't know what makes me laugh harder, *wash your hands* or *uniform.* Tears form at the corners of my eyes from choking down my giggles. Brayden doesn't care. He just lets loose.

"Get out of here, Brayden. Go find something to do. I think your father is shooting pool with Kent in the game room. Go join them. We'll have this dinner whipped up in no time."

"It's going to take a few hours," Mama says.

"A few hours? Hmmm . . . maybe I should change my shoes."

Oh, my goodness, this lady thought she was going to cook an entire holiday meal while wearing Jimmy Choo pumps. I help her unbuckle the straps and hand her a pair of flip-flops from her bag.

"Now I'm ready," Marilyn says. "Let me at that turkey."

"I was thinking you could start with the vegetables. They need to be chopped," Mama says.

Marilyn eyes the pile of celery, onions, and bell peppers with contempt. "That seems incredibly boring."

"Oh, but it's the most important part," Mama says. "We have to have good dressing for the turkey, and that doesn't happen without the veggies."

"But I want to stuff the turkey," Marilyn says.

"We won't stuff it, because it takes too long to cook that way, and sometimes it dries out," Mama says. "But we'll make a nice pan of dressing to eat on the side. It'll be wonderful."

Marilyn seems to be warming up to Mama, like I knew she would. Mama is going to make Marilyn think she really helped cook this meal.

"You're a makeup artist to the stars, huh?" Marilyn asks as she waves me over and hands me a knife and a cutting board.

I start chopping a bell pepper while she chops celery.

"To a few stars. I hope to get some major clients, and maybe go on tour with a musician or band."

"Well, I'd like for you to do my makeup tomorrow evening. Joseph and I have a party, and I'd like to make an entrance."

"You want to slay all the other women in the room?"

Marilyn laughs. "Yes, girl. I want those other hussies to ask themselves if I've had work done."

"You want me to take some years off, then? I've got you. My contour game is solid. They will think you had Botox and a face lift."

"You might just be my secret weapon. How much is your deluxe package?"

"Oh, I couldn't charge you. You can get the family discount."

Marilyn pauses her chopping as if she's considering this. Then she starts again.

"Family?" she asks.

"Brayden feels like family to me, and you're his mother. So, yes, you get the family discount."

"All right then. I'll take it."

I think we've just turned a corner. An olive branch was offered and received. We've got a long way to go, but chopping vegetables together and me doing her makeup is a very good start.

Chapter 23

I didn't think I'd become a football fan just by watching Brayden play. I thought I'd become a Brayden fan. But now I watch the games even when I'm home in Atlanta. I even watch the highlights on the cable sports networks.

So I'm here at this playoff game, not just as a girlfriend, but as a fangirl. I read the stats on the other team, and they are favored to win. The Dallas Knights are underdogs, but I want them to win.

The game starts off tough. First quarter, Brayden makes a completion, but then fumbles. It's recovered by the opposing squad's defense, and they score a touchdown.

The Los Angeles Stars' fans scream and cheer, because that touchdown puts their team up twenty-one to three. But I'm not concerned with them. I'm too busy staring down at my man on the field. I've never seen him this upset.

Their head coach pulls him over to the sidelines and tries to talk to him, but he stares straight ahead. I wish I could go down there and talk to him. Shoot, I almost wish his mama was here. Maybe she'd know what to say to him.

Brayden stays on the bench for the next couple of drives, and then he's finally back in. But he's still not on his game. He doesn't complete another pass even though the quarterback throws a few to him. Something isn't right.

A few moments before halftime, he finally catches another pass, but he fumbles it again. This time the Stars' defense doesn't recover the ball, but the damage to Brayden is the same.

He storms off the field and kicks the water cooler. When the rest of the team goes into the locker room, Brayden stays on the sideline. I hate that I can't text him, or reach out to him, or soothe him. I can't do anything except watch this unfold.

"Brayden's gotta get his head in the game today," Trudy, one of the Dallas Knights' wives says.

I don't know how to respond. Is she saying this because she wants me to agree, or is she just merely making a rhetorical statement? It's the first time one of the wives has approached me with any conversation about Brayden specifically.

"He'll have a stronger second half."

"I sure hope so, else we'll all have some bitter men on our hands this evening."

Okay, first of all . . . football is a team sport. This isn't just on Brayden. I don't even know who her husband is. He's probably a kicker or something. Shoot.

Second half is worse than the first, because it's not just Brayden dropping passes and fumbling, it seems like the entire team is off. The quarterback gets sacked multiple times. The kicker misses two field goals in a row.

The Dallas Knights aren't just losing this game. They're giving it away.

Final quarter the score is thirty-five to ten, and the Knights really don't have much of a chance to turn this around. It doesn't seem to stop them from trying, though. They rally on the last drive and almost score a touchdown.

But they don't. And now the Stars are taking a knee and letting the clock run out. Just like that, it's over. The Dallas Knights are out of the playoffs.

This time, there are no happy and joyful hugs after the game. Most of the players trudge out of their exit, eyes not leaving the ground. I don't see Brayden at first, but finally he comes out, with his head held high. There are no fans back here, so he doesn't need to do that. I mean, if he wants to be broken about this loss, he should allow himself to feel broken. Wait. I hope he isn't doing this for me.

I run up and throw my arms around his neck. His hug back is weak in comparison to the last time we were here. He doesn't lift me off my feet and spin me around, either. I compensate for his lack of warmth with all the heat I can muster in this January cold.

When he lets go of our embrace, I notice that his eyes are wet. Not filled with tears, but spent. The tears were there; he's just strong enough to hold them back now.

It seems like a man crying over a football game would be a turnoff to me. Like if someone asked me if a man crying over sports is masculine, I would probably say no. I mean, before tonight. But looking at Brayden who has the strength to hold it all together when he wants to break down—this is the epitome of strength. And it is definitely masculine and hot.

I just want to climb him like the chocolate tree that he is.

"I'm sorry, babe. I don't know if I still want to go out. Can we just stay in for the night?"

"Yeah, baby. Let's stay in tonight. We can stay in all day tomorrow, too, if you want."

He wants to nurse his wounds. I get that. Except he can leave his wounds to me. I'm gonna be the nurse, the doctor, and the cure.

Chapter 24

When we wake up in the late morning (almost noon), our clothes litter the floor in Brayden's enormous master bedroom. I shiver from the January chill that's in the air, even with the heat on in the house. But Brayden stands staring out the window wearing only a pair of snug boxer briefs. I can see his facial expression from his profile. His eyebrows are pulled together in a frown, he holds his lips tight, and a vein throbs at his temple.

Clearly, my man is stressed.

We made love all night, and he's still not back to himself. Well, I'm not back to myself, either. I'm sore like I went to the gym last night.

"Baby, what's wrong?"

He turns to me and relaxes his frown. He doesn't quite make it to a smile, but he does stop frowning.

"I made so many mistakes last night. I keep thinking about things I'd do differently if I could go back in time."

I climb out of the bed, dragging the blanket behind me. I close the space between us. As I stand before him, he stares down at me, hunched over a bit to bring his face closer to mine.

With both hands, I reach and pull him into a kiss deep enough to erase his uncertainty.

"Next year you'll be better," I say. "Now, all you can do is rest. So, come back to bed."

"What if there isn't a next year?"

"No next year? I don't think they're going to cut you for what happened, Brayden. You're not the only one who wasn't at his best last night."

Brayden laces his fingers through mine as he kisses my throat. The blanket slips down a little because I forget to hold it up. I forget everything when Brayden is kissing me.

"What if they do cut me? Is there still an us? Are we still a thing?"

I feel myself frown at this question. It's insulting, really, that he continues to wonder if I'm in it for his status.

"There's an us, as long as you can survive not being a baller."

Brayden chuckles. "I don't even know what that looks like."

"Well, one day you won't be playing anymore, so it'll look like retirement."

"Not there yet."

"I know you're not, so why are we having this conversation?"

He lifts me into his arms and carries me back to the bed wrapped in the blanket. I feel the warmth between my thighs start to reignite, as I bury my face into his neck and inhale his perfectly masculine scent.

He lays me down and unwraps the blanket like he's opening a gift on Christmas Day.

"I love you."

My heart skips. He's said it before, so I don't know why it makes me emotional today.

"I love you, too, babe."

His eyes ask me if he can partake. My smile tells him yes.

Then he eases down and kisses my forehead.

"Go shower, and get dressed," he says. "I want to take you on a road trip somewhere."

I'm trying to figure out why we can't have this road trip after he takes me to the top of the mountain. Because I'm ready for the mountain.

"Can we go later?" I ask in a whiny voice.

He chuckles then nuzzles my neck. "We can finish *this* later. I want to take you somewhere that's special to me. It's going to be dark when we get there."

"Do I need to pack a bag?"

"A change of clothes is fine, but we won't be going out on the town. You don't need your whole suitcase."

Wherever we're going must not be very far, because I have to be back in Atlanta in a few days and he's not telling me to bring my suitcase. I guess Miami Beach is out.

Wait.

I am getting used to being a baller's girlfriend. I don't know if I would want to give all of this up. And how in the hell can I date another guy after Brayden? This better be forever. Shoot.

I climb out from under Brayden and hurry into and out of the shower. When I step back into the bedroom, Brayden has showered, too, in the spare bathroom.

I don't want to put on clothes now. I want to snatch his towel off and crawl back into bed.

"I promise we'll finish later," Brayden says, just like he's reading my mind. "I don't want to drive in the dark."

"Okay. Shoot."

Brayden just smiles at my impatience and grabs the little backpack with my overnight things.

This better be good.

Chapter 25

This was going to be good—no, great. Brayden glanced over at Chenille as she dozed in the passenger seat of his SUV. She'd wrapped herself in a little blanket and turned on the heated seats, so Brayden knew that her conversation wouldn't last long, and it didn't. She was asleep before the end of the first hour. It was okay, though. He needed time to think.

Brayden was taking her to his cabin in Hot Springs, Arkansas, and they would be there soon. He touched the lump in his jacket pocket: the ring he and his mother had picked out at Tiffany and Co. He was going to propose.

Chenille was beautiful as she slept. An ebony angel, inhaling the stale air inside the car and exhaling fairy dust and magic. Brayden touched her face. She stirred, but snuggled farther down under the blanket.

He wanted to spend an entire lifetime with her and beyond, but the hold she had on him was frightening. The idea that she might ever leave him, or fall out of love with him, was unfathomable.

Brayden was starting to understand why men got cold feet, and why Chenille put up such a fight in the beginning. Being in love like this meant giving away all power. It meant putting your heart in the palm of another person's hand and hoping they didn't squeeze too tightly.

But he had to do this.

He had to make her his own. Two had to become one flesh, and not just physically. They'd already joined in that way. He wanted the rest. Her soul and spirit.

He pulled into the drive of his cabin. He thought about the preparations that he'd made and wondered if they were corny or too much. It was too late now to rethink it, though.

"Wake up, babe. We're here."

Chenille stretched like a cat and slowly opened her eyes. She squinted and looked around.

"Where is here?"

"Hot Springs, Arkansas."

"Arkansas? Oh, wow."

"What were you thinking?"

"I can say that Arkansas did not pop into my mind at all. You surprised me."

Brayden grinned. "This is my cabin. I love it here. It's the most peaceful place I know. Let's go inside. It's cold out."

Brayden grabbed his and Chenille's small bags out of the trunk and walked them both up to the front door of the tiny, rustic cabin. It wasn't anything like his other properties, and that was the point.

"Close your eyes," Brayden said.

"Why am I closing my eyes?"

"Obviously, there is a surprise inside. I'm putting a blindfold on you."

"Okay."

Brayden led Chenille through the front door. When they stepped inside, he bent down and untied her shoes.

"Wait. What are you doing?" Chenille asked. "Can I take this blindfold off?"

"Not yet, babe. Just trust me."

"Okay."

"Step out of your shoes."

While Chenille took her shoes off, Brayden did the same.

"What? You got a chinchilla carpet or something?" Chenille asked.

"Nope."

Brayden pulled Chenille to the middle of the room. She wiggled her toes around.

"Is this . . . sand?"

Brayden smiled and removed the blindfold. Chenille covered her mouth with both hands, but the squeal made it out anyway.

"You like it?" Brayden asked.

"I cannot believe you did this. How long have you been planning this?"

This was Brayden transforming his entire cabin into a little version of Jamaica. The hardwood floors were covered with sand, and big-screen televisions covered the wall with a scene from Negril's Eight Mile Beach. There were even palm trees, hammocks, and beach chairs.

"From the day I met you in Jamaica, my life hasn't been the same."

Brayden dropped to one knee, and Chenille burst into tears. Her hand shook in his, and he kissed it tenderly.

"I am going to love you forever, Chenille Abrams. I would love for you to be my wife. Please say yes."

Chenille put both her hands on Brayden's face and pulled his lips to hers.

"Yes, yes, yes."

Brayden stood up and lifted Chenille off her feet. He carried her over to the hammock and laid her down.

"Shall we continue what we started earlier, future wife?"

"Abso-freaking-lutely, future husband."

Chapter 26

One year after the wedding

"There are a million different directions we could go with this. Say the word and I'll have you guys on every blog and morning talk show."

Brayden looked for any signs of affirmation in Chenille's face. All he saw was indifference and boredom. Yes, Brayden's manager, Drake Mills, wasn't the most exciting human being on the planet, but he was talking about branding opportunities. Making money shouldn't be boring.

Drake sat down at his desk and crossed his arms over his chest. "I'm waiting on y'all."

"No. We're waiting on Chenille," Brayden said.

"I'm not holding anything up."

"You two have been the NFL's fairy-tale romance since the photo spread of your wedding in *People* magazine."

Brayden wished Drake hadn't brought up that photo spread. It wasn't Chenille's idea for those pictures to be in a magazine. Brayden had made the deal without asking her about it, and she'd been mad as hell.

"That was over a year ago," Chenille said.

"Exactly," Drake said as he slammed his palm down on the

desk. "We've been leaving money on the table for an entire year."

"Maybe if you tell Chenille some of the offers we've received."

"A cooking show on the Food Network. *Cooking with the Carpenters.*"

"Seems like we should've gotten an offer from HGTV. *Carpentry with the Carpenters.*"

Chenille laughed at her own joke, but she laughed alone.

"I can make that happen. Is that what you want? A home improvement show?"

"I don't want to be on TV."

Brayden shook his head. "Why not? You can promote your makeup artistry."

"How, by looking pretty while I stand next to you? Or what? I'm gonna say, 'That was a yummy-ass bundt cake, now let me come and do your eyebrows.' How does that even go together?"

Drake tapped his chin. "What if . . . what if we do a signature lip gloss for you? I was thinking of doing a Dallas Knights wives club makeup collection, and you could have your own gloss."

"How about if it's just me. Not the rest of the wives. I could put together an entire line of lip stains and glosses with custom colors."

A smile teased the corners of Brayden's lips. Chenille completely transformed when it came to talking about makeup. She had a hundred ideas for that space, but no passion for any of Drake's other schemes.

"How do we make Brayden a part of it, though?"

"I have a few skincare items I mix for men. Mostly moisturizers, and shave cream. I could add some of that to the collection."

"I can see that," Drake said. "We can call it Carpentry. Your beauty building blocks. I am a genius."

"Don't like it," Chenille said.

"Why not?" Brayden asked. "It's perfect."

"Carpenter is your last name."

"It's yours, too."

"Yeah, but it's not my given name. I'd rather do something with my first name. Maybe Shades of Chenille, but spell shades with a c."

"Let me shop this around to a few people," Drake said. "I'll let you know in a few weeks. Are you two going to the Knights' Thanksgiving Charity Ball?"

Chenille rolled her eyes, although she was going. Brayden had asked her to turn down a gig so that she could be on his arm for the ball.

"Yes, we're going," Brayden said. "With the rest of the team."

"I will send a stylist over with dresses and shoes for Chenille."

"A stylist? How much is that going to cost?" Chenille asked. "This is supposed to be for charity. I don't want a stylist. I have dresses and shoes."

"You're killing me, Chenille. Let me do what I do," Drake said. "It is for charity, but you need to be red-carpet ready. Designers will let you wear their dresses, shoes, and jewelry for free as long as you look good in it. Media will be there."

"I'll be ready. And I'll look awesome. Without a stylist."

Drake's cell phone rang, and he glanced at it. "Oh, I need to take this. Give me five minutes?"

"Take ten," Chenille said.

Drake stepped out of his office and closed the door behind him. Brayden turned his chair around to face Chenille.

"Why are you being so difficult today? Attitude on one hundred."

Chenille shrugged. "I don't know. Drake is getting on my nerves, though. I do know that."

"He's getting on your nerves trying to make us household names?"

"You're already a household name."

"You don't want to wear a free designer dress on the red carpet?"

"I don't want to walk the red carpet."

Brayden sighed. One of the things he loved about Chenille is that she had no desire to be in the spotlight. She wasn't posting selfies on her social media pages every day, and she stayed away from the places that paparazzi trolled.

Although Brayden loved this private quality about Chenille, he owed it to his fans to give them something, a little taste of his life. Chenille was a part of that.

"What do you want in exchange for this?"

Chenille lifted an eyebrow. "In exchange for this stylist red-carpet foolishness?"

"Yes."

"Ooh, you're not going to like this one."

"Go ahead, hit me with it."

"I want a Marilyn-free Christmas. We spent our first Christmas with her. This one I want just me and you."

"You want to go away for the holiday?"

"Nope. I want Christmas in our home. With just the two of us."

Brayden's nostrils flared as he thought about how he might make this work. If they were not on vacation somewhere, Brayden didn't think his mother would appreciate being banned from his home on Christmas.

"Yep. You're going to have to tell Marilyn she can't come over."

"Babe."

"Not sharing you with her."

"Okay, I'll tell her."

Chenille squealed, jumped out of her seat, and gave Brayden a kiss that was more appropriate for their bedroom than his manager's office.

"What else do I need to uninvite my mama from?" Brayden asked.

"That's it. When Drake comes back, you can tell him to send his stylist to our house. I'll have Kara help me pick out my dress."

"Pick a hot one. Low-cut and snug. I want all those curves on display."

"Really?"

"Yes. I'm proud of my baby. I want every other brother there to be jealous."

Brayden was sure they would be jealous, too, and not just because his wife's body was perfect. They'd be jealous because of everything they had together. The perfect marriage and the perfect partnership.

Chapter 27

I'm so glad I talked Brayden into a Marilyn-free Christmas—not because I don't like his mama. I do like her, and I'm starting to love her. But she smothers Brayden, and wants to be number one in his life. As soon as I became Mrs. Carpenter, I took that slot. She's still adjusting.

This is just another lesson.

Brayden insisted that we not stay home for the holiday, even though I know this is only because he wanted to let his mama down easily. At first, I objected, until he told me that we were invited on a yacht to the Amalfi Coast and the island of Capri with an elite group of celebrities.

I don't give a damn about the celebrities, but I do want to see the blue waters of Capri. That is a bucket list trip for me. Or it was until I married a football player and the bucket list went away and everything became possible.

In fact, there's a party going on right now, on the top deck of the ship, but I'm below in our cabin, because I feel strange. I've never been seasick before, but I'm nauseous with every little bump the boat takes. I decide that I need rest, so I lie across the bed looking out at the ocean through the little porthole. Above, Taneeka sings her newest ballad, and the scent of marijuana seems to come through the air vents.

Brayden probably doesn't even know I'm not up there. I can hear his laughter bellowing out every few moments. He's enjoying himself, and I'm glad that he is. It isn't the holiday that I wanted, but it is Marilyn free.

I wish Kara was here. She'd enjoy this more than I am. When I told her about it, she practically salivated. I do feel blessed to have a friend like her who isn't jealous of all this.

"Babe."

I sit up in the bed and feel a wave of vertigo. Brayden stands in front of the bed with a smile on his face and a drink with an umbrella in his hand.

"I brought you a drink."

"Oh, thanks babe, but I don't think I want anything to drink."

Brayden cocks his head to one side and gives me a strange look.

"What?" I ask.

"I've never seen you turn down a tequila sunrise."

"My stomach feels kind of queasy."

"Oh no. I hope you aren't about to get your period. I still have to get some booty on the top deck after everyone is asleep."

"I'm not about to get my . . ."

My voice trails off because terror fills my core. I can't remember the last time I had my period.

"Why aren't you upstairs enjoying the concert with everyone else?" Brayden asks, clearly not catching the shift in my mood.

"I'm enjoying it down here. Taneeka sounds amazing."

"She does. Talented girl, but a total jerk."

This makes me chuckle. "She's getting better. Used to be a lot worse than that."

"So, you gonna come up and chill with me?" Brayden asks as he puts his hand on my lower back and pulls me close to him.

"This is your world, babe. I don't really want all that."

"What would you like to do right now?"

I kiss Brayden's neck. "I'd like you to get in bed so we can snuggle."

"Just snuggle?"

"When do we ever just snuggle?"

Brayden laughs. "Okay. I'm down."

Brayden takes my drink and sits it on a deck table. He kisses me deeply and makes me forget that anyone else is on the yacht.

But he doesn't make me forget that I haven't gotten my period this month. And now that I think about it, I don't remember getting it in November either.

My mind races, while I try to recall the last two months. We've been having lots of sex. Great sex. That reckless, without abandon, honeymoon sex. Did Brayden knock my IUD loose? Is that possible?

"Babe, you know what? I'm sleepy. Maybe I should lie down."

Brayden touches my forehead. "You don't have a fever, but you do look a little strange."

"I just need a nap."

"I'm going to climb in bed with you. I can hear the music just fine from here too."

Brayden gets into the bed with me and cradles me in the crook of his arm.

"How are you feeling about the playoffs? Think you guys are going to go all the way this year?" I ask.

"Not gonna say. Don't want to jinx it."

"You football players are so superstitious."

"Yeah we are."

"Well, I'm going to say what I think. I think you're going all the way this year."

Brayden smiles and kisses the top of my head. This is how he starts. He says he's only going to snuggle and cuddle, but then he starts kissing and rubbing. Once the fire is started there's only one way to put it out.

And that's exactly why I'm lying here wondering whether or not I'm pregnant.

Brayden's kisses go south from the top of my head to the small of my neck. I feel my second wind coming.

"You sure you're sleepy?" Brayden whispers in a husky voice between kisses.

"Mmm-hmmm . . ."

Brayden slips his hand under the thin material of my sundress and strokes my breast while his kisses continue. I squirm beneath his touch. The heat in the room having nothing to do with the warm Mediterranean breeze.

"What about now?" Brayden asks. "You awake?"

He pulls me back in and kisses me again. The taste of him intoxicates me more than the drink left on the table.

"I'm awake."

"All right, then. Let me get out of this bed and give you your Christmas present."

"I thought this was my everyday present."

"It is, but this is gonna be the Christmas edition."

I can't deny him even if I wanted to, and I don't want to. I'm not going to lie, the loving is one of the best things about being married to him. But the loving makes babies, and babies steal careers.

I let out a long sigh. Brayden probably thinks it's a sigh of pleasure, and it is, but it's also an apprehensive sigh. A worried sigh. Because what am I going to do if I'm already pregnant with a gut full of human?

Chapter 28

Weeks after the Marilyn-free Christmas and I still don't have my period yet. Shoot.

I am never late. Since I was twelve years old, my monthly visitor shows up like clockwork. Every twenty-eight days. I know this means I'm pregnant. I just don't want to admit it.

And it's not just the lack of my period. My body is changing too. My breasts are heavier and sore all the time. I can barely smell anything cooking without a wave of nausea overtaking me.

Brayden would've noticed if he wasn't so wrapped up in his work. The Knights are going to the Super Bowl, so that's all he can think about. I wish I could share his excitement.

It's time for me to find out for sure, but I am standing in the bathroom, unable to go through with it. Once I know for sure, I can't trick myself into being optimistic about this anymore.

This is the worst possible time ever, too. Taneeka just asked me to go on her world tour in four months and command a team of makeup artists. That is completely next level, and I'm gonna have to turn it down, because by my calculations, I'm almost three months pregnant—if it's true.

I cradle the pregnancy test in my hands. I don't even want to open the box. Because if I open the box, then I have to take it, and if I take the test, then I'll know the truth.

I let out a massive sigh and then unbutton my pants. Might as well do it while I've got the courage.

Taking the test is awkward. I hover over the toilet and try to urinate in a straight line. Pee splashes all over the toilet seat. I hope I got it over the hole on the test. *Hold in urine stream* is just about the most useless instruction ever.

I put a piece of toilet paper on the sink and place the imperfectly saturated pregnancy test on top of it. Then I wipe myself, fix my clothes and sit on the edge of the bathtub.

The test takes three minutes to be sure, the box says, so I don't touch it for three minutes. I stare at it: a little piece of plastic that's holding my life hostage.

I hear Brayden in our bedroom. He's finally awake. The television is on ESPN, because that's the only channel he ever watches. Every morning, he blasts ESPN while he's getting dressed.

I grab the test before he has a chance to burst into the bathroom. Brayden doesn't believe in privacy. He'll be in here in a minute, giving zero cares as to what I'm doing.

"Shit."

That's the only word that comes out of my mouth, and it sums up every emotion I have. Panic at the thought of even being pregnant. Then, more panic at the thought of having an abortion. I could never abort our child.

It's early. Maybe it won't stick. Maybe I'll miscarry.

Shit! What kind of monster am I? Who wonders if they'll miscarry their first child?

I burst into tears. Can't contain them anymore. In my mind, I just see my career going up in smoke. I wish I was like those gospel singers Mary, Mary. They were popping out babies left and right, singing on the stage and then going right on into labor the same night. I remember watching their reality show in awe, thinking if I get pregnant, I'm doing that. I'm working until this baby falls right on out, and then I'm gonna scoop it up, put it in a stroller, and keep on working.

The only wrinkle in this working mother's fantasy is my very wealthy husband. He will ask me to put my business on hold, because we don't need the money. He will insist on me staying home and sitting down until our baby is born.

I refuse to sit.

He jiggles the doorknob, and I snatch the test off the sink. I wrap it in tissue and stick it in my pocket, then I toss the unused ones to the back of the medicine cabinet. I'm not ready to tell him yet. I don't know when I'll be.

"What are you doing in there?" Brayden asks. "Can I come in?"

"Yes."

Brayden opens the bathroom door and heads for his sink. He takes out his shaving equipment and lines it up on the counter.

"You're about to just come up in here and set up shop, huh?"

"What? We can share this space. It's huge."

"I know. I was just enjoying being alone with my thoughts. With you in here, it's no longer quiet."

I need time to think and strategize without Brayden's input, because, let's be real, I already know what his input will be. He wants me fat, pregnant, and home. Period.

I sit quietly on the edge of the tub while he brushes his teeth. His perfectly sculpted body is always pleasing to look at, but lovemaking is the last thing on my mind this morning. Our coupling like rabbits is what got me into this mess.

"You okay?" Brayden asks.

I must look crazy, like I've seen a damn ghost. I have. The ghost of my career floating right out of this bathroom. The ghost of careers past.

"Just have a headache this morning. Not sure why."

"Maybe you're about to get your period. You always get a headache right before."

Brayden is just like a man. He thinks he knows my body so well, but he doesn't. He's up here talking about my period, and I'm pregnant as all get out.

He goes back to brushing his teeth and humming. It's some gospel song he likes to sing.

"You're in a good mood," I say. "You have good news?"

He sets his toothbrush down and grins. "I thought you'd never ask. I'm getting my own shoe. With Nike. It's going to be a limited edition, to see how it sells. Us going to the Super Bowl and now this! God is blessing us right now."

"Really? That's awesome, honey. I get to rock my man's shoes at the big game."

"Yep. I'm getting them for you in every color."

"I hope they're super comfortable so I can wear them on the set this spring."

He has questions in his eyes, so I guess I'll just go ahead and tell him. I was trying to wait until after the football season was over, but this baby will complicate things anyway.

"I'm going on tour with Taneeka. Remember I told you I was meeting with her manager?"

"Where's the tour going?"

"It's a European tour. She has concerts planned in Germany, England, France, Spain, and Italy. I can't wait. There will be a whole team of makeup artists that I'm supervising, so it's really a great portfolio builder."

"I thought we might do some traveling during the off-season."

"We can. Why don't you do the tour with me? That'll be fun. You can be my fan for once."

His eyebrows shoot up. "For once?"

"You know what I mean."

"No, I don't. I've been your fan since the day we met."

It's not like he's going to let me travel to Europe without him after he finds out about the baby. He'll be stuck to me like glue, and more than likely we'll be stuck together stateside.

He takes a swig of mouthwash, swirls it around in his mouth, and spits. When he looks up at me, there is a string of saliva hanging off his bottom lip and into his beard. The sight of it makes my stomach turn.

Next thing I know, I'm kneeling in front of the toilet bowl and vomiting my guts out. Luckily, I haven't had breakfast, or this would've been worse.

Brayden's attitude immediately fades. He's at my side in an instant, dabbing my face with a cloth.

In all the ruckus, the pregnancy test slid from my pocket and is now on the floor next to the toilet. We both see it at the same time, but he's quicker than I am.

"Is this what I think it is?"

I nod. "I wanted to make sure before I told you. This is the first test I've taken."

He picks it up from the floor, and an even bigger smile spreads across his face. "We're having a baby. We're having a baby!"

He jumps up and nearly knocks me backward into the tub. Then he's all over me hugging, kissing, and cradling me.

"Did I hurt you?"

"No. No, I'm fine."

He's inspecting me, looking for bumps and bruises, I suppose. I can tell that he's going to get on my last nerve with this pregnancy. He's already doing too much.

"Are you happy? You don't seem happy."

"I haven't decided how I feel yet."

"But, we've wanted a baby . . ."

"You've wanted a baby."

"You don't?"

"I don't not want a baby. It's just a bad and inconvenient time to be pregnant. With the tour and everything."

"You won't be able to do the tour pregnant."

"I'm definitely still doing the tour."

I was on the fence about doing the tour pregnant until just now. Until he tried to put his foot down and tell me what I'm not going to do.

"How? You're not going to be able to travel to other countries that don't have good drinking water."

"You act like I'm going to the jungle or somewhere. I'm going to Europe in April. If I conceived when I think I did, I'm not going to be due until July. It'll be safe."

"We have the best doctors here. In Dallas. I want you to see a doctor here."

"And I will, but I will see a European doctor in Europe if I need to. This isn't up for debate, Brayden. Pregnancy is not a medical condition. It's a normal part of life."

"What if you need bed rest?"

"We'll cross that bridge when we get to it, but, babe, really? I'm in my twenties . . ."

"Late twenties."

"Twenties still. I am fit, strong, and healthy. This pregnancy is going to be fine."

"What about when the baby gets here?"

"What about what?"

"Are you going to quit working then, and raise our child?"

Anger overrides my nausea, and the queasiness in my stomach is replaced by fire.

"Are *you* going to stop working?"

"That doesn't even make any sense. I take care of us."

"So only my life changes when we have a baby? Yours stays the same."

"Our life changes. We're both going to be raising our child."

"But you just asked me if I was going to quit working and raise our child."

"You know what I mean."

"We've talked about nannies in the past. Let's revisit that."

Brayden's jaw drops as he stands to his feet, like I've just said the most ridiculous thing he's ever heard.

"Most women would be happy to be able to stay home and care for their child. They go back to work because they have to, not because they want to."

"I'm not most women. I didn't sign up to be just like your mother."

"My mother did work. And she set a strong foundation for me. But I bet if she could've stayed home and raised me, she would've chosen that option instead."

"Well, then you know working mothers produce well-functioning, well-adjusted adults."

"No nanny is going to raise my child."

"Then you quit working and stay home with the baby."

"You're just trying to win the argument."

"No, I'm not. I just want you to hear how crazy you sound every time you ask me to give up what I love. This baby will be healthy and fine, and it will be raised by two loving, working parents."

Brayden looks completely frustrated, and who doesn't care is me. One day he's going to understand that my career doesn't stop for him, the NFL, or babies, either.

"Just promise me that if the doctor doesn't want you to go on tour that you'll stay home."

"I promise that I'm going to do everything to keep our child safe. I shouldn't have to promise that, though. You should know that I would keep this baby safe."

"When are we telling our parents? Both of our mothers will be excited."

"After we confirm things with a doctor. This could be a false alarm."

"And you'd be happy if it was."

Should I respond to this? I wouldn't be unhappy if it was a false alarm, that's for sure. I just hate that he's trying to make me feel like a horrible person for it.

"If it was a false alarm, I wouldn't be upset. I would think that it wasn't the right time yet, and that we'll have a baby when it truly is our time."

This mini-speech is an exercise in futility. I know I'm pregnant. I don't need a doctor to tell me what my body is already communicating. But what I do need is a mediator between me and my husband, because he's already on my nerves. There is no way I'm going to be able to deal with this for nine months.

Chapter 29

This pregnancy is taking me out. Between the nausea, vomiting, vertigo, and lower back spasms caused by this little symbiont growing and resting its body on my spinal cord, I'm pooped. And nothing is glowing. Not my face, hair, nails, or anything that the old wives' tales swear improve when you're with child. In fact, my dentist just told me I have a cavity that needs a root canal, probably because the baby is sapping up my body's calcium.

Of course, Brayden is beaming. You can't wipe the smile off his face. He's telling everyone that he's having a son. I sure hope he's not disappointed when he finds out today. It doesn't make any difference to me. Baby boy or baby girl is going to spend at least two years in stinky diapers, spewing bodily fluids from both ends, and being basically helpless, so I don't have a preference. I just want a healthy baby.

Today we're not going to see the doctor, just the ultrasound technician. Then, we go back to get the results from the ultrasound explained by the doctor. And yes, each visit requires a co-pay. I swear this stuff is a complete sham. I bet I only really need to go to the doctor in the last trimester of pregnancy, when everything is huge and the symbiont is trying to burst out of my belly like the monster in the *Alien* movies. All these other visits are completely unnecessary, yet here I am, lying on this cold table, on a thin strip of paper that doesn't even cover the width of the table, waiting for us to get this ultrasound show on the road.

"It's too early to determine the sex, I think," Brayden says from his too small stool next to the examining table.

"Where'd you read that?"

"In the baby book I bought you."

I should ask *which* baby book, because besides grinning and bragging about this baby, Brayden has been buying stuff. And not just books. He's bought infant football gear, boots, and other shoes. He bought a book about labor, a book about delivery, and a book about labor *and* delivery. I've got breastfeeding manuals, potty training guides, and a bunch of other things I'll probably never read.

Thank goodness the ultrasound technician comes into the room, so I don't have to hear any more pregnancy facts. I don't need to hear about what I might feel or what I should expect— I'm actually feeling the stuff, whether I expect it or not.

"Hi, Mr. and Mrs. Carpenter. Are we here for a full ultrasound today?"

"I think so. Is that what it says in my chart?" I ask.

The ultrasound technician nods. "Yes, it does. My name is Cindy, and I'm going to be taking photos of your baby today."

"My son," Brayden says.

"It could be a girl," Cindy says.

"Nah, I talk to my son every night. He communicates with me."

"You're ready, huh?" Cindy asks as I snatch my blouse up, revealing my belly.

There's no baby bump yet, but I am already weary of being pregnant. I am sick all the time, but I'm also always ravenous. I can't stop wolfing down food and then throwing it up again. I feel like I have an eating disorder. I've gained two pounds in fourteen weeks. Nowhere near what I need—according to Brayden's books.

I flinch when she spreads the cold gel on my tummy.

"Sorry," she says, "I should've warned you."

"I'm good."

"So, let me just say that I won't be able to tell the baby's sex today with certainty, but there is a study we've been a part of that helps us with a good guess. Do you want me to guess?"

"Absolutely. My son is ready to meet us!" Brayden says.

"I feel for your heart if this is a girl," I say.

Brayden ignores me and stares at the little screen, waiting to hear what he thinks he already knows. Meanwhile, Cindy is going crazy with the goopy and cold gel. How much does she need?

Finally, she places the little tool on my belly. It slides around in the gel.

"I'm going to measure all of the vital organs, the skull and extremities, and of course try to determine the baby's sex, by looking at the position of the placenta. If it's to the right of the uterus, more than likely it's a boy. To the left means a high probability that it's a girl."

Cindy zooms in and starts taking pictures.

"Which side is it?" Brayden asks.

"Right side."

Brayden jumps out of the chair and pumps his fist. "I knew it! A son!"

"I don't think you were this happy on our wedding day!"

"I was, but this definitely matches that feeling."

"Ten fingers. Ten toes," Cindy says.

"I am gonna be the best peewee football coach."

I squeeze Brayden's hand. "Yes, you are, babe."

"Skull is perfectly developed," Cindy says. "Right on track for fourteen weeks."

"Perfect skull for his perfect brain," Brayden says. "My son's got good genes."

I watch Cindy hover her mouse over the baby's heart. She squints at the screen and makes a note that I can't understand. It's in code.

"What does that mean?" I ask.

"Oh, well, Dr. Peters will discuss the results of the ultrasound with you. I'm just noting the measurements."

"What do you think it means?"

"I'm not an expert," Cindy says. "You should wait to talk to the doctor."

I turn to look at Brayden. "Something's wrong with his heart."

"What? Is that true, Cindy?"

"Oh, I might be mistaken, so I don't want to say anything for sure. That's why you should wait and talk to the doctor. It's probably nothing."

The look on her face tells me that it's not nothing. They only say wait for the doctor if there's something wrong. Only a doctor can share negative news with a patient. I know it's something bad, and she's not going to be the one to break the news to us.

Brayden and I both fall silent. I don't know exactly what he's feeling, but suddenly my maternal instincts awaken. I feel protective of this little person, and beyond anxious to know what is wrong with him.

We can't get to the doctor fast enough.

Chapter 30

Brayden gripped Chenille's hand as they sat in their obstetrician's office. He told himself that he did it to give his wife moral support, but his hand was the one clammy and trembling. The ultrasound results were in, and he was afraid.

"Did I congratulate you on that playoff win?" Dr. Peters asked.

Brayden forced a smile. "Thank you, Dr. Peters, I didn't know you were a football fan."

She chuckled. "Everyone in Dallas is a fan when the Knights are in the playoffs or at the Super Bowl."

"That's true."

"What are the results?" Chenille asked, abruptly cutting off the small talk.

Dr. Peters cleared her throat and sighed. Not a good sign. There was never a pause when there was good news to share.

"Your baby has hypoplastic left heart syndrome. It means that the left side of his heart is not functioning properly."

"Prognosis?" Chenille asked.

"He will be in for some surgeries right after he's born. If those surgeries are successful, he will live, but he probably won't play football, Dad."

Brayden didn't care if his son never played sports. He just wanted to hold his baby in his arms and hear him say "Da-Da."

"He can be an engineer, then," Brayden said.

"If," Chenille said. "You said if. What if the surgeries aren't successful? What are the chances that they will be successful?"

"It really depends on how severe his defect is at birth. There is no cure for this disorder, but there are steps we can take to help him have his best chance at survival."

"Don't mince words. Dr. Peters. What are the chances that my child will die?"

"Out of the three surgeries your baby will need, the first one is the most dangerous. About half of the infants that have the first procedure don't make it. But if your son is strong enough to make it through the first surgery, he'll have much better odds of surviving the other two."

"Will the surgeries cure him?"

Brayden had barely digested the first part of this. Their baby had a heart condition that would require three surgeries. He could barely contain his emotions or even breathe, but Chenille pressed on with interrogating the doctor.

"The surgeries won't cure him. He may end up needing a heart transplant at some point in his life."

"A heart transplant." Chenille repeated the doctor's words. "A heart transplant."

"Listen, we caught this early enough that your son is going to have an excellent chance of survival into adulthood."

"Just survival? What will his life be like? Will he need constant care?" Chenille asked.

Dr. Peters gave Brayden an uncomfortable glance, but then trained her attention back on Chenille.

"All infants need constant care."

"Sick infants need more."

The doctor let out an exasperated sigh while Brayden sat horrified, listening to his obviously selfish wife. She was probably sitting there thinking about how inconvenient all of this would be to her business plans.

"There is still time to terminate, Mrs. Carpenter. It does take an exceptional amount of patience and fortitude to care for a child with this severe of a heart defect."

"I lack neither. I just want all the facts, so I can consider all my options."

"Don't you mean our options?" Brayden asked.

"I said what I meant. Thank you, Dr. Peters. I wish you'd had better news."

Brayden followed his wife out of the office, fuming. His blood was damn near boiling. And Chenille strutted like she wasn't carrying his legacy in her womb. Head up, shoulders back, heels clicking against the pavement.

They got to the car, and as always, Brayden opened the door for Chenille and closed it for her. There was a peaceful look on her face, and that worried Brayden. How could she be peaceful after the news they'd just heard?

"Where are we eating lunch?" she asked as Brayden slid into the driver's seat. "I'm hungry."

"Do you really think we're not about to talk about what happened in there?"

He pressed the button to start the car, but made no attempt to put it into reverse. They were going to discuss his concerns whether she wanted to or not.

"What do you want to talk about? The fact that only half our son's heart works? Or that a surgeon is going to cut him open right after he's born? Or that if he survives the first surgery then we've got to get him through two more, and he still might need a heart transplant?"

"None of the above. I want to talk about how you think everything is your decision."

"Until this baby leaves my womb, it is my decision."

"So I don't get a say when it sounds like you want to have an abortion?"

"Oh, I already know your thoughts on the matter. Give birth to a sickly child. Stay my ass at home like a good mama should and nurse him to health. Watch him struggle to breathe, and be terrified every time he takes a nap that he might not wake up. Bake cookies and throw elaborate birthday parties full of kids he doesn't know and doesn't play with, because HE CAN'T PLAY. He can just watch all the other kids throw water balloons and play catch with his NFL daddy. His hero. While I'm nobody's hero, just a mother who has to bury her son before he graduates high school."

Brayden blinked rapidly, mostly from the shock of Chenille's intense emotions. He could feel the pain in her trembling voice. He'd confused her interrogation of the doctor with being selfish, but this wasn't that. This was fear, from the core of her being.

"Babe, I'm scared, too. You think it doesn't break my heart to know that I will never cheer for my son while he's sprinting down a football field? That is my dream! But I know my grandmother always says that if God brings you to it, He'll bring you through it."

"Why would God do this to us?"

Brayden couldn't answer that. Just like he couldn't explain why he was born with physical gifts and the next person was not. Was it God's plan or sheer luck? If it was luck, then his had certainly run out.

"We have the finances to give our son all of the help he needs. Full-time nurses and nannies. This will not be your burden."

"Like hell it won't. No one will judge you if you keep working with a sick son, but I will be scum to your mama, my mama, and everyone else."

She was right, but how could he respond in a way that would be helpful? He wasn't going to quit playing football.

"What if you confine your work to my off-season? When I'm playing, you're the FTP."

"FTP?"

"Full-time parent. And when I'm off, I'm the FTP."

Chenille was quiet for a long time, like she was weighing the pros and cons of this strategy. It wasn't perfect, but Brayden thought it could work.

"When do we get to be husband and wife?" Chenille asked in a quiet voice.

"It's only for a little while, until our son is out of the woods."

"Okay."

"Okay?"

It was set, then. A game plan. Chenille was a good teammate, even when things were falling apart.

And even though he hid it with a smile, Brayden had never felt more broken.

Chapter 31

I can't stop crying. Every time I think of my son having surgery right after he's born, I damn near have a nervous breakdown. And Brayden's not here, so we can't break down together. He's gone to some pre-Super Bowl practice. Since the Super Bowl happened to be in Dallas the year the Knights advanced to the big game, Brayden's free time outside of practice is consumed with meeting fans and taking interviews.

He has a distraction and doesn't have to think about our baby. I don't. All I can do is lie on our couch, eat ice cream, and think about our son.

It's funny, I didn't even think about him as our baby until I found out that he's deathly ill. He was just a miniature vampire sapping all my energy, and now he's someone I need to protect, nurture, and cherish.

My cell phone rings, and I look at the caller ID. Kara. Not in the mood. She can go to voice mail.

And she does. But she calls right back.

I send her to voice mail again.

She calls back. Damn!

"Hello?"

"Heffa, are you screening your calls?"

"Not really. Okay . . . yes, but it's only because I'm tired."

"You sound like you been crying."

"I haven't."

It's okay for me to lie. I'm not ready to share this with the world yet. And with her big mouth and compulsion to make everything a status on social media, sharing with Kara is like sharing with the world.

"You haven't? Well, what's wrong with the baby?"

For a long moment, I'm silent. How does she know there's something wrong with the baby? Or maybe she doesn't, and she's guessing.

"What are you talking about?"

"Girl. Brayden is on ESPN, talking about he's about to play this game for his sick, unborn son."

"He's what?"

"Turn on the TV. He's still on."

I scramble from my place on the couch and grab the remote from the coffee table. I turn on the TV, and of course it's already on ESPN. It's always on that channel. And Kara is right. Brayden is in his practice gear, talking to Sherri Levy, his favorite reporter.

"You have a red band around your arm," Sherri says. "Tell me what that's for. Is it for your son?"

Brayden nods. "Only half of my son's heart works. He's going to need a team of surgeons when he's born, and I thank God that I have the resources to get my son the best medical care."

"Everyone here at ESPN will keep you and your family in our thoughts and prayers," Sherri says.

"Thank you. Like I said, I'm playing for my son tomorrow night. I'll be thinking of him with every pass and on every drive."

I stand still with my arms at my side, phone in one hand and remote in the other. I can't move. Disbelief has me paralyzed.

We haven't told our family. Our mothers. Why would he tell the entire world without telling the people we love first? I can hear Kara's voice squeaking out of the phone, so I lift it to my ear.

"What?" I ask.

"Tell me what's wrong with the baby," Kara says.

"You heard him. Half of his heart doesn't beat."

"Can they do surgery on him while he's still in your womb? They do it on *Grey's Anatomy* all the time."

"The doctor didn't say anything about doing that."

"That's 'cause y'all are black. They never give black people the best options."

"Our doctor is black, Kara. We've got the best options."

"What did your mama say? Is she coming to stay with you?"

"Let me . . . let me call you back."

As soon as I disconnect the call with Kara, my phone is buzzing again. My mother. Of course. I don't answer. I can't talk to her right now. She'll be in panic mode, and I don't feel like panicking. I need to try and feel calm.

I do send Brayden a text, though. *Really? You did a damn TV interview about this?*

I stand there and stare at the phone until he replies, because it better be immediate.

Sorry.

One-word response. Ugh.

Sorry? That's it?

I wait again. This time I'm waiting too long. I press his name on my recent calls list.

The phone rings three times. Too damn many. Then finally he answers, but says nothing.

"Brayden."

"I know you're pissed. It just came out."

"You better answer the phone when your mother calls. I don't want her calling me."

"Are you coming to the game?"

"I was. I'm not now."

"Wow."

"Brayden, are you kidding me? You just made it to where I can't come out the house without paparazzi and reporters swarming me. I don't want to talk about our son's medical issues to anyone."

"People will support and pray for us. This doesn't have to be a bad thing."

I feel my upper lip curl into a snarl, and I press end to disconnect the call. I cannot believe he did this to me.

I clutch my phone to my chest and plop back down onto the couch. I wonder if we have enough groceries so that I don't have to go outdoors until after the Super Bowl. My mother calls again. I close my eyes, exhale, and go ahead and answer it. Might as well. She's just going to keep calling back, and this will never, ever be an easy conversation to have.

"Chenille?"

It breaks my heart to hear my mother's voice crack like this. She sounds as scared as I am. My mama isn't supposed to be afraid. She's supposed to be the one who keeps me together. I need her to be brave.

"Yes, Mama."

"My grandbaby's heart doesn't work properly? Tell me how to pray. You know we will pray for a healing."

I rub my hand across my face with frustration. I knew she was going to put her prayer circle on it, and it's not that I don't want them to pray. I just don't want them involving me, and asking for updates and testimonies.

I do want them to pray, though. We need them praying.

"He has a birth defect, Mama. Saw it on the ultrasound. They're gonna start fixing it as soon as he's born."

"A grandson. Well, hallelujah, God can fix the baby's heart while he's still in the womb."

I don't respond to this. Not that I don't think God can do it. I just don't want to start hoping that He's *going* to do it, because if He doesn't, then what? Who do I get to blame? Do I get to be angry?

"Don't tell Daddy."

"Too late. He's the one who saw Brayden on TV. You know he's watching every second of the coverage. He's in there packing his things for the game now. I wasn't going to come to Dallas with him, but now I think I will. You need me there with you."

"Mama, please don't travel on account of me. You don't have to worry about me or the baby right now. He's a long way from being born."

"But, I want to be with you, honey."

How do I tell my mama that I don't want her here, and that I just want to be alone?

I don't.

"Okay, you can come, but I'm sure I won't be very good company."

"You don't need to be company at all, baby. I'm not coming as a guest. I'm coming as your Mama. And as a prayer warrior."

As much as I don't want to admit it, I need her here. Tears start to pour from my eyes as I think of her wrapping me in her arms and squeezing. My mama has the best hugs. And I can ask her to make chicken and dumplings. My mama has the best food.

She also has the best prayers. I think we need those more than anything.

Chapter 32

B rayden sat in the team locker room, trying to focus. This was the first time the Knights had made a Super Bowl appearance in his football career. He was one of the most important playmakers on the team, and he should be stoked and ready to get the entire victory—his first Super Bowl ring.

He couldn't think of plays, though, or how he was going to be one with the football. All he could think of was his unborn son.

And the fact that Chenille wasn't coming to the game.

Seeing her in the stands cheering for him was the best feeling in the world. He wanted to pull her on the field when they won. He wanted to share this moment with her.

"She's gonna come, bro," Jarrod said as he sat next to Brayden on the bench. "But you can't worry about it right now. You're making the entire team nervous."

"What? I am?"

"Yeah. Even though you're playing the game for your son, they're thinking maybe you're going to be too distracted by your troubles to make the right plays."

"I'm good. For real."

"Well, come over here with everybody else, and give us one

of those pep talk speeches that you always do before big games."

Brayden looked over at the rest of his teammates. Some were starters, and some wouldn't play at all, but they were still all counting on Brayden.

"All right."

Brayden stepped into the center of the circle of players. They gave him a round of applause as he came.

"I know y'all heard about the things I have going on in my personal life. The challenges I have to face real soon, with my first child being born sickly. He will be in my heart while I play this game today. But, hear me when I say . . . I will play this game today with everything in me. We've nearly made it to the pinnacle of success, and today may be the day we achieve the biggest victory in some of our careers. Today, we are one team. Let's go out there and show our fans that we appreciate their adoration, and that we feel blessed to be able to make more than an honest living doing what we love."

One of the players, a rookie, clapped slowly, and soon they all joined in. Slow claps that got louder and louder, until it sounded like thunder in the locker room.

"Today we are knights in shining helmets! Today we are victors! Dal-LAS!"

"KNIGHTS!" the team chanted in response.

"Dal-LAS!"

"KNIGHTS!"

Brayden watched his teammates get hyped, smack each other on the backs and beat their chests. The adrenaline surged through his body, giving him the push he needed to run out on the field and fight for a win.

The Knights' defensive coordinator who was also a pastor led the team in their pre-game prayer, and then they burst out of the locker room onto the field. The fans yelled and screamed and let out a battle cry that seemed to fuel the energy of the team.

But Brayden was only looking for one person. He only needed to see one face.

He glanced up into the owner's box, where Chenille always sat with her jersey and jeans—her lucky charm outfit.

Brayden spotted Chenille, standing in front by the glass window, like she always was. He blew her a kiss, and she blew one back.

Chenille would never leave Brayden hanging. It wasn't who they were. It wasn't what they did. She was here for him, and he would be there for her when the baby was born, and for whatever came after.

The whatever came after part left Brayden feeling more vulnerable than he'd feel standing in front of the opposing defense with a football in his hand, without helmet or pads. But there was no earthly armor or helmet Brayden could put on for this battle.

They had no choice but to do it afraid.

Chapter 33

There are two weeks until this baby's due date. I have never been more miserable in my life. I've got the last trimester blues. Or, I should say, the last trimester plus bed rest blues. Or should I say, it's the last trimester, plus bed rest, plus annoying husband and mama blues.

My mama and Brayden are taking turns at being the most irritating, and although I know they're trying to make me comfortable, I just want to escape. But I can't go outside. My feet won't even fit in shoes. I can only wear socks.

Who can escape in socks?

"What do you want for breakfast, baby?" Mama asks.

"Blueberry pancakes, eggs, and bacon," I reply, my mouth watering as the words leave my lips.

"Oh, I don't know, sweetie. The last time you ate like that you got constipated. How about some oatmeal with blueberries and flaxseed?"

Why did she even ask me what I wanted to eat if she was just going to tell me no? I wish I wasn't on bed rest so I could make my own food.

Brayden comes into the bedroom with his workout gear on. Shoes and everything.

"Are you going to the gym?" I ask.

"Yeah, babe. I have to, since I'm probably not going to make it to training camp. I want to make sure I'm in top shape when real practice begins."

He's laser focused on the game, I see, instead of what's about to happen with our baby. Everything is about to change for us, but ever since the Knights won the Super Bowl, football has become more of a priority than it's ever been. Brayden's itching to do a repeat of last year, and so is the rest of his team.

"We haven't decided on a name yet," I say as Brayden tightens the laces on his sneakers.

"I know."

"Why not make him a junior? That's the easiest."

Brayden shook his head. "Imagine him having to grow up with my name, and not ever being able to pick up a football. That's not fair."

That's true, but I can't help but think he wants to save his name.

"Well, I can't think of anything else."

"Why don't you wait until he's here?" Mama says. "Some babies choose their own names with the looks on their little faces."

"Maybe. What about the crib, though? Did you finish that, Brayden? I can't get out of bed to make sure the nursery is all right."

I burst into tears before I can stop myself. Brayden sits down on the side of the bed and holds my hand.

"Babe, the room is perfect. I'm gonna go in there right now and FaceTime with you so you can see everything. It's okay, honey. Everything is okay."

"Everything is not okay. As soon as the baby is born, they're going to cut into him. He might die. How can you say everything is okay?"

"My faith tells me it's okay."

"Well, I'm scared. I'm not going to lie and tell you I'm not. I hate to say this, but I want this pregnancy over with. I want to know what's next."

"Next is that we raise our son. Together."

"Says the guy who's going to the gym while I'm stuck in this bed with a remote control."

Brayden takes his shoes off and kicks them across the room. He gets in the bed with me, climbs under the comforter and stretches out.

"Gimme that remote."

"Brayden, what are you doing?"

"Until you give birth to our son, *we're* on bed rest. I could use some rest anyway."

"Go get ready for the season, Brayden. I was just feeling sorry for myself."

He shakes his head and clicks over to ESPN. "No. Mom, can you take my phone and go into the baby's nursery."

Mama grins as she comes and takes the phone from Brayden's hand.

"I get it. You support me. Thanks, babe," I say as Mama leaves our bedroom. "Please don't have Coach Wyatt calling me and acting a fool."

Brayden ignores me and FaceTimes his phone from my phone. Mama answers, and we see the bottom half of her face.

"Mom, turn the camera around, so she can see the baby's room," Brayden says, trying to contain his giggle.

"How do I work this thing?"

"Do you see the tiny picture of yourself?" I ask.

"Yes, I do. Lord have mercy, I shoulda put some powder on my face today."

Brayden and I both burst into laughter. She doesn't need powder, but she could zoom out a little on the camera.

"Press the little camera icon that's inside the square with your picture."

"Oh, there it is."

Mama finally figures out the phone, and the first thing that comes into view is the baby's crib, decked out in the comforter set that I chose, with the little Elmo mobile hanging at the top. A huge smile spreads across my face. It looks exactly how I thought it would.

"Show her the mural," Brayden says.

"Mural?"

"It was going to be a surprise, but since you're feeling down, I think you should see it now."

Mama turns the camera to show the wall across from the crib. There is a wall painting of me, in a rocking chair and nursing a baby. It is an outdoor scene, and the rocking chair is in a beautiful meadow covered in purple, orange, and gold flowers. I'm wearing a gold colored dress and gold bracelets that go all the way up my arm. In the painting my afro is huge and has gold and purple ribbons tied across the front to hold the hair back. I'm gazing down at the bundle at my breast with such love and adoration.

I look like Mother Africa and our baby is her progeny.

After I finally exhale (because I've been holding my breath since my mother turned toward the mural), I burst into tears.

"B-Brayden, it's so beautiful."

"If you weren't on bed rest I couldn't have hidden it."

"I haven't seen the outside of this room in weeks, not even walking down the hall."

"It also helps that you sleep like a log."

"Snores, too," Mama adds.

"Mama."

"Well, it's the truth. You couldn't hear anything over all that rattling you do while you're sleeping."

Now my tears turn into laughter.

"Shoot. Now I've got to pee."

I slowly ease my legs over the side of the bed and slide my feet into my bunny slippers. It takes me a few moments to get into the bathroom, and more than a few to use it. This belly gets in the way of everything.

"You need help?" Brayden asks.

"No, I'm fine."

When I'm done, I slowly make my way back to the bed. My belly is hanging too low for me to take entire steps, so I lift my foot and then slide as I place it on the floor. This movement propels me forward, ever so slowly, back to the bed.

Brayden chuckles as he watches me do my step slide.

"What is so funny? You'd be walking like this too if you had an entire human hanging in your belly."

Brayden jumps out of the bed and runs up next to me. He links his arm into mine.

"It looks like you're doing the Cupid Shuffle."

"Shut up!" I say.

"Slide to the left, slide to right, right foot now, y'all. Slide again," Brayden sings.

I give a sidelong glance to our bedroom's full-length mirror. I'm wearing a Beyoncé t-shirt and the bottom of my belly slides beneath the bottom of the shirt. My shorts are fine, just regular black spandex, but my legs are incredibly ashy. They look like I jumped in a bag of flour and rolled around.

I shake my head and pick up my foot to do my step slide again.

"Slide to the right," Brayden says as my foot is suspended midair.

The image in the mirror of my foot perched to make a landing, Brayden's singing face, and my ashy legs is too much. The laughter bubbles out of me like a volcano from a sixth grade science experiment.

"Oh, shoot. I have to pee again," I say.

I try to rush back to the bathroom, but there is no such thing as rushing when you're nine months pregnant and your belly is between your knees.

"Oh, my goodness!" I say. "I think I'm having an accident."

Brayden's eyes widen. "Let me help."

As the stream of liquid goes on for way longer than I'm used to, something occurs to me.

"Wait . . . I don't think I'm peeing, Brayden. I think my water broke."

"Your water broke?"

He runs into the bathroom and comes back out with a few towels, and starts cleaning up the mess.

"Are you in pain?" Brayden asks. "Are you having any contractions?"

I shake my head. "No. Nothing. Is that normal?"

"I don't know!"

"I thought you read the baby books."

"I didn't get to this part."

Thankfully, my mama comes back into the room, because we have absolutely no idea what we're supposed to be doing next.

"Did I hear y'all say her water broke?" Mama asks.

"Yes," Brayden says. "Do we need to go to the hospital if she's not having contractions?"

"Sure do. Once the water breaks, bacteria can get into the birth canal and harm the baby."

"I'll go get the car, and the baby bag," Brayden says. "Mama, can you help her get into some more comfortable clothes?"

"Yes, chile. Go get the car."

As my mama and my husband stand here making decisions about what happens next, like I'm not in the room, I feel a surge of excitement. I get to meet my son soon.

Then, the surge of excitement changes over to a feeling of fear. Our son is about to meet his mommy, his daddy, and his heart surgeon.

Chapter 34

Brayden was a bundle of nervous energy in the labor and delivery suite. Dr. Peters had informed them that their son would be fine when he was first delivered, and that they could hold and cuddle him right after birth. The problems with his oxygen and blood flow wouldn't start until the blood vessel that connects both sides of the heart closed.

Still, Brayden couldn't make himself calm down about his son's arrival.

He looked over at Chenille. Her hair was slicked into a high bun on top of her head, and little rivers of sweat trickled down her forehead. Brayden rushed over to dot her head with the cool towels that the nurses provided every few minutes.

"Are you sure you don't want some anesthesia?" Brayden whispered. "I don't like seeing you in this much pain."

"No . . . drugs."

The decision to try natural childbirth with no drugs had been mostly Chenille's decision, although Brayden supported it. Dr. Peters had told them both that the drugs they give women while they're in labor could make their son lethargic at birth.

Chenille's breathing was even and slow until the monitor showed a contraction. Then she concentrated, gripped the bed rails, and gave quick, shallow breaths until it passed. Brayden took her hand, and she snatched it away.

"My skin feels weird," she said.

"It's okay, hubby," Nurse Jessica said. "This happens to a lot of women during labor. Hypersensitive skin. Just keep dabbing her forehead with the towel."

"Water," Chenille said. "I'm thirsty."

"Let me get your ice chips," Brayden said.

He picked up the cup from the bedside table and fed a few chips into Chenille's mouth. She looked grateful.

"Where's my mama?" Chenille asked. "Is she still here?"

"Yes, all four of our parents are in the waiting area."

"Can you have my mama come in here? Just for a little while."

Brayden swallowed and put the towel down on the table. Why did she need her mama? Wasn't he enough? He already didn't feel like enough with her not letting him touch her.

"I want her to sing something, Brayden," Chenille said. "If you had a better voice, I'd ask you. I need a distraction."

That made him feel a little bit better, although he would rather she listen to the playlist of music that they'd brought to the hospital. It was part of their birthing plan to listen to Lauryn Hill and Jazmine Sullivan.

Brayden stepped into the hallway, and all four of the parents jumped to their feet, all probably wanting to be first to see their first grandson.

"Is the baby here?" Marilyn asked.

"Not yet. Her contractions are very close now, though, and Dr. Peters says she's dilated nine inches."

"So, almost," Charlene said.

"Mama Charlene, she wants you to come in the room," Brayden said.

"Absolutely."

Marilyn frowned. "What about me?"

Brayden knew his mother was going to take offense at this, but there was no time to smooth over her feelings. Not when his wife was giving birth.

"She asked for her mother," Brayden said. "She wants to hear some singing."

"I sing," Marilyn said with a pout.

Marilyn *did* sing. That was a completely accurate statement. She sang in the choir at her church, with all the other women of a certain age who had zero high notes in their range. She augmented the men in the tenor section who also didn't have any high notes.

Mildly put, Marilyn's singing wasn't what anyone would request while they were going through the worst pain of their life.

"Mama, I promise I will come and get you when the baby is born."

"He has to bond with all of us," Marilyn reiterated.

Joseph gently pulled his wife back down into her seat. "Marilyn, this is not about you today. We want Chenille to be at peace, so that this baby comes out like warm butter. Lord knows he's already got a struggle ahead of him."

"Mama, please just send up some prayers. Right now, the baby isn't in any distress, and he'll be here soon."

Charlene pushed past Brayden and marched into the labor and delivery suite like he'd just tagged her into a wrestling match. Brayden followed her inside and watched Chenille's face light up a bit when she saw her mother.

"What you want me to sing, baby?"

"I don't know. Maybe a gospel song."

Charlene smiled and opened her mouth to sing. "Lord I will lift . . ." Her voice was angelic as she launched into the sweetest version of "Total Praise" that Brayden had ever heard. Another contraction began, just as she reached the climax of the song.

Chenille gripped the bed rails again, closed her eyes, and let out a low moan.

Nurse Jessica rushed to the side of the bed. "Don't forget to breathe, Chenille. You're holding your breath."

"I . . . need . . . to . . . push," Chenille said.

"Okay, honey," Nurse Jessica said. "I'm going to get Dr. Peters. Just hold on a minute. And breathe."

I take Jessica's place next to Chenille, and finally she grips my hand. Hard.

"It's like . . . one long contraction now."

"Hold on. We're almost to the end zone."

Chenille narrowed her eyes and shook her head. "Really, Brayden?"

"My bad. No football today?"

"Nooo . . . ahhh!"

Chenille squeezed Brayden's hand so tightly that for a split second he thought he heard bones crunching. But then everything became a blur, because Dr. Peters ran in and took over. They pushed Brayden out of the way to check the monitor.

"You and Mrs. Rodriguez across the hall decided to push at the same time, huh?" Dr. Peters said as she rolled a tiny stool to the foot of Chenille's bed.

Chenille closed her eyes and nodded. It seemed that was all she had enough energy to do.

"Well, you've been a champ, sweetheart," Dr. Peters said. "Let's get this baby boy born."

The two nurses swirled around Dr. Peters, following her instructions. Brayden and Charlene stood on either side of the bed, waiting to help.

"Okay, Dad and Grandma, let's each hold one of Mom's legs back to give her leverage for this big push. The baby's head is already crowning. Three big pushes, and we've got a baby boy."

Brayden and Charlene did as they were told, and it seemed that Chenille ran straight off instinct. Dr. Peters wasn't giving her instructions at all. It was like her body knew what to do on its own.

"It's a boy!" Dr. Peters said, but Brayden listened for the scream.

Their son didn't scream. Dr. Peters held him up for both parents to see. The baby opened one eye and let out a howl. It was like someone had disturbed his sleep, and he was mad about it.

Brayden exhaled, and tears fell as he watched Dr. Peters lay the baby on Charlene's bare chest while his umbilical cord was still attached.

"You don't have to cut the cord?" Brayden asked.

"It's fine to wait a few minutes," Dr. Peters said. "Let's let him acclimate to his new surroundings first."

"He's beautiful," Chenille says. "Look at him, Brayden. Isn't he beautiful?"

"He's amazing."

He was amazing, and the most unbelievable part of it all was how healthy he looked. His little face was bright red from hollering and the sound level that he got on those screams didn't seem like he was missing out on any oxygen.

"Dr. Peters, are you sure that this baby has a heart problem?" Charlene asked. "He looks healthy to me."

"He will be fine for a few days, and then his heart will start to have trouble pumping oxygenated blood to the rest of his body," Dr. Peters explained. "While he is breathing fine, we're going to get him some of that awesome mommy breast milk, to build up his immune system for surgery."

"Mama, can you go get Daddy and Brayden's parents?"

Dr. Peters said, "We're going to have Dad and the grandparents all put on little hospital gowns and masks. We need to be extremely careful, because little man is going into surgery in five days. Until then, he'll be in the neonatal intensive care unit."

"What are we going to name him?" Chenille asked.

"For some reason, when he looked at me with that one squinty eye, I thought Quincy. Quincy Carpenter."

"Middle name should be Byron," Chenille said. "Doesn't that sound like a power name? Quincy. Byron. Carpenter."

"Right. Like he's going to be a billionaire or something," Brayden said.

"He is. If he's got this much of a struggle ahead of him just coming out the womb, my son is going to be incredible. Destiny has spoken."

Brayden stared at his beautiful son as he squirmed in his wife's arms trying to find a breast to nurse. Inside he said a prayer, that no hurt, harm or danger come to his son, and that he was going to live up to his powerful name.

Brayden's heart said amen.

Chapter 35

Today is my baby's first of three surgeries. The Norwood Procedure. It doesn't sound like something that could fix a heart that only worked on one side. It sounds too plain. Too simple.

But there is nothing simple about what they're going to do.

The two cardiac surgeons, Dr. Benjamin and Dr. Panesh, are going to basically reroute Quincy's blood flow so that the right side of his heart can do all the work.

My son looks like a little brown angel in his tiny bassinette. He hasn't even had surgery yet, but already there is an IV pumping something into his little arm. His hands are balled into tiny fists, as if he is protesting what is about to happen. I'm protesting it, too. I wish that the healing everyone has been praying for had come through.

"Look at him," Brayden says as he strokes Quincy's tiny foot. "He looks like me."

"He does look like you, but I see me in there, too."

"Not much. This is my son."

I laugh as my heart swells with love for my baby and my man. I never thought I could feel so much love at once. It's overwhelming.

But even as we bask in this love, Brayden and I are nervous wrecks as the nurses take Quincy down to prep him for surgery.

"Let's chat in the hallway for a moment," Dr. Benjamin says.

My own heart races. Is there something wrong? Is Quincy not a good candidate for the surgery now? I feel myself panicking. Brayden's hand is on my back, patting me, but it's going too fast, like he's in autopilot mode and doesn't recognize his strength.

"Brayden and Chenille, I know you know all the risks of this surgery. We've talked about them all."

"Yes. Quincy's heart is tiny, about the size of a quarter. All the parts of his heart are tiny. The vessels, the aorta, the chambers. A millimeter mistake could cause him to bleed out," I say almost by rote.

"Some babies have cardiac arrest during surgery," Brayden says, picking up where I left off. "About one in five don't make it, but if he makes it past this one, the other two are easier."

"This is what I want you to try to do," Dr. Benjamin says. "Prepare for the worst, but hope for the best."

What the hell? He's supposed to be telling us that our son is going to come out on the other side of this okay. And how in the hell do you prepare yourself to lose your child? Already, in five days, he means more to me than my own life.

"Dr. Panesh and I have done this surgery hundreds of times. We've done it more than any other surgical team in the country. You have the best. But we are not gods. We have lost some of our patients. Our percentage is way higher than the national average. Ninety-eight percent of our babies survive."

"Better odds," Brayden says.

"Absolutely. Trust us to do everything in our power to keep your little angel alive."

"We do," I say. "We have no choice."

"I just need to ask you to send prayers the whole time we're in there. The surgery takes several hours, and I need you to pray the entire time."

"We will," Brayden says.

"There's nothing more powerful than a parent's prayers over their baby," Dr. Benjamin says and then hugs me. He shakes Brayden's hand.

And then he's gone, down the hallway to the operating room, with our child's life in his hands.

Out of the corner of my eye I see Brayden's lips moving in what I know is a silent prayer. I do the same.

No, not Dr. Benjamin and Dr. Panesh's hands. God's hands.

Chapter 36

The waiting was the worst part. Every forty-five minutes or so, a nurse came to tell Brayden and Chenille that the surgery was still going well. It helped to get those updates, because outside of their prayers, they both felt helpless.

It was also a comfort to have their parents present, even though Marilyn was mildly annoying with her frantic pacing. She was a distraction, though, from the praying and the helplessness.

"Mom, you're going to wear yourself out," Brayden said. "You've walked about twenty thousand steps in an hour."

Marilyn cut Brayden a serious glare. "Don't interrupt me when I'm talking to Jesus about my grandson."

"You hear how she says *her* grandson," Joseph said. "You'd think there weren't three other grandparents in this waiting room."

"I am a glamparent. There's a difference."

Charlene glanced up at Marilyn, shook her head, and went back to her Bible. She obviously didn't care about Marilyn's made-up words, and neither did anyone else.

"Marilyn, sit down," Joseph said. "You're putting everyone on edge. Relax."

Brayden was glad when his mother took her seat without arguing with his father. On any other day, their sparring was entertaining, but not the day his five-day-old son was lying on a cold operating table with his chest open.

"Do you think Dr. Benjamin has enough stamina to be doing this type of surgery?" Chenille whispered to Brayden. "He's over fifty. He's been on his feet for hours."

"It's kinda late to be asking that, don't you think?"

"Yeah, you're right."

"I wonder if he was nervous about something. Do you think he tells all his parents to pray like that? That was kinda weird, wasn't it?" Brayden asked.

"What are you two whispering about?" Charlene asked.

"They're two married folk, Charlene. They can whisper if they want," Kent said.

"Nothing, Mama," Chenille said. "We're just worried. That's all."

"You can't give something to God and then worry about it," Charlene said.

Brayden noticed Chenille's sigh, even though she didn't say anything to dispute what her mother said. Sometimes, church folk gave the most useless advice ever. Even grandmothers who meant well. He and Chenille were trusting God on everything, but they were still worried as hell about their baby.

After the third hour of Quincy's surgery, everyone started to get antsy. Chenille broke down and cried a few times. She went through an entire box of tissue. Brayden had shed a few tears, too.

"Shit," Chenille said as she looked down at the front of her shirt. "I'm leaking milk everywhere."

"You didn't put on the pad things?" Brayden asked.

"I did. Soaked through."

Brayden went up to the nurses' station. "My wife is leaking milk. Do y'all have a dry shirt she could put on and one of those handheld breast pumps?"

"I've got a hospital gown back here, and we can ask over in Labor and Delivery if they have a breast pump."

"Thank you so much."

"Hey, aren't you the football player?" the nurse asked.

"Yeah."

"That was your little baby going back there for surgery? Awww . . ."

Brayden didn't know how to respond, which made this a very awkward moment. Did he say thank you? For the *awwwww*? He wasn't sure if that was sympathy or blessings or what.

"Can I get the hospital gown?" he asked.

"Oh, yes. I'll have someone bring over the breast pump in a minute."

Brayden rushed back over to Chenille with the hospital gown, and she gave it a skeptical look.

"I guess that'll work," she said.

"It was all they had."

A few minutes later a nurse from Labor and Delivery brought over one of those plastic handheld pumps. Chenille took it and disappeared into a little room, and the Labor and Delivery nurse sat down next to Brayden.

"Is that your wife?" she asked.

Brayden nodded. The nurse bit her bottom lip and looked to the left and to the right, like she was about to cross a busy intersection.

"I don't think I pictured a man like you with a girl like her," the nurse said.

"What?"

Brayden guessed that his voice sounded harsh, because the nurse jumped back in her seat.

"I didn't mean to offend you. I just, well, when I see ballplayers they're usually with a different type of girl."

"Yeah, well, she's what I like, so yeah."

The nurse lowered her voice to a whisper. "If you ever decide you might like something new . . ."

"I'm his mother-in-law," Charlene said as she pushed herself out of her seat and marched toward the nurse with her index finger pointed directly at the nurse's face. "And if you don't get yo' triflin' ass outa here while this man is trying to pray for his son—"

The nurse jumped up. "I'm so sorry. Didn't know you were waiting for someone in surgery. Bad timing. Sorry."

It was more than bad timing, and Brayden would be pissed if he didn't want to burst out laughing at Charlene cussing the girl out. Even though she'd only said one curse word, to Charlene that was cussing someone out.

"Ole triflin' bird," Charlene said as the nurse walked away.

Marilyn scoffed and shook her head. "My son knows how to handle his fans. He's had to deal with girls like that since high school. You're making a countrified scene."

"And I would've caused an even bigger one if she didn't carry her behind on."

"Don't argue, y'all," Brayden said. "It's fine."

"It wasn't fine. She was being very disrespectful to your wife," Charlene said.

"I won't let it happen again."

Chenille emerged from the examination room wearing the hospital gown and holding a container of breast milk.

"Do you feel better?" Brayden asked.

"Yes, I do. Mama, what's wrong? Why do you look upset?"

Charlene glared at Brayden and shook her head. "Nothing, baby. The devil is busy, that's all."

"We can't have that. We trying to get some prayers through, right?" Chenille said.

Charlene nodded and walked slowly back over to her seat. Chenille looked at everyone, but no one said anything.

"Okay . . ."

"I think we're ready for another update on Quincy," Brayden said. "It's been a while."

"Yeah, it's been more than forty-five minutes. Maybe they're almost done."

Brayden sent up another prayer, because they'd gotten distracted for a moment. Dr. Benjamin asked for them to pray the whole time, but here they were arguing over a groupie. Maybe Charlene was right. The devil was busy.

Finally, Dr. Benjamin walked down the hallway instead of a nurse. Chenille stood up and walked to meet him. Brayden followed her, but by the time he got out of his seat she was running toward the doctor. She stopped just short of barreling into him.

"How is my baby? Did he make it?"

Chenille's voice was shrill and desperate as she asked the questions, but Dr. Benjamin took both her hands.

"He made it. He did better than make it. Quincy is strong."

Brayden almost collapsed as the relief washed over his body. He realized that he hadn't eaten or slept in over twenty-four hours, and before that he'd had only snatches of rest and snacks instead of meals.

"He's still in recovery with Dr. Panesh. We had to bring him up from the anesthesia slowly, to manage his pain. But your son is going to heal from this surgery."

"When can we schedule the next one?" Chenille asked.

"We've got a long road ahead of us," Dr. Benjamin said. "First, we've got to get Quincy's chest closed. I'd like to try it in five days, because if he's intubated too much longer than that he'll lose his sucking reflex. I want to try to get him back to bottle feeding, and possibly back on the breast."

"What do you mean possibly back on the breast? I absolutely want to keep nursing my son."

"It might be an option, depending on how he heals. It is really for the best. It will help him with pain management, and he will be getting all the nourishment he needs."

"What do I need to do?"

"Make sure you drink lots of liquids and pump with an electric pump on the same schedule as the baby's feedings. For now, we will put breastmilk in his feeding tube."

"Okay. I can handle that."

Brayden felt relieved that all of Chenille's focus was on Quincy. Chenille hadn't even mentioned her business since Quincy was born.

She was being a mother and mothering. Brayden had known she'd catch the bug as soon as she held her baby in her arms. And he was glad that she was finally all in, because although Brayden couldn't say it out loud, he was scared to death of losing his son.

Chapter 37

Two Years Later

I am up to my neck in birthday party planning for Quincy. We didn't get to celebrate his first birthday the way we wanted to, because he was in the hospital and not even really eating solid food. Now that he's turning two and is finally healthy (relatively speaking), we want to really make it a huge event.

Of course, Marilyn wants to be a part of the planning as well. She just wants me to sit down while she plans the whole thing. I invited her over for lunch on our patio to talk about our party concepts.

She's currently inspecting my pasta salad. She always has something to say about my cooking, even though she can't cook without burning or ruining something. I hope she doesn't see me roll my eyes.

"Was that a black olive I saw in there?" Marilyn asks.

"Yes, I put black olives in my pasta salad."

"I see."

She painstakingly removes both olives from her plate. I am just going to ignore that. I'm not about to let her get on my nerves. Not today.

"What do you think of the plans? Quincy loves animals, so I thought having his own little zoo in the backyard would be awesome."

"It's going to smell. All I can think of is the odor," Marilyn says.

"We can get around that by serving the food inside here on the patio. The children can go outside to see the animals, and then come inside for lunch and cake."

Marilyn nods. "That might be a feasible compromise. What will you be serving for the meal?"

"They're children. So hot dogs, baked beans, macaroni and cheese? Kids' foods."

"Oh, good heavens."

"What! That is the menu of all of the kiddie parties I've been invited to."

"I am inviting all of my Jack-and-Jill friends, Chenille. We are not serving them hot dogs."

"Well, what do the Jack-and-Jill friends eat, Marilyn? I'm not aware."

"You would be if you would accept my invitation to join."

So, here's the thing. I don't object to Jack and Jill. They have these children out here doing lots of volunteer activities and they also give out scholarships. I'm on board for all of that. What I'm not on board for is Marilyn controlling my life and my social circle. She wants to mold me into a miniature version of herself, and that is not about to happen.

"Marilyn, what would you like to serve at the party?"

"Maybe we can do a nice barbeque. We can have hot dogs for the children. Brisket and chicken for the adults. Maybe even some salmon, and a salad table. We'll have cupcake stations, bottomless mimosas, and a candy table as well."

So we're going to have a bunch of drunk women at my son's birthday party.

"Bottomless mimosas? It's a children's party."

"Well, it's a children's party, but it's also a coming-out party for you. It's time you joined Dallas's society, Chenille."

"I'm not a socialite, Marilyn. I have a business. I work."

"But you could host the best fund-raisers. With yours and Brayden's story with Quincy, you should be helping raise money for heart disease in children."

"We donate lots of money to that cause."

"But being a millionaire in the black community comes with certain responsibilities."

I let out a huge sigh. Marilyn is such a broken record.

"Chenille, you're leaking again . . ."

I look down at my blouse and groan. I've been so busy today that I haven't nursed Quincy yet.

"Let me text the nanny to bring Quincy downstairs."

Marilyn clears her throat and shakes her head. I already know what she's thinking. I don't want to hear it.

"You know, I've read that prolonged breastfeeding could turn a young man into a homosexual," Marilyn says.

I squeeze my hands into fists and then release them. I've heard her reasons for not nursing my son. Multiple times. But I'm not listening to them.

Quincy will wean himself when he is ready. He's been through so much pain. So many surgeries. His chest has been opened and shut three times in two years. Dr. Benjamin and Dr. Panesh think that nursing him helped his healing process.

So, basically, I don't give a damn what she says.

My nanny, Lisa, walks in with Quincy on her hip, and she hands him to me. I plant kisses all over his chubby brown cheeks. He hugs me around my neck and showers me with kisses. Then he gets comfortable and helps me lift my blouse.

"Oh, good heavens. I can't watch this."

Marilyn stands and snatches her purse from the table.

"Call me later about the party plans," I say, completely un- bothered by Marilyn's judgmental attitude.

"I'm not inviting my friends if you're going to have your nip- ples hanging out during the party."

This makes me laugh out loud. Quincy stops sucking and looks at me, probably trying to understand what's so funny.

"If my son is hungry, he's gotta eat. Although I'm sure he'll be too distracted by the animals and cupcakes to want to nurse, though."

Marilyn storms out of the patio area, and I keep laughing. Louder. I want my laughter to follow her all the way to her car.

"I think it's great that you keep nursing him," Lisa says.

"Thank you for saying that."

I don't really care about who supports or who doesn't support this decision. So, while I thank Lisa for her words of support, I don't need them. Brayden has tried on a couple of occasions to persuade me to wean Quincy before he's ready—at his mother's request—and I promptly cussed him out.

Quincy kicks his feet happily as he nurses, and even hums a little. I stroke the top of his head as he falls quickly into a nap. He never nurses for a very long time, and he does eat real food. It's just like any other toddler who'd have a glass of milk a few times a day. And outside of his heart troubles, he's never sick. He doesn't have ear infections or colds or anything.

Brayden walks up as Lisa takes Quincy from my arms and takes him into the house.

"It's too hot outside," Brayden says, as he sits down at the patio table and plunges into the pasta salad.

"Yes, it's July in Texas. Hot is expected, babe."

"I thought my mama was coming over today? She left already or not here yet?"

"Left already."

Brayden lifts his eyebrows. "Everything good?"

"You know your mama, huh?"

"I know my wife, too."

"What's that mean?"

Brayden laughs. "Y'all would argue about whether or not ice water is cold. I'm not getting in that."

"Smart man."

"So how much is Q's birthday gonna cost me?" Brayden asks.

"It's going to cost us maybe ten thousand dollars."

Anytime we make a big purchase, Brayden refers to our money as his. I don't think he notices that he does it, but I do, and it's annoying as hell. This is the reason why I will have my own job, and my own business, no matter what anyone says.

"Well, I'm here for it," Brayden says. "My son deserves to have a big party in his honor. I'll have some of the team members bring their kids."

"Jarrod gonna bring his daughter?"

"Alleged daughter."

This cracks me up. Jarrod has some drama going on in the blogs about some girl claiming that he's the father of her three-year-old daughter. Brayden has automatically sided with his boy. I'm not so sure. I think the girl is pretty believable.

"Just so you know, about two weeks after the party, I have a gig in New York City."

"That's when training camp starts."

"Yes, I know."

"Are you taking Quincy with you?"

"No, Lisa's going to keep him. I've been freezing milk ahead of the trip."

"That's probably not necessary."

"Yes it is. He doesn't drink cow's milk at all, Brayden. What will he have in his cereal and oatmeal?"

"Oh, well, I guess whatever you feel is best, then."

I tilt my head to one side trying to read Brayden's mind. "Why does it seem like you have a problem with my gig?"

"Because I don't like for our son being left with a nanny and neither one of us are in town."

"Lisa is trained as an emergency room nurse. She'd be more helpful if something happened than I would."

"I still don't like it."

"Well, how about you take off the first week of training camp. I'm sure Coach Wyatt would understand."

"Not happening."

Well, then, he can change the subject, because as far as I'm concerned, it's over.

"Don't you want to know who my gig is with?" I ask.

"Who?"

"Designer Klein Newton is having an exclusive fashion show, and I'm doing all of the models."

"Klein Newton? For real? You about to be big time, then."

Sarcasm is dripping from his tone.

"Do you know who Klein Newton is?"

"No. Sure don't. I don't care, either. I care about my son having a parent with him."

"You don't care enough to take time off from your job. All these years you been playing for the Knights, you don't have any sick leave?"

"This is our third year in a row that we are favorites in our conference to go to the Super Bowl. How would it look if last year's MVP didn't show up for the first week of training camp? What message would that send to the rookies?"

If I hear Brayden refer to himself as the MVP one more time I'm going to vomit. Yes, the Knights won the Super Bowl two years in a row. And Brayden was the key aspect of their win the second go-round, so yes, he got the MVP honors. But right now, we are not on the football field or having an interview on ESPN. We're in our home, talking about our family.

So why do I care about what message anything sends to the rookies?

"Listen, if you want, I'll ask my mother to stay on after the birthday party. Quincy will have his grandmother."

"I guess I don't have a choice. This is what you're doing," Brayden said.

"It's what you're doing, too. I go to work, you go to work."

"We keep having this same conversation."

"We do. Let's have a different conversation. We're having a zoo theme for Quincy's birthday. He likes lions and tigers, but he's gonna have to settle for a baby goat, a pony, and lizards."

"Lizards."

"Yes, he likes lizards, too."

"Well, I'm looking forward to the party. My son has been blessed to make it this far."

Brayden wouldn't know what Quincy likes. He doesn't know his favorite book or his favorite t-shirt. He's here, but Quincy and I are secondary right now. The surgeries are over, and we're just the Dallas Knight MVP's backstory.

So I'm about to write my own story where I'm the lead. This Klein Newton fashion show is just the opportunity to make it happen.

Chapter 38

It was almost the perfect day for a birthday party. The sun was blazing and the few clouds in the sky looked like they were placed there by a perfect outdoor set designer. The only thing that took away from the beauty of the day was the stifling Texas heat. Brayden wiped beads of sweat off his brow as he moved one of the outdoor tables to a different spot at Chenille's request.

"Is this how you want it?" he asked.

She cocked her head to one side and frowned. "I think it's still crooked."

Brayden mumbled curses under his breath as he looked around for one of the hired staff that was supposed to be on hand to do this type of thing.

"You're trying to have me smelling like a bag of onions by the time the guests arrive," Brayden said as he dragged the table to the left.

Brayden didn't know why Chenille was stressing so hard over this party anyway. It was a children's party. Their son's first time having a birthday party, yes, but it was for a bunch of kids.

"Here comes your mother," Chenille said.

Brayden looked up as Marilyn crossed the back lawn and stepped onto the patio.

"Why is it so hot in here?" Marilyn asked.

"Hello, Mama," Brayden said as he gave his mother a small hug.

"You smell like manual labor. Chenille, I thought we were going to have the patio doors closed and the air-conditioning on in here."

"We will," Chenille said. "As soon as we finish loading in all of the equipment."

Marilyn nodded. "The table linens look nice, don't they? Aren't you glad we didn't go with the plastic?"

"I'm sure it wouldn't have made much of a difference for me," Chenille said.

"I'll be glad when you can admit that there are some things I'm right about, daughter-in-law."

"After you, mother-in-law."

Chenille then turned her attention back to Brayden. "Thanks, babe. The table is fine. I'm going to go and check on the catering. I think they're about to start setting up."

Brayden watched Chenille as she waved at the chef. He still enjoyed watching her walk away. He gazed after her for a few moments, noticing the deep sway of her hips that had become even deeper after she'd had Quincy. Child-bearing hips. But not children-bearing hips. She wouldn't hear a word about having another baby.

"Where is my grandson?" Marilyn asked.

"He's inside, Mama. We don't want him to see everything. He's already excited, though."

"Today is his day. He should feel like a little king."

Watching his mother spoil Quincy was like Brayden reliving his childhood. His mother might've been meddling and nosy, but no one could ever say that she didn't always want the best for him. Now that same caring and consideration was extended to Quincy. Brayden was grateful.

"I'm going to go indoors and see my little man until there is air-conditioning on in here."

Brayden's cell phone buzzed in his pocket. It was Coach Wyatt.

"Coach."

"Brayden. Chenille got you over there blowing up balloons and hanging piñatas?"

Brayden chuckled. "Not yet. She just made me move a table, though."

"Did you let her know about the camera crew?"

Brayden winced and groaned. He'd forgotten to tell Chenille that ESPN wanted to send cameras here to get footage on Quincy's birthday. They were interested in doing a mini–reality show on their family and how they'd overcome the challenges with Quincy's birth and heart disease.

"You didn't tell her."

"I forgot. I don't think she'll mind, though. She's in a great mood, and she's turned our entire backyard into a zoo carnival or something."

"Just tell her she can plug Chenille's Party Planning on film. She'll be okay with it then."

Coach Wyatt laughed at his joke, but Brayden didn't join in. It wasn't a secret to anyone in their circle how obsessed Chenille was with being known as a successful businesswoman. The Dallas Knights Wives Club had invited her to help run fundraisers and host charity events, and she didn't want any part of it. Brayden was almost embarrassed by it, but he couldn't complain. Chenille's ambition had always been one of the most attractive things about her.

"It's too late to tell her now. I'll just deal with the fallout later," Brayden said.

"I wouldn't even want to be a fly on the wall for that beatdown she's gonna serve you."

"I've got my ways, Coach. She can't resist me when I turn on the charm. And I'll hold the baby while I tell her. She's got an even softer spot for Quincy."

"We all do. Julie and I will be there in about an hour."

"Okay, see you then."

Brayden thought an hour was just enough time for him to butter Chenille up before the ESPN cameras arrived. He walked over to the chef's station where they'd set up a temperature-controlled tent and the start of a buffet.

"So, we're going to be able to put these cupcakes out and they won't melt? That's what you're telling me?" Chenille asked.

"We're going to put the frosting on them closer to the time the party starts. We made it with shortening instead of butter," the chef said.

"What? The frosting? We're serving Jack and Jill and the NFL Crisco frosting?"

"It'll be fine. They won't know the difference."

"Promise?"

"I promise, Mrs. Carpenter. No one is going to complain about the cupcakes."

"Can I borrow my wife for a moment?" Brayden asked.

Chenille spun around and Brayden snuck a kiss on her lips. She lifted a mischievous eyebrow, and shook her head.

"You can do more than borrow her, Mr. Carpenter," the chef said. "Please take her off our hands so we can finish setting up."

Brayden burst out laughing, and Chenille narrowed her eyes and glared.

"I'm in your way?" Chenille asked.

The chef nodded. "Yes, Mrs. Carpenter. You are in our way."

Brayden pulled Chenille out of the chef's tent and toward the house. She pretended not to be coming willingly, but the grin on her face said otherwise.

"Well, babe, there is something I had wanted to show you inside," Brayden said. "It's of an urgent nature."

"Oh, really?"

"Yes, it's quite urgent."

"Well, your son's party is about to start soon," Chenille said with a playful lilt in her tone.

"That is more than enough time for us to handle this particular business."

"You're nasty."

"That's why you married me."

Chenille laughed. "That is not why I married you. That was just an extra benefit."

"Well, I want to be beneficial to you right now, my sweet goddess."

"This better not take more than an hour, Brayden."

Brayden still got excited when he was about to see his wife in all her ebony glory. Giving birth had done nothing but enhance her sexiness. The extra curves that she had developed post-pregnancy drove him to the brink of madness.

He continued to pull Chenille into the house, but now she came willingly.

Until they got inside the house, and the camera crew had already arrived.

"What the hell is this?" Chenille asked.

Brayden looked around the room to see who'd let them in. Of course, his mama. She was already in the makeup chair getting prepped by the makeup artist.

"We're the camera crew from ESPN, ma'am."

"I mean, I can clearly see who you are. There are big cameras that say ESPN on the side of them, so that makes sense. My question is why are you here today?"

"Babe," Brayden said.

"This you, Brayden? Do you have an interview today? You working on the day of our son's birthday party?"

"Not exactly."

"Well, someone needs to tell me what's going on here."

Marilyn shook her head. "You're causing a scene."

"I will cause whatever I want to cause in my own house."

Brayden took Chenille's hand, and she snatched it away. He sighed.

"Can we go and talk in the study?" Brayden asked in a calm tone.

Chenille's nostrils flared, but she didn't say anything else. She led the way into the study. Brayden followed her inside and closed the door behind himself.

"What the hell, Brayden?"

"Lower your voice."

"Don't tell me to lower my voice. Tell me why an ESPN camera crew is here on my son's birthday."

"Coach Wyatt . . ."

"Oh, so this is on Coach Wyatt. This was his idea?"

"Can you let me finish?"

Chenille rolled her eyes. "Finish."

"ESPN had reached out to Coach Wyatt about doing a mini– reality show on some of the team members and their chal- lenges. You know, to kind of personalize us to the fans."

"And you invited them to Quincy's birthday party?"

"We're inviting our fans to celebrate that our baby is healthy. They've been with us the whole way, Chenille. We've got fans that have been praying for our son since before he was born."

"Only because you got on TV and told everyone our busi- ness."

"I am a public figure, Chenille."

"Only because you want to be. I don't see a lot of your team- mates posted up on TV like you. They play the games, go to practice, and go home to their families. You always want to bring the fans home with you."

"What is the issue, Chenille? Like what is really the problem?"

"This is *our* celebration. With our friends and family. Yo mama's friends and family."

"They won't encroach on our fun, I promise."

Chenille sighed and shook her head. "Why didn't you tell me about it? Why do I always have to be surprised about stuff? Why can't you respect me enough to do that?"

"I do respect you."

"No. You love me. You don't respect me. You don't care about what I think about things, especially when it comes to football. When it's about the NFL, I don't have a voice."

"That's not true."

"It is true. Listen, let me go nurse Quincy, and then I'm gonna get dressed."

"You don't have to nurse him right now. We were gonna spend some time together, I thought."

Chenille scoffed. "Really, Brayden? Just go. Go and film for your fans."

Brayden wished he hadn't forgotten to mention the camera crew to Chenille, but now he wished even more that he'd turned down the request to do it in the first place. She didn't understand that sometimes he also felt like he didn't have a choice in the matter.

Brayden would handle Chenille later, after they celebrated their son. It was Quincy's day, and Brayden was going to make sure it was unforgettable.

Chapter 39

"You look cute," Kara says as I put the finishing touches on my makeup for Quincy's birthday party.

"Had to put on more than I typically would for a children's birthday party."

"'Cause of the cameras downstairs?" Kara asks. "I was wondering about that."

"You know how Brayden turns everything into a Dallas Knights moment. I was just hoping today could be about my baby and not about his career."

"I saw little man when I came in with his little seersucker shorts on. I just love my godson."

"Mmm-hmmm, but you don't come through when I need a babysitter."

Kara clicked her tongue and flipped her blond wig. "Chile, y'all got too many rules and too many schedules. I can't keep up with all of that."

She's right. Watching Quincy for even a few hours is drama for someone unfamiliar with his routine. That's why I limit who keeps him to Lisa and my mother. Shoot, Brayden doesn't even know what time to administer Quincy's medication.

There's a knock on the bedroom door, and Kara jumps up to answer it. Lisa brings Quincy in.

"I wanna see the animals, Mama," Quincy says.

"Animals? What animals?"

I scoop my baby up in my arms and kiss him. His light blue-and-white shorts match my light blue sundress.

"Grandma says a pony!"

"She did? Grandma sure likes to say things, doesn't she?"

Kara giggles into her hands, and Lisa struggles to hold in her laughter. I can't believe Marilyn ruined the surprise for Quincy. Why in the hell would she tell him about the pony?

"Well, I don't know about a pony, but I bet there's birthday cake."

"Cake."

"Because it's someone's birthday."

Quincy giggles. "It's my birthday."

"It is, big boy. How old are you?"

"I'm two!" Quincy points to himself as if there is another toddler in the room with a birthday.

"Let's go downstairs with Auntie Kara and Ms. Lisa and see what else we can find outside."

It is time for us to make our entrance, so I wait for Brayden to come out of his study. I took his clothes to him so I could get dressed in peace, without him trying to apologize for the camera crew or trying to get me to have sex with him.

"Lisa, can you go knock on the door to the study, to let Brayden know we're ready to go outside and greet our guests."

After a few moments, Brayden emerges from his study with a contrite look on his face. I don't care how sorry he looks. I'm still mad as hell, and that feeling isn't going anywhere for a while.

He does look nice in his white linen pants and his light blue shirt that matches the shade of my dress perfectly.

"You look beautiful," Brayden says.

"Thank you."

"You gonna smile at the people or mean mug them?" Brayden asks. "'Cause right now you look like you might cuss the guests out."

"I'm gonna cuss your mama out."

Brayden laughs. I don't know why he's laughing. I know I don't look like I have good humor on my face.

"Why? What did she do? She's out there being the perfect grandmother hostess. Your mother is just sitting there sipping iced tea."

I lift my eyebrows damn near close to my hairline. "That's all my mama gotta do. That's all I asked her to do."

"I'm just saying. What are you mad at my mama for this time? All she's doing is helping us put on this party."

"And ruining the surprise for my baby."

"Grandma said it's a pony," Quincy whispers to Brayden like the rest of us can't hear him.

Brayden shakes his head. "That's not a big deal, babe. Come on. Let's not be mad the rest of the afternoon. Let's have fun."

"Let's look perfect for the cameras, right?"

"We don't have to look perfect. We just have to be the happy family that we are."

I don't react to this, but I do take Brayden's extended arm as he guides me out the kitchen entrance of our house. We walk down the cobbled path to the patio and pool area. Not even a breeze disrupts this oppressive heat. We should've had a pool party, because right now, I feel like stripping off my dress and jumping right in the crystal clear, blue, cool water.

When we approach the patio, someone gives the DJ the signal that we're arriving. He cuts the music.

"Ladies and gentlemen," the DJ says, "please make way for the man of the hour, the birthday boy, Mr. Quincy Byron Carpenter!"

Everyone stands and gives a round of applause as we step into the room. Quincy's eyes are wide, and his little mouth is in the shape of an "o." I think he realizes that all of this is for him, that everyone is clapping for him.

One of the party staff runs up and puts a little party hat on Quincy's head. She also slips a little candy ring on his finger.

"Mama, can I eat it?"

"Yes, baby."

And then Quincy gasps with excitement, because off in the distance he sees the pony and the goat.

"A pony!"

He squirms to get out of my arms, and Lisa is right there ready to take him out to the other children and the zoo friends.

I wish I was going with him, but I've got to entertain the socialites and the cameras. Coach Wyatt waves to me and Brayden, so I guess that means we're going to eat at the table with them.

"Guests, please direct your children to go with our friendly staff in the red shirts. They're going to be taken through the petting zoo, and to their dining area, which is adjacent to this patio in the tent with the red top," the DJ announces.

Brayden leads me to the table where Coach Wyatt has gotten up. He extends his arms like he wants to hug me, so I play the role. I put on a big fake smile and walk into his waiting arms.

"I swear, Chenille, you look prettier and prettier every time I see you."

Julie, Coach Wyatt's wife, blows me a kiss. "She does get more gorgeous. That's what they call black girl magic these days. You've certainly got a healthy helping of it. Come and sit."

I graciously go and sit next to Julie, but I'm irritated by the cameras that aren't even a little bit inconspicuous. They're just out in the middle of the floor like they have invisible equipment or something. No. We *all* see you, and it's taking away from the aesthetic of the party.

"So, I was thinking, since the season is starting again," Julie says, "that we could start doing some girls' outings. Like wouldn't it be fun to do a wives' trip when they do an away game?"

I give her a fake smile. I hope it looks real on the camera. Wait, no, I don't. I don't care how it looks.

"Where do the wives want to go?" I ask. I play along with this, even though I wish someone had given me the script.

"Maybe Cabo. Somewhere we can let our hair down, have too many cocktails, and not care about the boys trying to keep us in line."

I feel myself blinking, because I don't even know what to say to this. I don't want to drink too many cocktails with this woman, or any of the Knights wives. Why? Because they're not my friends.

"Cabo sounds nice. I love a good beach, and a good cocktail," I say.

My improvisation skills are excellent. This is going to make some good TV, even though it's not real.

Marilyn takes one of the empty seats at the table with us. I notice that Joseph decided to stay over at the table with my parents. He's probably trying not to be on TV, too.

"Julie, do you think there's any room for team moms on this excursion?"

Julie laughs. "Only you Marilyn. You're hardly a mom. You're one of the girls."

"We haven't had a girls' day lately, but I'd like for you and I to go to a spa and have facials sometime soon."

"I feel like there's a hidden agenda there," Julie says. "I know you, Marilyn."

I snicker under my breath. I don't think this was part of Julie and Coach Wyatt's script, but no one is going to put a TV camera within a hundred feet of Marilyn and her not figure out a way to make it about her.

"Not a hidden agenda. I want us to partner again. You know I'm so passionate about research for heart disease in children these days, because of Quincy."

"Oh, absolutely," Julie says. "I'm so glad you brought that up, because I want to talk to Chenille about this very topic. The Knights wives are dedicating our fall fund-raiser to heart disease. We're going to do a twilight walk through downtown Dallas. I think we can raise at least two million dollars."

"That is fantastic," Marilyn says.

I don't say anything, although both of them are looking at me. I don't care. They're just going to have to edit this part out.

"We'd like for you to be the hostess," Julie says.

"Who, me?" I ask.

"Yes, you, dear."

"Oh."

My petty level is on extraordinary right now. I try to make eye contact with Brayden, who is off camera talking to Coach Wyatt about something. Did he know they were going to do this to me? Was this his idea?

I stand, because I'm about to go and ask him.

"I'll be right back," I say.

"But the fund-raiser," Julie says.

"I'll be right back."

In my mind, I start composing the words with which I'm going to tell Brayden all the way off. I've strung together a very exciting and creative group of curse words that I'm going to lay on Brayden's entire being, because he and his crew have turned my baby's birthday into a circus, and I'm not here for it.

I can almost feel the cameras on my back as I take wide strides in Brayden's direction. Hopefully they're getting a good shot of my booty, because I've been working out.

But then, one of the red-shirted party staffers comes running through the patio door, and she damn near knocks me over. The alarm on her face chills me to the core.

"It's Quincy. He's collapsed. Lisa is doing CPR and the paramedics are on the way."

Everything is forgotten. Cameras, Brayden, Julie, Marilyn. Nothing matters except my son.

I take off running.

Chapter 40

Brayden's heart pounded so loud that he was sure everyone around him could hear it. But drowning out the sound of his thudding heartbeat was Chenille's scream. Brayden didn't have enough breath to let out a noise, but Chenille covered for both of them.

Quincy was in Lisa's arms when Brayden and Chenille approached. Quincy was drenched with sweat, his breathing labored (at least he was breathing), and his little limbs hung limply.

The other children, who looked traumatized by the chaos, were being herded into the children's tent.

"What happened?" Chenille yelled at Lisa. "You were only gone for ten minutes."

"H-he was fine. He was feeding the goat a handful of the little food pellets, and laughing with all of the other children. Then, in the next moment he collapsed. At first, I didn't feel a pulse. I thought he had cardiac arrest. Then, I did CPR, and his heart and breathing started again."

"His heart stopped?" Brayden asked. "You think his heart stopped?"

"I couldn't find a pulse."

The paramedics arrived in a flurry of activity, putting a stop to Brayden and Chenille's interrogation of Lisa. Not that they were angry with her. Whatever happened wasn't her fault, and she had probably saved Quincy's life.

"Do you want to ride in the ambulance with him?" Brayden asked Chenille.

Chenille didn't reply. She didn't seem to be listening to him at all. She was on autopilot, and all she seemed interested in was what was happening to her son.

Chenille climbed inside the back of the ambulance without asking for permission or being invited. She probably would've fought anyone who tried to keep her from getting in there next to Quincy.

There wasn't enough room for Brayden, so he ran back toward the house to get his truck. He had to pass the patio, so Marilyn screamed out his name. There was no time to stop and explain things to her. She had to find out what was happening later. Besides, he had nothing to tell her. He had no idea what was happening himself. He just knew that he needed to get to the hospital.

When Brayden got to Baylor University Medical Center, the same hospital where Quincy had had all of his surgeries, he went straight to the emergency room. No one had to give him directions. He knew this hospital like the back of his hand.

Chenille was standing in front of the admission desk. There were chairs there, but Brayden knew she wouldn't sit. She wouldn't relax until Quincy was okay.

"Babe . . ."

Chenille spun around and stared at Brayden. She had a wild look in her eyes. "This is my fault. He was so excited about the p-party. I shouldn't have had all of those activities. It was too much. He can't take too much."

Brayden encircled her in his arms. "Shhh . . . we don't know what happened yet. It's not your fault."

Chenille sobbed into his chest. "It's supposed to be over, Brayden. He's supposed to be okay now. I can't keep going through this."

"We're going through this together, babe. Me, you, and Quincy. We're going to be fine, you'll see."

Brayden finished the paperwork for admittance, and as he led Chenille to the waiting area, Dr. Benjamin met them. He was wearing what looked like golf pants under his lab coat. He'd probably had the day off, but that was ruined now. Duty called. He answered.

"Brayden and Chenille, I sure hate to see you all under these circumstances."

"Same here, doctor. Do you know what's wrong with Quincy? Did he have a heart attack? Cardiac arrest?" Brayden asked.

"I'm still running additional tests, but from what I've already seen, I don't think he had a heart attack or cardiac arrest. I think Quincy has an arrhythmia."

"What is that?" Chenille asked.

"Sometimes his heart skips a beat. The ten-minute test I just ran on the heart monitor seems to confirm this, but I want to be sure to make the diagnosis."

"So, what is the treatment for an arrhythmia? Does he have to have more surgery?" Brayden asked.

"Maybe not. Depending on the severity, we can monitor it without surgery. Sometimes even without medication. You'll just have to be mindful and watchful. If it is severe enough, then it could require a pacemaker."

"Another surgery," Chenille said. "You're going to crack my baby's chest open again. Can he get any peace in his life? Oh, my God!"

"Try to stay calm, Chenille," Dr. Benjamin said. "Remember what I asked you about your prayers? They're still important. Even now. The last thing I want is to open Quincy's chest again. He's had enough pain in his life."

"Prayers? Prayers?" Chenille shrieked. "Why won't anyone answer this question for me, huh? Why did God do this to *my* baby in the first place? I'm gonna keep praying and God's the one who did this?"

Again, Chenille sobbed into Brayden's chest. Unlike his wife, Brayden was still praying. He didn't know how long he'd have to keep asking God the same thing, but he wasn't tired of asking yet. He'd have to send up enough prayers for them both.

Chapter 41

Brayden sat in Coach Wyatt's office, nervous about what he was about to say, but knowing that he had no choice. Brayden was going to take several months off from football, whether Coach Wyatt liked it or not.

"Coach, my son is sick again. I'm going to miss training camp, and probably several games."

Coach Wyatt closed his eyes and sighed. "Brayden, you know I support you, and I've been praying for little Quincy every day—"

"I appreciate you."

Brayden cut Coach Wyatt off mid-sentence because he could hear the "but" coming. There shouldn't be a "but." There should only be, *Go ahead, Brayden. Take all the time you need.*

"But the team needs you," Coach Wyatt said. "We've got young, young running backs on the bench. None of them are ready to step up and fill your shoes."

"I'm aware of that, Coach Wyatt."

"We're on our way to another Super Bowl."

Brayden inhaled sharply and exhaled. "Aware of that, too."

"Are there not doctors taking care of Quincy around the clock? Do we need to bring in another expert? Another cardiologist?"

"No. Dr. Benjamin is the best in the country. He did all of Quincy's surgeries. He's the reason my son is alive today. No one is better than him."

"Why don't you just sit out training camp and see what happens? Don't make the decision to miss any games quite yet. Your son may get better, and then we won't even have to have this conversation."

"All of this is hard on Chenille, Coach. She needs me by her side for all of it. She needs to know that I'm going to be there."

"And what about the team? What about our Super Bowl hopes?"

Brayden stood firm. "I have no greater responsibility than to my family, Coach. I would support you if you had to make a similar decision."

"That's the difference between me and you, son. Football makes my life possible. My whole family knows that."

Silence stood between the two men like a thick fog. Neither gave an inch in their perspective on Brayden's very personal choice.

Finally, Brayden spoke. "Coach, I will let you know my son's progress. Perhaps you'll want to send cameras to the hospital. Maybe you'll want the fans to see how much you support me in *this* time of need."

"Once you quit on the team, the fans quit on you. If we don't make it to the Super Bowl this year, because of your little hiatus, the fans will never forgive you."

"Well, since I don't lie down every night next to them or wake up to their beautiful faces, I'm going to have to say, I don't give a damn about being judged by the fans. Not this time."

Brayden stood, wishing he had a better feeling about the outcome of things. He would be a free agent next season, and while his future with the Knights had never seemed to be in jeopardy before, he couldn't tell what might happen now.

Coach Wyatt's attitude made Brayden regret all the times he'd risked Chenille's anger by doing something Coach Wyatt wanted. This man didn't seem to care about Brayden or what was important in his life.

No, that wasn't correct. Coach Wyatt did care, but his concern had at least one condition. That was Brayden putting the Dallas Knights first.

Unfortunately, this time, that was a condition that Brayden was unable to meet.

Chapter 42

Brayden sits at the edge of our bed, staring at the TV. His least favorite channel these days: ESPN.

Today, he goes back to practice and rejoins the team, halfway through the season. Right now the Knights have three wins and five losses, and are last in their conference. It's gonna take a miracle for them to come back and go to the playoffs now. They'd have to win the rest of their games.

The entire season seems to be resting on Brayden's back. I don't like it. I thought football was supposed to be a team sport. How can one person make or break an entire season?

The reporter on the TV is asking the same thing.

"Will Brayden Carpenter be able to save the Knights from an embarrassing season?" the voice blares from the screen.

Brayden shakes his head. "Did Quincy nurse this morning?"

"Yes. Like a champ."

"Good. I'm glad he's finding some comfort in it."

I don't tell Brayden this, but Quincy has been nursing more since he collapsed during his birthday party. Several times a day now, almost as many times as he did before he started eating solid food. I never deny him, but I think something beyond physical happened to my baby that day.

It was like the first good thing that ever happened to him was snatched away before he even got a chance to enjoy it. I think it hurt him physically, mentally, and emotionally. Nursing him seems to be the only thing that keeps him calm.

"Do you think everything is going to be okay with the team?" I ask.

Brayden shrugs. "Maybe. Maybe not. They're playing like trash. Wilson is throwing interceptions left and right. Jarrod and the defensive line are terrible, too. It's like they all decided to take a break when I took a break."

Maybe there was something to what Coach Wyatt had said when he'd called me on the phone, begging me to help him change Brayden's mind about taking time off. He'd said that Brayden was the heart and soul of the team. Maybe he was.

But he was the heart and soul of our family, too, so I refused Coach Wyatt. For once Brayden was choosing our son over the team. He thought he was supportive before, but I've been carrying the burden while he played football.

Maybe that's why he was so good. He left all his stress on the field, and that equated to wins.

Luckily, Quincy hadn't needed surgery. Dr. Benjamin said the arrhythmia was not as severe as he initially thought and that it was probably more the heat and excitement of the day that made Quincy collapse. Yet Dr. Benjamin still wanted to monitor Quincy for a few months to see if he deteriorated. If he did, they would consider putting in a pacemaker.

"How do you feel about going back to work?"

Brayden sighs. "You know a few of the guys are angry with me for taking time off. I think the only friend I have left on the team is Jarrod."

"They'll be cool as long as y'all start winning again."

"Right."

Brayden turns around and rubs my ankles and calves. It makes me glad that I didn't get out of bed and get dressed yet. I'll take a spontaneous massage anytime.

"How do you feel about *not* going to work?" Brayden asks.

This is a tough question to answer. I do miss work. I've been thinking about the lost opportunity with Klein Newton, but I'm okay with being here for now. I keep thinking about what might've happened had I been in New York when Quincy collapsed. I just am not ready to be apart from him yet.

"Eventually, I want to go back. Kara has been maintaining some of my Atlanta clients, and I am thinking of ways to move more to product development as opposed to doing the artistry. That will keep me home. Luckily, Dallas is a good location to make that happen."

"Thank you." Brayden crawls up to the top of the bed and kisses me. "I have to go. I know reporters are going to be at practice. Wish me luck."

"You don't need it."

"You're right. I'm blessed."

He always says that. No matter what we're going through, no matter what happens to Quincy, he says we're blessed. I don't know if I necessarily share this same opinion.

While the status of our blessedness may be up in the air, there is one thing that no one can dispute. We are survivors.

Chapter 43

The Dallas Knights didn't make the playoffs. Brayden felt like everyone blamed him: the fans, Coach Wyatt, and even his teammates. Usually, the team had a getaway after a losing season to try to regroup and figure out how to start again for the next year. But not this year. Coach Wyatt was so heartbroken about not having a shot at another Super Bowl ring that he didn't host the getaway.

Jarrod seemed to be the only one left on Brayden's side, so he was over visiting Brayden's man cave like old times. Before marriage and sick children.

"Man, I'm glad this season is over," Jarrod said as he cracked open his bottle of beer.

"I know. I just keep feeling like it's my fault we didn't go to the playoffs."

"And that's exactly what Coach Wyatt wants everybody to believe, but it ain't your fault. What if you had gotten hurt? That bench was trash."

"I felt guilty as hell every week when I watched the games."

"One player leaving shouldn't turn a winning team into a losing team. This season is on all of us. And if one of his kids had almost died, he would've done the same thing."

"You think so?"

Jarrod took a swig and slammed his beer down on the table. "He sure would. 'Cause he's a damn human and father. But you don't get to be a human. You belong to the Dallas Knights."

Brayden shook his head. He hadn't even viewed it from that perspective. He'd only thought Coach Wyatt's thirst for winning was the impetus for him trying to block Brayden taking leave from the team.

"I don't belong to them. Not anymore. You either. We're free agents."

Jarrod nodded hard. "Damn straight. And I'm weighing all my options. Especially since I got my Super Bowl rings. I can go wherever I want. To whatever team gives me the fattest paycheck."

Brayden had never even thought about playing anywhere else besides Dallas. He'd been a Dallas Knights fan since he was a little boy. He'd only wanted to go to college in Texas, because he'd have a better opportunity to get face time with the Knights.

"Playing for the Knights has never been just about money for me, though."

"You better start thinking about them the way they think about you," Jarrod said. "I've got a sports agent that you should meet."

"I've never needed an agent for the Knights. Only for endorsements and outside stuff."

"Because you've always only taken what they handed you. It's time for you to make some moves."

"Maybe."

"Think of it this way. You making more money is not just for you. It's for Quincy, and it's for Chenille, too. And there are a lot of teams who would want to get their hands on the Knights MVP."

Brayden clicked on ESPN on the TV in the man cave. Looked like maybe Cleveland was going to win the AFC championship. No one saw that coming at the beginning of the season.

"There's Coach Wyatt now, looking like he just sucked a lemon," Jarrod said.

The reporter asked Coach Wyatt what his thoughts were on the postseason, and what plans he had to make sure the Knights had a winning season next year.

"You know we've maybe got the opportunity to make some roster changes in the off season. A few contracts are up for renewal, and we . . . well, we just have to evaluate all situations, and make sure we are doing what's best for the team."

"Are you referring to the fact that Jarrod Green and Brayden Carpenter are both free agents this year?"

"I'm saying that we're going to evaluate every area of the team and make sure we have the right players in the right positions."

For the first time all year, Brayden switched to a different channel. Jarrod laughed and shook his head.

"I told you, man."

The idea that Coach Wyatt might be implying on national television that he was done with Brayden, just because his son had gotten sick . . . Well, that was just unacceptable.

"Give me his number," Brayden said.

"Whose number?"

"The agent," Brayden said. "I'm gonna call him."

Chapter 44

I can tell Brayden has something to tell me that's going to piss me off, because he's been walking on eggshells since he woke up this morning. I watch him carefully and neatly hang his towel on the towel rack instead of throwing it on the floor. Then, he puts all of his shaving equipment in the correct places. He even wipes the sink dry.

Yes, he's absolutely going to get on my nerves this morning.

"You want to meet for lunch today?" Brayden asks as he steps out of the bathroom with a towel wrapped around his waist.

No matter how many times I see him this way, I never get tired of looking at his perfectly sculpted physique.

"Can't do lunch. First, Kara and I are taking Quincy to breakfast. Then, we've got a meeting with a chemist about making some new lip gloss colors for my clients. They loved the eyeshadows that I put together on the fly, so we want to follow that up with some gloss."

He nods and chews the inside of his cheek—a sure sign of stress.

"What's going on? You got something you want to talk about?" I ask.

Brayden grunts a reply, but instead of sharing what's on his mind, he walks into our closet. I follow him. We're going to get this over with right now. I don't want to spend the whole day worrying about what he's keeping from me.

"Brayden."

He turns to face me and sighs. I grip the edge of the bed, because I know it's coming. The bomb he's about to drop.

"What is it?"

"It's good news, actually," he replies.

"So, lay it on me. I love good news."

"Well, the league just approved a new expansion team in Portland, Oregon. The Portland Beachcombers."

"What does that have to do with you?"

Brayden sits down next to me on the bed. He takes my hand. Aw, hell. This is worse than I thought it was going to be.

"The owners want me to be a franchise player. They're going to build the entire team around me."

"Why are you talking about this? The season isn't even over yet. It's only January."

"The season is over for us. Deals are already being made, and the Knights haven't reached out to me with any offers for a new contract. I can go wherever I want. Even Portland."

"If you accept the offer." I snatch my hand away.

"Why wouldn't I accept the offer?"

I can think of a host of reasons he wouldn't accept, but the thing I can't get past in this moment is the fact that he didn't even mention that he was considering this. I stand up and start pacing our bedroom.

"Because I don't want to move to Portland, for one," I say, finally answering his question.

"Don't move, then. Stay here with Quincy, and I'll go to Portland for the season."

I press my lips together into a deep frown. He already knows how I feel about us living apart, especially after what happened with Quincy.

"Do you know what it means to be a franchise player?" Brayden asks. "Do you have any idea what this will do for my career?"

"Your career."

"Yes, my career! The career that pays for all this."

Now he's pacing and waving his arms around the closet, lingering on my shoe collection.

"I never asked for all this."

"Being a franchise player means a higher salary, more endorsements, and a better future. A legacy for my son."

"Our son. And what about my career? My work isn't in Portland. I've already given up most of what I do. Now you're asking me to give up the last piece of it."

Brayden takes one hand and slides it down his face in frustration. "You and Quincy can stay in Dallas."

"What the hell are you giving up?"

"I gave up half a season with the Dallas Knights, Chenille. That's why we're here right now."

"We're not living apart, and we're not living in Portland. I say no to both of those."

"You don't get to say no to this. You don't get to take this from me, Chenille."

"So you don't mind only seeing me once a month?"

"It'll be more than once a month. We're millionaires. We can fly out more than once a month."

This is how it begins. We plan to see each other every other weekend. Then, one of us has a meeting or event, and we have to cancel. We FaceTime each other at first; then it tapers off. Then he meets a groupie at a game, and . . .

My mother told me about the groupie ho that just slid up to him while we were at the hospital during my son's surgeries. I thought it would stop when we got married. It never stops.

"You don't trust me," Brayden says. "You think that just because we'll be working and living separately for part of the year, that I'm going to fall in the first vagina that I see."

"Why are you seeing vaginas?"

"Come on, Chenille! This is about all the bad things you believe NFL players do to their wives."

"It's about all the things they really do, not just what I believe."

"And you think I'm like the rest of them."

"I think you're a man."

"Your husband."

"Where is all this coming from? Since when were you unhappy here? I didn't know that you were even thinking of doing this."

Brayden shakes his head. "Are you hearing what I'm saying to you? Dallas may not be an option anymore."

"I'm saying no to this, Brayden."

"I'm. Saying. Yes."

We stand for a moment, glaring at each other, neither of us willing to bend, neither of us willing to compromise.

I break first, spin around on one heel, and storm out of our bedroom.

Straight to Quincy's nursery. I pick him up out of his crib. He laughs and smashes his hand into my face like nothing is wrong.

Everything is wrong.

I grab Quincy's boots and shove them into his bag. I have to get out of here in a hurry. Toddler boots are the worst to put on. They never go on quickly.

"Chenille!"

I hear Brayden calling my name, but I ignore him. I'm not talking to him until he's saying something that makes sense. Not having a conversation with me until he says he's not going to destroy our family.

Quincy still giggles as I pile him into the car seat and toss his bag on the floor of the back seat.

"Want to go see Auntie Kara?"

Quincy claps. No objections from him. It's crazy how kids can be oblivious to drama going on right under their noses.

Brayden's saying yes? He's saying yes!

I speed down the driveway and try to get to the freeway as quickly as possible, because it's almost time for Highway 121 and Highway 114 to gridlock with the rush hour traffic and DFW airport traffic, and that's the quickest way to Kara's apartment.

Shoot. I'm wrong. It isn't almost time. It is time.

My phone rings on the car Bluetooth, and I roll my eyes when I see *NFL Bae* flash on the screen. That nickname is supposed to make me smile when I see it. Instead my eyes cloud with tears as I hit ignore on the touch screen.

How could he be considering this? Portland freaking Oregon. First of all, black people do not live in freaking Oregon. I don't know any black people there. It's too far from my parents. Shit, it's too far from Brayden's parents, too. Second, has he heard of the Cascadia Subduction Zone? Why would he move our son to a city that is about to fall in the freaking ocean?

The Bluetooth phone rings again. I hit ignore again.

His career is good in Dallas. It's great. We've got everything we can ever want. We've invested well. If he retired today, we could live like celebrities for the rest of our lives. Why does he want to destroy us? Why does he want to tempt himself? Groupies with build-a-Barbie body parts, looking like Kardashians-slash-strippers-slash-Instagram-booty-clappers-slash-models will swarm him like a bunch of angry honey bees forced out of their hive.

Third time the phone rings.

"What!" I yell. Quincy stops giggling.

"Chenille . . . I . . ."

"Why are you doing this to us? Why?"

"You have to trust me, honey. This is going to be good for us. You'll see."

"No, no, no . . ."

"How about, how about you take a year off from your makeup business. Just one year. Help me get established in Oregon . . ."

"No! NO! You don't get to do this!"

Tears pour from my eyes. I knew from the very beginning it would always come to this. His freaking NFL career was always poised to eclipse everything I do. I knew I would disappear into him, into *his* life. He's trapped me in Dallas. With a baby. With *him.*

I pound the steering wheel and scream at the top of my

lungs. I disconnect the call. Not answering again. I refuse to disappear.

Traffic is opening up again, so I accelerate. Gotta hurry and get through this day, so that I can plan. I need a strategy. How can I keep it all? My husband, my business, my freaking life. I want all of it.

No, no, wait! Brake lights. My foot slides to the brake a second too slow. And then my car is smashing into the one in front of me. And then another car hits us from behind.

I feel consciousness fading. It's too quiet in the back seat.

I struggle to turn my head and see, but the airbag is in the way. I can't see. My head is wet and sticky.

I close my eyes. I just need to rest a seco . . .

Chapter 45

Brayden moved through the hospital hallways on autopilot. He'd gotten the call that no one ever wants to receive, that his family had been in an accident and that he needed to get there as soon as possible. No details had been provided, so he could only think the worst. And their little family couldn't take anything worse.

"Where's emergency?" Brayden asked the first hospital employee he saw. "My wife and son are there . . ."

This was not Baylor. Brayden didn't know his way around this hospital.

The orderly's eyes lit up. "You're Brayden Carpenter."

Of course. He recognized Brayden. Who in Dallas wouldn't?

"I am, but right now I need to find my wife and son."

Perhaps the somber tone to Brayden's voice shook the orderly out of his fandom, because his facial expression changed to match the seriousness of Brayden's.

"The emergency department is on the north side of the hospital."

Brayden blinked a few times and then started to read the signs, because the orderly was less than helpful. On another less critical occasion Brayden might have given him a tongue

lashing, but he needed his energy. He couldn't waste it school-
ing a hospital employee on good customer service.

"Let me just take you there," the orderly finally said.

Brayden breathed a heavy sigh of relief. "Thank you."

Brayden followed the orderly through the hospital, silently
praying that the caller had been overly cautious when she'd
contacted him. He actually convinced himself of just that. Out
of an abundance of caution, because he was a celebrity, the hospital staff had made a big to-do about contacting him. Chenille
and Quincy were fine.

The orderly delivered Brayden to a nurses' station in the
emergency department.

"You should be able to get your answers now," the orderly
said.

Brayden didn't even open his mouth to ask a question. He
just gave a pleading stare to the nurse and hoped she didn't
make him go through any additional hoops to find out what
was happening with his wife.

"I'll call for a doctor," the nurse said. "Go ahead and have a
seat."

Brayden sat, but he couldn't relax. If everything was fine, the
nurse would've told him. She would've eased his mind, but she
looked nervous. People always gave themselves away with body
language. A person could always tell when there was bad news
coming.

"Mr. Carpenter."

Brayden turned around in his seat to face a very young looking doctor. Too young, in Brayden's opinion, to be a surgeon.

"I'm Dr. Torres, the lead cardiothoracic surgeon."

"Cardio? Are you working on my son? We have a surgeon. Dr.
Benjamin. He's been operating on my son his whole life."

"Yes. We've reached out to Dr. Benjamin. He's out of the
country on vacation, but he will be calling us for a consultation.
In the meantime, your wife is stable. She's going to need re-
constructive surgery on her fractured pelvis and surgery to re-

pair her broken ribs, but after some rehabilitation, she will be fine."

"What is happening with my son?"

"That is a bit more complex. When he was thrown from his car seat, four of his ribs shattered, puncturing the good side of his heart."

Brayden's hands shook involuntarily. Quincy only had half a heart to begin with. What kind of twisted fate would allow the good side of his heart to be destroyed?

"Is he going to make it? Please tell me my son is going to make it through this."

"We've examined his surgical options. It doesn't look good without a heart transplant. We've put him on the transplant list."

Brayden nodded with his lips pressed in a grim line. A heart transplant. Dr. Benjamin didn't want to crack Quincy's chest open again. He had been hoping the arrhythmia would resolve itself and that he wouldn't need a transplant. Now Quincy no longer had a good side of his heart.

"He's high on the list, but if a heart doesn't come available in the next few days, he is going to have some severe issues. His heart defect and previous surgeries have already compromised his other vital organs to a degree."

"Can I see him?"

"Yes, but he's unconscious. He's on bypass and in a medically induced coma. A healthy child could survive on heart-lung bypass for weeks, but Quincy cannot last that long."

"So if we don't get a heart, he's going to die?"

"Yes, but we are near the top of the list now."

"Can I give him my heart?"

"Even if you were a perfect match, we couldn't harvest your heart and give it to your son. You need your heart to live."

"I don't want to live if my son dies."

"UNOS, the organization that regulates the transplant list, decides who gets hearts, so they might direct your heart to another person, even if we would take your heart—and we wouldn't. That is assisted suicide, which is illegal."

So many thoughts went through Brayden's mind. Could he commit suicide in a way that could give his son a heart? What if he shot himself in the head? Right in the hospital, so that they could take the heart right away. Or maybe slit his wrists in the emergency room.

"I know what you're thinking," Dr. Torres said. "Most of the methods of suicide would destroy the heart and not give us a viable organ. And again, we probably wouldn't be able to use your adult heart in his chest. The best thing for you to do is pray that a heart becomes available soon."

"So I'm supposed to pray that someone else dies? I'm praying that someone else's child doesn't wake up tomorrow? How in the hell can I pray for that?"

"I know it sounds crazy, but you are a man of faith. I've heard you talking about it on TV. I thought it might give you some comfort. Come and sit with your son. Maybe being in Quincy's presence will help."

Brayden followed Dr. Torres to the cardiac intensive care unit. He put on a gown and mask and prepared himself for what he was about to see.

But nothing could have prepared him for this.

Brayden had seen his son post–heart surgery before. Since birth he'd had tubes running through his nose and an incision down his rib cage. But this was different. Quincy looked battered.

Both of Quincy's eyes were puffy black and swollen. His lips were swollen, cracked, and tinted blue. That meant he wasn't getting enough oxygen—Brayden knew this from Quincy's previous surgeries.

"Why are his lips blue? He needs more oxygen."

"He's got as much oxygen as we can give him. The color will come back soon. He's adjusting to being on bypass."

Brayden sobbed. He couldn't help himself. He'd been avoiding the one thought that stayed at the forefront of his mind, but now he couldn't.

This was his fault.

He'd pissed Chenille off in the same way he always had, by

taking her contribution to their household for granted, by act-ing like who she was and her passion didn't matter as much as football. By trying to force her into being his football wife.

If he had apologized—no, if he had considered her before he made his decisions and made deals—none of this would have happened. His son would be breathing on his own. His son's heart would be beating on its own.

The surgeon touched Brayden's arm. "Do you need a minute? You can leave and come back. Take a few moments to collect your thoughts."

"I . . . Can you just have someone tell me when my wife is out of surgery? I need to be with her."

Brayden collapsed into the chair next to Quincy's bed and did exactly what the doctor had suggested in the first place. He prayed. For everything. A heart for his son, total healing for his wife, and that they would walk out of the hospital intact and whole.

And Brayden told God that if He was going to take Quincy and Chenille to go ahead and take him, too, because Brayden didn't want to live in a world without his wife or his son.

Chapter 46

I wake up screaming.

Two nurses run into the room and it hits me. I'm in the hospital. I've been in an accident. My whole body hurts, and I can't move.

"Her morphine drip is disconnected!" one of the nurses yells at the other.

I'm still screaming. It feels like someone shoved a broken bottle into my midsection.

"Where's my baby?" I wail as they reconnect my IV.

"Just try to relax, Mrs. Carpenter," the yelling nurse says. "Take deep breaths. The morphine will take effect soon."

"My baby!"

"He's in the cardiac intensive care unit," the other nurse says.

Finally, I breathe for real. He's alive. Cardiac intensive care is nothing new for my baby.

"He needs my breast milk. He needs to nurse. That will help him get better."

"Mrs. Carpenter, even if he could nurse, you have too many drugs in your system."

Brayden can go and get the milk from the freezer at home. There's plenty of milk in the freezer.

"My husband?"

This comes out shaky and whispery. I'm starting to feel drowsy.

"He's here. With the baby."

Then I remember I'm furious with him. This pain I'm in is his fault. My baby is back in intensive care because he . . .

Because I didn't strap him in his car seat all the way.

Tears pour from my eyes. Then the medicine kicks in. Dosage must be high, because I can't hold on to consciousness. My eyes droop as I struggle to stay awake.

"Get some rest," the first nurse says. "You need it."

Sleep is coming, but not rest. Rest won't come until my baby is back in my arms.

Chapter 47

Brayden's eyes flickered open. He'd fallen asleep next to Quincy's bed. What roused him from sleep was the sound of beeping on one of the monitors.

Brayden stood to go find a nurse, but he didn't even take two steps before the room was flooded with doctors and nurses. They pushed him out of the way.

"Mr. Carpenter, please step outside," Dr. Torres said.

"What's happening?"

"Please! Outside!" one of the nurses yelled. Brayden ignored her and stayed put.

"Looks like your son is having a stroke," Dr. Torres explained. "If it's a brain bleed, we need to find it, and I can't do that and hold a conversation with you."

Brayden backed out of the room and into the hallway. He watched the door swing closed as the doctors worked on Quincy's lifeless body.

"Mr. Carpenter?"

Brayden whipped his head toward the nurses' station. "Huh?"

"Your wife is out of surgery. Would you like to go and sit with her, while they work on your son?"

"Is she okay?"

"Yes, it appears so. She's sedated."

"Then no. I want to stay here until they tell me my son is okay."

The nurse nodded and went back to working on her papers and charts.

Brayden stared at the closed door that separated him from Quincy. He heard the chaos and noise happening behind the door, but hoped that meant they were saving his life.

Then, the door burst open, and the whole surgical team was pushing the bed and all of the equipment to the elevator.

"What's going on?" Brayden asked.

"I've got to get him to an operating room. He's had two strokes. We've got a brain bleed on our hands, and I have to stop it," Dr. Torres said.

Brayden watched helplessly as the hospital staff rushed his son into an elevator. The doors closed, and Brayden tried to swallow back his fear, but the sobs came anyway. One of the nurses, Brayden didn't know which, led him to a group of chairs where he could sit and do nothing.

"We're praying for your baby, Mr. Carpenter," the nurse said. "It's in God's hands."

Even though he was a praying man, Brayden found no comfort in the words. They'd prayed so many times over Quincy, starting from birth. What if they'd finally run out of answered prayers? What if it was Quincy's time?

Brayden slumped in the chair and sobbed some more. He looked down at his wedding band sparkling on his finger. He remembered his vows. In sickness and in health. They'd had sickness. More than enough for any union to withstand. For better or for worse. When was better coming?

Hours passed before the surgeon reappeared in the waiting room. The dejected look on his face communicated his message before he even opened his mouth.

"Just tell me," Brayden said.

"Your son had two brain bleeds. We got one before it did too much damage. The second one was more difficult to find, and by the time we did find it, Quincy's brain had swollen considerably, cutting off oxygen to his vital organs."

"Is he going to make it?"

Dr. Torres sighed. "It looks like the time without oxygen was too long, and it appears that he is brain dead. We are running tests for brain activity to be sure, but you should begin to consider donating the few viable organs that he has left."

Brayden broke down. He didn't hear anything else Dr. Torres said. He felt arms and hands on his shoulders and rubbing his back—he didn't know whose—and tissue being placed in his hands. These things were no comfort.

Then he remembered. Chenille.

"I . . . I have to tell my wife."

Chapter 48

This time when I wake up, I'm not in pain. They have the meds right, thank God. But Brayden is sitting next to my bed. His eyes are puffy and red, and a different kind of pain hits me.

"Quincy," I say.

Brayden nods. "He's not going to make it."

I struggle to sit up in the bed; pain forces me to lie still. I grip the bed rails and glare at Brayden.

"What do you mean, he's not going to make it?"

"Babe . . ."

"No. What the fuck happened?"

My chest hurts when I speak, but I push the words out anyway.

"Broken ribs punctured his heart. He had two brain bleeds. Surgeon said that it was a complication from him being on bypass. They couldn't find the second bleed fast enough."

All I feel is disbelief. I need more details. All of them.

"He's just gone?"

"He's on life support, but they can't find brain activity. Wanted to wait for you before we take him off life support."

I shake my head. "We're not taking him off."

"Babe . . ."

"Stop fucking calling me that! We're *not* taking him off life support."

"If we wait, his organs will fail, and maybe they can use some of his organs to . . . help someone."

In spite of the pain, I lunge at Brayden. He easily evades my swipe. If he were any closer, I would've clawed his face.

"How the fuck are you so calm about this? You're telling me my child is brain dead, and you want to take his organs? He never did get anyone to give him a healthy heart, but you want me to parcel up his body for someone else? Get the fuck out of my room."

"Chenille."

"No! This is your fault! Everything is all about you! I bet you have cameras in the hospital lobby. They gonna document you flipping the switch on your son?"

Those words were meant to break Brayden, but I just broke my damn self. The sounds coming from my body don't even seem like they belong to me. I sound like a wild animal. I feel like one.

Brayden jumps up and stumbles away from my bedside. His expression is a mix of shock and horror. And sadness. He looks as broken as I feel, but I don't give a damn.

The nurses run into my room, probably in response to my growls and screams. One of them pushes Brayden out into the hallway. The other one goes straight to my intravenous drip.

"No! I don't want to be put under. Last time I was out, my son had a brain bleed. Let me stay awake!"

"Mrs. Carpenter, you just came out of major surgery yourself. You have to rest."

"I cannot. I cannot rest while my baby is on life support. I gotta get up. I gotta see him."

I try to sit up again, and the entire room starts spinning. This heifer gave me the medicine anyway. I struggle against it, but my eyes are heavy again. I swear I'm gonna beat her ass if I never see my child alive again.

I open my eyes again. This time my vision is blurry, but there's nothing cloudy happening in my brain. I am fully aware of what's happening. My son's life is over.

And Brayden's ass is sitting in my room again, this time out of arm's reach. He sits up, noticing that I am awake.

"Chenille."

"Is my son still alive?"

"He is still on life support."

"Good."

"Nille . . ."

"Why aren't you praying like you prayed when I was pregnant? When he was having all of those surgeries? Where are your prayers, Brayden?"

"I've been praying since we got here."

"Do my parents know?"

"Not yet."

"Does your mama know?"

Brayden doesn't reply. Of course, he told his hateful-ass mama, and not mine.

"Call my parents. Fly them here. They should already be here, praying over their grandson."

"Babe . . ."

"Stop calling me that."

"Chenille." Brayden's voice cracks when he says my name like his throat is tired. "My parents are here, but I can send them home. It's just me and you. I think we need to do this alone."

"If you don't get my mama on a plane here, I swear to God, when I get up from this bed, I'm gonna claw your eyes out."

"I just thought we'd be there for one another and say good-bye to our son together."

"You've given up. Why you praying if you've given up?"

"If you saw him, Chenille, you'd let him go, too."

I close my eyes and let out a low moan. My breasts are heavy with milk. Quincy's milk. The let-down reflex makes my nipples start to tingle when I think of my son. It's long past time for him to nurse. He's never going to nurse again.

"Get my mama here, Brayden."

I close my eyes, because I can't stand to look at him. I feel the hospital gown moisten with a combination of my tears and Quincy's milk.

"Chenille, I'm sorry this accident happened. I'm sorry this happened to us."

"It didn't just happen, Brayden. You did what you always do. You made a decision without caring about how it would impact us."

"I made you angry. I apologize for that, but you didn't have to leave like you did."

"You made me angry. You are the cause. *This* is the effect."

"You didn't strap my son in the car seat."

His son. Not our son. *His* son. And he's trying to lay the blame for this at my feet. I already know what I didn't do. I will never forget or forgive myself for that. But this fool thinks he's blameless.

He isn't. If he'd put me first and his son first—before fucking football—my son would be just fine. Laughing. Playing. Living.

I'll never let him get away with this.

Chapter 49

Brayden met Chenille's parents in the waiting area outside Chenille's room. He'd given them details before they'd gotten on the plane, so Charlene's eyes were red and puffy. Kent's jaw was locked and his mouth turned down. Both of them looked like they'd already started the grieving process.

Charlene ran up to Brayden and hugged him tightly. Her wails broke the floodgates of his own tears.

"How could this happen?" Charlene cried. "How could the Lord take my grandbaby?"

Brayden didn't answer her questions, because he didn't have any answers. He was asking himself the same questions.

"I want to see my daughter," Kent said.

Brayden led them to Chenille's room, where she was mildly sedated. Her eyes were open, but she wasn't screaming like she'd been doing for the past three hours.

"Daddy," Chenille croaked.

Her voice sounded scratchy and raw, and Chenille didn't look at Brayden. Only her father.

"Aw, baby," Kent said. "We're here now. We've got you."

His father-in-law's words stung Brayden. *He* was here for *his* wife. He loved Chenille and Quincy more than his own life. He wished he was the one lying on the table without brain activity and that his in-laws were supporting Chenille in turning off his life support.

"Are your parents here?" Charlene asked.

"They're in with Quincy. Praying over him."

"I want to see him," Charlene said.

"Mama," Chenille asked. "Can you go to the nurses' station and ask if I can go, too?"

"You haven't seen the baby yet?" Kent asked, glaring at Brayden.

"She just had major surgery," Brayden explained. "They wanted to make sure she was stable."

"She should see her son," Kent said. "A mother's touch is healing."

"Exactly, Daddy. Please ask the nurses to take me to him."

Brayden followed Kent out of the room as he stormed over to the nurses. Then he stopped and turned to Brayden with a snarl on his lips.

"How did you let this happen? You're supposed to protect them," Kent said.

"Sir, it was an accident. You don't think I blame myself? You don't think I'd trade places with my son? With Chenille?"

Kent's face softened, but not much. He turned to the nurse.

"My daughter would like to see her baby. Is that possible?"

"She was frantic earlier," the nurse replied. "Her heart rate and blood pressure were too high. Seeing her son is going to be traumatic."

"Not seeing him is worse," Brayden said. "Just for a little while, and if she can't take it, we can sedate her again."

The nurse nodded. "Okay. I'll have her transported down to the pediatric intensive care unit."

Kent pushed past Brayden and went back into Chenille's room. Brayden felt unwelcome and unloved. Instead of waiting for the transport, he went ahead and walked to where his son was being kept alive.

Inside Quincy's room, Marilyn stood at the foot of the bed.

Joseph sat in the corner of the room, dabbing his eyes with a tissue every few moments.

"Mama."

"I'm waiting to hear from God, son. But I don't think Quincy is going to live here with us anymore. I think his spirit has already gone home."

Brayden didn't know why his mother's words gave him comfort, but they did. It made the decision to turn off the life support easier to swallow, although it wasn't easy at all. It was the hardest thing he would ever do.

An orderly pushed Chenille into the room in a wheelchair, with an IV unit attached to the side. Tears streamed down her face, but she didn't scream or yell. Brayden walked over to her and took her hand. She didn't snatch it away, but she didn't squeeze back.

"My baby," Chenille whispered. "Push me closer. I want to see him."

The orderly pushed the wheelchair to the head of the bed, where wires crowded Quincy's nose and throat. Chenille stroked Quincy's unmoving hand. Brayden touched her shoulder and squeezed. It wasn't just for Chenille's benefit. Brayden needed to feel connected to his wife. She wasn't the only one broken.

"We can take him off life support now," Chenille said. "My baby is gone."

Brayden exhaled, but it wasn't relief that he felt. It was resignation. Soon they'd be burying their son. After the miracle that had been Quincy's healing, now he was gone.

Charlene's quiet sobs were the only sounds in the room, outside of the buzzing of the machines keeping Quincy's body alive. Kent turned to leave, but Brayden couldn't move. His feet felt glued to the floor, his eyes trained on what was left of his son.

A few moments later, two doctors entered the room. Dr. Torres, the one who hadn't saved Quincy's life, held a clipboard in his hand.

"Mr. and Mrs. Carpenter, I'm very sorry for your loss," Dr. Torres said. "But your son's life can still have meaning. His corneas will give sight to a toddler who has been blind since birth."

"Sign the paper, Brayden," Chenille said.

Brayden took the clipboard from Dr. Torres and signed without reading anything. Dr. Torres nodded and gave silent directions to the staff who had suddenly appeared in the room. Nurses and doctors quickly moved to turn off monitors that showed Quincy's heart rate.

Brayden cried uncontrollably, but Chenille's tears had stopped. She watched, with dry eyes, as the hospital staff disconnected Quincy from the machines.

"He may take a few breaths when we take him off the ventilator," Dr. Torres said. "That is normal. It doesn't mean that he should go back on the equipment."

"Understood," Chenille said.

There was silence in the room after the hospital staff left. Brayden, Chenille, and the grandparents stared at the bed where Quincy's tiny body remained still. He did not take any breaths when the machine was turned off. Like Marilyn had said, Quincy's spirit was already gone.

Chenille put Quincy's tiny hand to her mouth and kissed it. Then she laid his arm across his chest. Brayden kissed his forehead.

"Take me back to my room," Chenille whispered.

Brayden touched the back of the wheelchair, but Chenille shook her head.

"Not you. Daddy, can you take me back?"

Brayden stepped to one side as Kent wheeled Chenille out of the room. Brayden swallowed hard, trying to subdue the sobs that wanted to rack his body in two.

"She's just hurting right now," Charlene said in a trembling voice, "but she needs you, Brayden."

Marilyn looked up from her grandson's body. There was a hint of anger in her eyes, but not enough to overcome the sadness.

"My son is also hurting, and he needs his wife, too."

Marilyn's words were true. Brayden needed Chenille now more than he'd ever needed anything or anyone. But he feared that she was as far away from him as Quincy's departed spirit.

Brayden grieved the loss of them both.

Chapter 50

My son's funeral is a damn circus. I didn't plan any of it. Couldn't. Marilyn took care of the entire freaking thing. She picked out the photos we would use. She chose the suit that they put on Quincy's lifeless body. I'm not upset that she did it, either, but from the number of reporters and media here, it looks like she probably sent out press releases.

We pull up to the church in a long white limo, the two of us, my parents, and Brayden's parents. Under our heavy winter coats, we're wearing blue—Quincy's favorite color. He loved blue so much, because Brayden always wore blue. The Dallas Knights wore blue. My son never left the house without wearing something blue.

As much as my son loved that color, you'd think the sky would cooperate. But no, it is a dark, dreary, gray January day. That color matches my mood.

I haven't cried again since we left the hospital, but I don't feel any peace. I don't feel anything. I'm just here. Maybe it has something to do with all the pain medication I'm on. That's why I couldn't help plan anything, really. I spend the majority of the day in a drug-induced blur. I'd rather things be blurry than clear these days.

They gave me medicine to stop my body from producing Quincy's milk, but I haven't taken it yet, so my breasts feel like rocks beneath my dress. I pumped a bit before we left the house, so that should get me through the service and the burial.

I'm not going to any repasts, parties, or anything else where they try to shove food down your throat and tell you everything is all right. Because that is a lie. Food doesn't make anything all right. Especially the kind of food they give you at repasts. They call it comfort food.

"Are you ready?" Brayden asks. "You don't have to talk to the reporters. Just act like they're not there."

"Why are they here?" I ask.

"You know why they're here," Marilyn says. "You're married to a celebrity. He is one of the most beloved men in Dallas. He brought the city two Super Bowls."

"They don't know you're leaving the team yet, do they? They wouldn't love you so much then."

"He's not leaving Dallas," Marilyn says.

I am surprised she doesn't know. Marilyn usually knows our business before I do, especially when it comes to football.

"I haven't made a final decision about that, Chenille."

"You might as well go. It cost our son his life."

"Your anger . . ."

Brayden's daddy put a hand on his shoulder, and he relaxed. Yeah, he better. He doesn't want to go there today. Blaming me today is not what he wants to do.

"Don't worry. I won't tell your adoring fans."

I slide my sunglasses onto my face and wait for the chauffeur to open the door. I still can't walk without a walker, so they've got a wheelchair waiting for me. I stare at the ground as Brayden and my father lift me into the chair. I hear the crowd gasp when they see me, and I also hear the cameras flashing. I'll be making the blogs this afternoon.

Kara is waiting right inside the entrance to the church. I wish I was happy to see her. I'm not.

Kara gives me a rough hug. I guess no one told her that three of my ribs are broken. She stops when I flinch.

"Did I hurt you?" Kara asks.

"A little, but I'm doped up, so I should be okay."

Kara hugs Brayden next and kisses his cheeks. She doesn't know what happened on the day of the accident. All she knows is that I got into an accident on my way to breakfast with her. If she did know what Brayden did, she'd be punching him in the face and getting hauled out by security. I'll tell her later when it's safe, when the cameras aren't around.

Brayden pushes my wheelchair up to the front of the church. I don't need to see my son's lifeless body again. I've already said goodbye. But this is a thing that's done. People go to the body and take one last look.

Quincy doesn't look the same. His skin is too dark. His mouth is turned downward when he was always smiling. He even looked like he was smiling in his sleep. That's how I know his spirit is long gone. Quincy's spirit smiled.

I hear Brayden's sobs behind me. He's leaning into the wheelchair. I can feel the pressure of his two hundred thirty pounds bearing down on me. The chair is holding him up.

Instead of a pew, the church has set up a row of chairs in the front, I guess to accommodate my wheelchair. Marilyn thinks of everything.

I am glad Kara sits next to me in the church. Brayden is on one side, Kara's on the other. He takes my hand in his, and I almost feel something. Then it goes away. I know he's in pain, but I don't care. His pain isn't worse than mine.

Brayden's teammates are all wearing blue suits with turquoise shirts and white roses on their lapels. They're all going to be pallbearers, even though Quincy's casket is so tiny. So tiny that it doesn't need all of them to carry him out.

A body that small isn't supposed to be in a casket.

I don't hear anything the preacher says. I mean, I hear noise, but I don't comprehend any of it. The church choir, for some reason, is only singing upbeat music. Praise songs. They're dancing and shouting like everybody's about to get the Holy Ghost.

I look down at the program in my lap. It says "Celebration of

Life," but my baby is no longer living, nor did he ever get to live, so what is it that we're celebrating?

The people who come to funerals just to get a show, to watch people cry and grieve, are getting a great performance from Brayden. He's on his feet now, hands lifted toward the sky. The sound of his wails almost rises above the singing.

His mother and some of the older women in the church surround Brayden. They rub his back, hand him tissues, and hold his hands while they pray for him. No one seems to care about my grief, except maybe Kara.

I glance over my shoulder at my mother. She's in bad shape, too, just as bad as Brayden. Unlike us, though, my father has his arm around my mother. He rocks her back and forth and dabs her eyes with tissues.

I dab my own eyes.

Some of the preacher's words start to break through my haze and float down to my ears.

He says, "We might have been caught off guard by young Quincy's home going, but God wasn't caught off guard. He was ready to welcome this young soul on home."

I think these words are supposed to be comforting, but they break me. A flood of tears flows from my eyes as I imagine my baby in heaven. I don't want him there. I want him with me.

Kara hands me a pill and water. I shake my head at her and try to hand it back.

"It's just Valium. It'll take the edge off, but you'll still be awake," she says.

I hesitate before putting the pill in my mouth. I don't want to get used to taking the edge off, but right now my legs won't stop shaking, and my throat is raw from crying, so I take the medicine.

I close my eyes, shiver, and wait for it to kick in. I still hear the preacher hollering at the top of his lungs. He's preached himself into a frenzy now. I feel Brayden's hand encircle mine. When I open my eyes, he's seated again. He pulls my hand up to his mouth and kisses it, wetting my hand with his tears.

Finally, I feel something for my husband. His pain is thick

and heavy, maybe heavier than mine, because he doesn't seem equipped for sadness. All of this crying and wailing seems alien to Brayden.

The Valium starts to kick in right as the pallbearers, Brayden's teammates, line up on either side of the tiny casket. Thank goodness for the medically induced mellow mood, because without it, I don't know if I could watch them carry my son's body out of the sanctuary.

Brayden pushes my wheelchair behind the pallbearers, and again I feel his weight on the chair. Without the support of the wheelchair for balance Brayden might be crawling up the center aisle.

The cemetery is only a mile or so away from the church, but the drive seems to take forever. There is an endless procession of cars behind us. There's no way all those people fit inside the church.

The car is silent outside of Brayden's sniffs and whimpers. I doze in and out of sleep because . . . Valium plus my pain medication. I wish I'd taken two or three. Maybe I'd be able to sleep through the rest of the day.

The car finally stops on the grass in front of a secluded plot in the cemetery. We must've purchased the celebrity special plot, so that our baby doesn't have to decompose with regular folk.

Hordes of people pile out of their cars, reporters included, to watch us put our baby in the ground. This really is too much for anyone. It's against the natural order of things. Quincy should be burying me. But it seems he was never meant to be here long. God didn't even give him a whole working heart. If it wasn't for modern medicine he would've died before he was a month old.

Dr. Benjamin is maybe here somewhere. I spied him at the church, but I don't know if he made it over to the cemetery. I wonder if he thinks this is a waste of his handiwork, his and Dr. Panesh's perfect trio of surgeries ruined by a car accident.

The hollering preacher is praying now. Except he's not hollering now. He's barely speaking above a whisper. At first I struggle to hear him, then I give up. It doesn't really matter what he says anyway. It won't take the sting out of this for me.

Nothing will.

My dress is wet. I can feel the warm, sticky liquid under my coat. My body's last-ditch effort to save my son. Trying to give him sustenance on his way into this hole in the earth.

I ignore it. Let it run. Let it drench my clothes, drip down my feet, and into the ground. Let Quincy's milk meet him in the afterlife. Isn't that what the old people say about heaven? It's like the promised land; flowing with milk and honey.

They don't lower the casket into the ground after the prayer. I guess they do that when the family is gone. Maybe it's too much. I can see how that makes sense. It is too much.

It's just that in the movies, they lower it into the ground, and inevitably someone tries to jump in. That would be Brayden. I don't want to see that. The bloggers would love it, though. Click bait.

Someone else is pushing my wheelchair back to the limo. It's not Brayden, because he has collapsed onto the ground. His teammates are helping him to his feet.

"I sure hate we're going through this, baby girl."

My daddy. I should've known that he would be the one taking care of me. He always takes care of me.

"Me too, Daddy. I miss my baby so much."

Saying this out loud breaks me again. These sobs are loud, ugly, and painful. Daddy pushes the wheelchair quickly, getting me away from the prying eyes.

Inside the limo, I hide behind the tinted windows. I go from feeling nothing to feeling everything all at once. I prefer the nothingness.

I reach in my purse for a pain pill. I double the dose, close my eyes, and wait for sleep to steal the next few hours.

Chapter 51

It had been two weeks since the funeral, and Chenille still hadn't said a word to Brayden. If it hadn't been for Marilyn, who had decided to set up shop in their home, and not leave until her son was okay, Brayden would've been living in complete silence.

He stared down at the breakfast in front of him. His mother's apple pancakes. His favorite, because it was the only thing she cooked well. But his appetite had not yet returned, so he ate only because he knew that his body would suffer without food.

"I took Chenille some breakfast. She neglected to thank me," Marilyn said.

"Mama, she's not talking. I don't think it has anything to do with you."

"I know what it has to do with. I understand losing a child. I had a miscarriage before we had you."

Brayden didn't correct his mother or explain the difference between losing a toddler and an unborn child. One, because he had no idea how much his mother had grieved that loss. Two, maybe that would help her relate to Chenille instead of pushing her away.

"I think she just blames herself for not strapping Quincy in that car seat," Marilyn said. "And it is her fault. I know if she could go back in time she'd change that."

Brayden shook his head. He'd already told Marilyn the reason Chenille had forgotten. And he'd placed himself at the center of Chenille's actions.

"So have you decided what you're going to do about this job offer in Portland?"

Brayden couldn't believe his mother had asked that question. Of course, he didn't know. He'd just buried his son and hadn't thought about what he might do for work. He hadn't decided what he'd do tomorrow, or the next day. He was living one minute at a time.

"I don't know yet. I know that I can't leave Chenille by herself. Not in this house, with all the reminders of Quincy."

"And what about you?" Marilyn asked. "You'll heal by throwing yourself back into your work. I think you should go."

"Only if Chenille is coming, too. I wouldn't leave her."

Marilyn gave an exasperated sigh. "I know. I raised the noblest son on the planet."

Brayden didn't know quite how noble he was, when the thought at the forefront of his mind was how to get Chenille to make love to him. He was going crazy with need, and the baby oil in the shower was getting old.

He knew Chenille's pelvis wasn't completely healed, but according to her doctor she was well enough for some contact.

Brayden was almost ashamed for feeling this way. What kind of oaf would be thinking about sex with his wife when they'd just lost their son and she was healing from an accident? But he couldn't help it. He wanted, no, *needed* her touch.

"Thank you for breakfast, Mama. I'm about to go and check on Chenille."

"Bring her empty plate back downstairs. I'll clean the kitchen, too."

Brayden couldn't remember the last time she cleaned anything. That was a job for the staff she hired. Brayden figured she was just giving herself a reason to linger in their home. He didn't mind. He was grateful for her presence.

Brayden stood in front of the master bedroom door. It was closed. It was always closed. Chenille had made it clear that she didn't want Brayden in bed with her, so he'd moved his residence to the man cave. But he wanted to go into his bedroom. He wanted to share the bed with his wife. They didn't have to have sex. He just needed to feel her warmth and inhale her scent.

He refused to knock on his bedroom door, although it felt as if he ought to. Instead, he pushed the door open slowly, to give Chenille the opportunity to react, holler, or scream. Maybe she'd even throw something in his direction. Any of that was better than silence.

Chenille said nothing as Brayden crossed the room. She looked straight through him when he stood at the foot of the bed. She pretended he was invisible.

"You can't do this forever," Brayden said.

She didn't respond. Maybe she intended on doing this forever, because she sure wasn't opening her mouth.

"Chenille."

She stared straight ahead. Even her blinks looked angry. They were slow and deliberate. She pressed her eyes shut tightly and sprung them back open again, like she hoped he'd disappear in the time she took to close and open her eyes.

Brayden walked over to the untouched breakfast plate and picked it up. Chenille had to be eating something, because she didn't look like she was losing weight, but she never touched anything his mother brought.

"These pancakes were good. You should've tried them," Brayden said.

She didn't respond, except to turn her head and look at the window. The curtains were closed, making the room dark outside of the artificial light from the lamp.

Brayden walked over and opened the curtains, letting sunlight spill in. Like a vampire, Chenille squinted and turned her face away.

"You need to go outside. It's really warm today. Too warm for

January. In the fifties. Maybe the nurse can wheel you outside for a while."

Still, Chenille gave no response to his presence in the room.

"You can't just keep ignoring me, Chenille. I am your husband. We have to face this together."

Brayden liked to think that he sounded confident in his declaration. She couldn't ignore him. He wouldn't let her. But Chenille's stubborn lack of acknowledgment spoke confidently, too. It said she could absolutely ignore him. Maybe even until the end of time.

Chapter 52

More than a month has passed since my son died. I still don't have much energy for anything other than my physical therapy, which is kicking my entire ass. It's not so much learning to walk again, but bearing the weight of walking. I really don't need to walk. Where am I going anyway?

My physical therapist, Becca, won't let me give up, though.

She leaves me sweating and tired after each session. She's determined to make me *want* to walk again. We're not there yet. My mobility still isn't at the top of my list of concerns.

Today, I think about pain meds again. I haven't been taking them. I'm growing dependent on them, so cold turkey it is. Don't want to have *drug-addicted* as an additional qualifier when people describe me. I've already got *grieving* and *bedridden* in front of my name.

Brayden comes in here every day. I hear him coming up the steps now. Freshly showered, I get settled into the bed to ignore him.

It might be easier to go ahead and talk to him and get it over with. I almost gave up the silent treatment until I heard him on the phone when he thought I was sleeping. Portland is still on the agenda. After everything, he's still planning to go there like it's an option.

It should've never been an option.

So I can't give in and let him think he's working his way back into my heart. Even if I'm talking to him, that's not going to happen.

This time when he opens the door, Brayden is holding roses, candy in a red heart box, and a little blue box. Right. It must be Valentine's Day.

And this fool is in here to ask me to be his Valentine. He's clearly lost his mind.

"Happy Valentine's Day," Brayden says in a cheery voice.

Cheery? How in the hell is he cheery? There is nothing to smile about here. No way he thinks he should be full of joy so soon after we buried our son.

I don't reply.

He walks over, uninvited, and sets the vase full of roses on the nightstand next to the bed. It takes all of my restraint not to knock it over on the floor. The only reason I don't is because then he'd clean it up, giving him another reason to stay in the room when I want him to just be gone.

"I got you a gift. From Tiffany's. I think you'll like it," Brayden says.

He sets the box down next to the roses, but I don't make a motion to open it. I don't care what's in that box, because I know Brayden is just trying to get back into this bed with me. I have zero desire for sex. Even if I wasn't sore from my waist down after my physical therapy, I still wouldn't want it.

For me, making love is more than just a physical act. It's emotional and spiritual. In those areas I feel like I'm floating in a dark void. Nowhere in there is the need to share anything with Brayden.

Since I don't open the box, Brayden does it for me. He clearly wants me to see whatever it is that he's purchased. I sigh and finally look in his direction. Maybe eye contact will help this move faster.

"It's a charm bracelet, with a pair of baby booties. Each bootie has a blue sapphire."

I take the bracelet from his hand and watch his facial expression go from cautious to optimistic. Next I close my hand into a fist around the bracelet.

Then I hurl it across the room with all my might, which isn't much. I wanted it to fly dramatically into the wall, but it just falls to the carpet with a small thud.

I don't want anything from him.

But I especially don't want anything from him that reminds me of my baby.

Brayden sighs and searches the floor until he has the piece of jewelry in his hand again.

"I know you hate me, but I don't hate you. I love you. I accept all of the responsibility for what happened to Quincy, but hating me won't bring him back."

Hating him wouldn't bring Quincy back. But loving him wasn't bringing my son back, either.

Why should he get to feel my love? Why should I wrap my arms around his neck and smother him with kisses? Why?

When my son's arms will never reach around my neck again.

I'll never feel his kisses on my face again.

I'm barely holding on myself. I have one foot inside this existence and one foot out. All of my energy is going to physical therapy and not taking all of my pills at once.

I don't have enough left for loving Brayden.

Chapter 53

Brayden sat at the foot of his bed and waited for Chenille to awaken. He was leaving for Portland, a month with the coach working through strategies and opening details for how Brayden would integrate with the team. Then training camp. He was going to be gone for months, and Chenille was still only giving him one-word answers when she did speak to him.

It had been five months since Quincy died. Brayden needed to talk to get through to Chenille.

She squinted and stretched. Then she rolled her eyes when she saw him in the room.

"What?"

"Good morning. Let's start there."

She grunted. It wasn't "good morning," but it also wasn't "get out."

"I leave for Portland today," Brayden said. "I'm going to miss you."

This garnered a laugh. "Why? I'm not even here anymore. Not really."

Three sentences. This was progress. She hadn't spoken three sentences to him since before the funeral.

"Because I miss us. Shit, I miss me."

"I miss my son," Chenille said. "Every hour, every minute, and every second of every day, I miss him."

"I know. I do, too."

Chenille scooted to the edge of the bed and got out slowly. She was walking much better now, with just a cane. In a few months she wouldn't need that.

She went into the bathroom. Brayden heard her flush and then the water running in the sink. She was washing her hands and then brushing her teeth. Chenille wouldn't go ten minutes in the morning without brushing her teeth. She said she hated the taste of morning breath.

Brayden found himself remembering every detail of her habits, and he yearned for her. He wanted to feel her minty fresh breath on his neck when she kissed him goodbye every morning.

"When does your flight leave?" Chenille asked when she came out of the bathroom.

"Four o'clock."

She nodded. She didn't look happy or sad about it, just seemed to acknowledge the fact.

"You know there's still time for you to come with me," Brayden said. "We can take some time off away from everyone."

"You're going to work."

This wasn't a no, so Brayden felt more hope spring forth.

"Yes, but I'll have plenty of downtime."

"I'll be fine here. Physical therapy, remember?"

"Right. You know we can find you one in Portland."

"Or one in Atlanta."

Brayden cleared his throat and sighed. He felt the hope evaporate.

"You're still thinking of moving back to Atlanta."

"Nothing keeping me here."

"Are we over?" Brayden asked.

"I don't know."

Brayden reached across the bed and tried to touch her leg. She recoiled as if he'd burned her.

"Don't touch me," she said. "My body. You need permission to touch me."

"Okay. I won't touch you. Just say you'll stay here until I get back."

"Why?"

"We've been through a lot. Maybe we're supposed to be together."

"I don't believe in destiny, because that means a cruel God destined my son to die. So I don't know what you mean by we're *supposed* to be together. People are together or they aren't."

"Right now we're between those two things."

"In between, but closer to aren't."

Frustrated, Brayden stood. He wanted to kiss her goodbye, but his touch was not welcome. He couldn't say goodbye, either. It felt ominous.

"See you soon."

She didn't reply. Maybe she wasn't planning on seeing him soon. Or ever again. Brayden's heart felt uneasy about leaving her there, but what could he do? He could be unwanted and unloved in Dallas or Portland. At least in Portland, he'd be distracted by work.

If Chenille was still here when he came back, then maybe they'd have a chance.

Chapter 54

Brayden hadn't known what to expect when he'd signed up for the support group his Portland coach recommended. But he definitely wasn't prepared for this: a room that felt like a conference room at the Four Seasons, but without a big table. There were only six leather chairs grouped in a circle. The big picture window was almost a distraction, or maybe it was the waterfall that rushed out of the side of a rock wall. Nature's decorating was always more breathtaking than man-made things.

Brayden glanced at the faces in the room. The support group was very small: four people, including the counselor. Brayden wished Chenille had come with him, or at the very least he wished she'd gotten on the airplane and come with him to Oregon. He wanted a new start with his love, but had no idea where to even begin with her. Maybe this counselor could help.

"I'm John," the counselor said to Brayden. "That's the way we introduce ourselves here. Just a name."

Brayden felt warmth emanating from the man. John wasn't smiling, nor was his voice especially cheery, but it was warmth and consideration that Brayden felt when John shook his hand.

"I'm Brayden."

It was an entire sentence, but Brayden had to resist the urge to say more. It was a relief, though, to sit in a room unrecognized. Or, at least, he thought he was. The woman in the room was barely engaged; she stared out the big picture window and hummed quietly.

"I'm Alan," the other participant said.

John walked over to the woman and touched her shoulder. She was startled.

"Oh. I'm Tia."

Tia's lips curled into a smile, but her eyes didn't do the same. Even though they were dry, she had the saddest eyes he'd ever seen. They were huge and heavily lashed, but red and puffy with dark circles underneath.

"Did you sleep last night, Tia?" John asked.

"No."

"Night before that?"

She shook her head.

"When did you last get any rest?"

"I took a nap before I came here. Or, I should say the nap took me. One second I was looking at my phone. Then, next thing I knew, I was waking up screaming. I think I was asleep about an hour or two. Not really sure."

"You need to sleep."

"I keep dreaming about her. How she might have felt when she died. I always wake up, though."

She blinked like she was about to start crying, but no tears came. Brayden wondered if she was dehydrated or just all cried out. Listening to her made him choke up a bit.

"I dream of my son, too," Brayden said. "But not about him dying. It's always random things, like him drinking a glass of milk or playing with his train set."

"And then you wake up and realize it isn't real," Alan said.

"Yes. That's exactly what happens."

"Do you appreciate the dreams or wish they'd go away?" John asked all three of them.

"If they go away, I lose touch with my baby," Tia said.

Alan scoffed and shook his head.

"You disagree, Alan?" John asked.

"I don't think I'm in touch with my son. He's gone, and the dreams are just memories of him imprinted on my brain. Nothing supernatural about it."

Tia rolled her eyes. "Maybe there's nothing supernatural about your dreams. You can't speak for me."

"What do you think, Brayden? Maybe you can break the tie."

"I don't know. I just know that I feel peace while I'm sleeping, but when I wake up, it's like I lose him all over again."

Both Alan and Tia nodded. Maybe they couldn't agree on the cause or purpose of their dreams, but the effect was the same.

"Write me a prescription, doc," Tia said. "Give me some good drugs so I can make it through the night."

"You know I can't write prescriptions, but I can give you a referral to a psychiatrist."

"I don't want your pills anyway. I want to stay in touch with my little Bella."

"You don't go to sleep, you'll be with your kid on the other side," Alan said. "That's what my doctor told me right before he gave me sleeping pills."

"How'd your son die?" Brayden asked Alan.

Alan traced the letters in the tattoo on his arm. Brayden figured it must be his son's name.

"Leukemia. I had it when I was a kid, but I beat it," Alan said.

Brayden looked at Tia, but she was staring out the window again, so he didn't ask her the question.

"My son was in a car accident."

"That's the worst," Alan said. "You can't prepare for that."

"Tell me about it."

"So, the next time any of you have a dream about your deceased child, write down as much of the dream as you can recall. Do this as soon as you open your eyes."

"Why?" Alan asked.

"To help you remember."

"What if it's the things I'm trying to forget?" Tia asked.

Brayden wanted to hug her. Or he wanted someone to hug her. Maybe physical touch wasn't part of John's therapy method, because no one moved.

"Let's talk about some relaxation techniques," John said. "You all need to learn how to go to a peaceful place in your mind when the grief comes."

Brayden closed his eyes and listened to John talk about deep breathing and meditation. This wasn't what he needed. Brayden needed Chenille.

But she wasn't in Portland, nor did she have any plans to be there. It wasn't as if she was well enough to travel. Brayden wondered if either of the other members of this group was married. Where were their grief partners?

Maybe it was a typical thing for spouses to grieve separately. Seeing Chenille did remind Brayden of Quincy. They had the same eyes, nose, and dimples.

The session ended, although John didn't really dismiss the group. He just told them good evening and left the room.

Alan left without saying another word to Brayden or Tia. Brayden almost wished that Alan had recognized him. He felt naked and ordinary without his celebrity status.

"Do you want to get coffee or something?"

Brayden heard himself inviting Tia out for coffee, and he wondered what made him do that. She wasn't friendly—at all— but he was lonely, and she was there. They had at least one morbid thing in common.

"Not coffee. Food. Haven't had a real meal in days. You buying?"

Brayden hesitated. Maybe she had recognized him and had gone straight to groupie mode.

"Where do you want to eat?"

She shrugged. "I don't know. Chili's?"

Brayden relaxed. She hadn't recognized him. If she had, she probably would've requested something more than Chili's.

"Sure. I like the chicken tenders."

"Yep. They're called crispers, and they're greasy and good."

Brayden chuckled as they walked out of the ballroom. "You look like you'd be a vegan or something."

"What makes you say that?"

Brayden motioned to her chunky box braids, flowery sundress, and flip-flops. "You've got a Solange, hippie vibe."

"Solange? Who is that?"

"Beyoncé's hippie sister."

Tia wrinkled her nose. "I'm sorry. I don't know who Solange is. I know Beyoncé, though. She looks like she eats meat."

That made Brayden laugh, and it sounded foreign and strange. He hadn't laughed since Quincy died.

"Did you drive here?" Tia asked. "I don't have a car."

"How'd you get here?"

"Lyft."

Brayden wished she had her own car. Something about arriving somewhere with a woman in his car worried Brayden. If this was Dallas, it would've been impossible. Tia's picture would be on the cover of every blog by morning.

But it wasn't Dallas. It was Portland. No one knew him here.

"Yes, I drove. Come on. You can ride with me."

Brayden walked Tia out to his rental, an Escalade, just like he drove at home.

"Wow. This thing is huge."

Tia was tiny, so it made the truck loom even larger. Brayden had to help her up into the passenger side of the truck.

When he got in on his side, Brayden watched Tia fiddle with the buttons and dials. It was almost like she'd never been in a car before.

"You never seen an SUV dashboard before?" Brayden asked.

"Not this kind. This is fancy and new. The Lyfts I get to ride in are usually small cars. I haven't been in a truck like this."

"Well, a lot of it is computerized and connects to smart phones."

Tia shook her head and snatched her hands away like the dashboard had suddenly become electrified.

"This is how they track you."

"They who?"

"The government. They're watching our every move."

Brayden let out that strange and foreign laugh again. "Let's go eat."

Tia stared out the window as Brayden pulled up the restaurant on his GPS.

"You from here?" Tia asked.

"Nah. You?"

"No. Los Angeles."

"Dallas for me."

Tia scrunched her nose again. "Texas is like its own country."

"Yep. I'm Texas born, Texas bred, when I die, I'll be Texas dead."

"That sounds stupid."

"Don't mess with Texas."

Finally, she laughed. "I don't think black guys from Texas are supposed to say those lines. I think that's for white guys only."

"Nuh uh!"

Chili's was only two miles away from the hotel where the sessions were held, and they'd missed the lunch crowd and beat the dinner crowd. They'd arrived during that witching hour when there was no wait for a table or a meal.

"You want a cocktail?" Brayden said when they sat down.

"No. I don't drink anymore."

"Recovering alcoholic?"

She shook her head. "Recovered."

Tia pushed her braids behind her ears, wrapped her arms around herself, and hugged.

"I've heard that a person never truly recovers from addiction. They always have to be vigilant."

"Not me. I am cured."

Brayden wanted to press for more details. It was like hearing someone else's problems helped him deal with his own. Or maybe forget his own.

"Well, no cocktails, then."

"It doesn't bother me if you drink. It won't tempt me."

Brayden wasn't much of a drinker, either, so cocktails were not a prerequisite to dinner.

"So . . . chicken?"

Tia smiled, and her face transformed. Her eyes tightened to little slits, and the apples of her cheeks reddened with . . . glee? No, that wasn't right. It was too fleeting. She quickly bounced back to her sullen mood as if she'd suddenly remembered some rule against smiles.

They placed their orders for the exact same meal. Chicken, fries, and corn on the cob.

"How long have you been going to the support group?" Brayden asked.

"A month."

"Does it help?"

"No. Not me."

Brayden wasn't sure that it would help, but hearing the words confirming that fact still took a moment to process.

"I don't think anything will make it better. Not even time," Tia said. "It's just pain you get used to."

Brayden woke up heavy. That's how his grief felt: like a large entity had centered itself on Brayden's chest. During the course of the day, the load didn't lighten. It wore him out. He was exhausted by nightfall, but couldn't sleep. Was she saying it would always be this way?

"You're married."

It was a statement and not a question as Tia motioned to his ring.

"Yes."

"How long?"

"Almost five years."

"Was the kid you lost hers?"

"Yes."

"But she's not here, in counseling with you?"

Brayden shook his head.

"She doesn't talk to me."

"Oh . . . how long has your child been gone?"

"Six months."

"She hasn't talked to you in six months?"

Brayden did not want to discuss this. Not with this stranger.

"What do you do?" Brayden asked.

"Do? Oh you mean work. I don't do anything. I am unemployed."

"Oh!"

Tia curled her upper lip. Brayden couldn't tell if this meant she was irritated or angry. He hoped he hadn't offended her.

"I'm sorry. I guess I just didn't expect you to say that," Brayden said. "Most people who are unemployed talk about the job they used to do or want to do."

"Not me. I stay in the now. Presently, I have no job. What do you do?"

"I . . ."

Brayden should have considered this line of questioning before he started it. She didn't know who he was, and she was unemployed, so he definitely didn't want her to know he was a ballplayer.

"I have a lot of investments. I own a restaurant back in Texas."

"Nice."

Brayden was relieved that she didn't want to dig any deeper. Surface level was better.

After a few minutes, their identical meals arrived at the table. They dug in ravenously, as if they'd just left from running a marathon and needed to refuel. An emotional marathon, maybe. And it wasn't over. This was just a rest stop.

"Why is the unhealthiest food always the most delicious?" Tia asked.

"I disagree with the unhealthy part. Chicken is protein. Potatoes are healthy carbs, and corn is just a perfect food."

"You have a nice face," Tia said as she chuckled. "Friendly. Like a person could trust you."

"I think I look too friendly. Every panhandler I see asks me for money."

"You need to work on your resting bitch face."

"I don't have one of those."

Tia laughed. Her braids swayed back and forth, as she tossed her head back and enjoyed the moment.

"Feels good to laugh."

"I know what you mean. I haven't found much to laugh about lately."

"You can laugh today."

Tia took Brayden's hand in hers and just held it. Her hand felt soft, although she looked hard around the edges. Her touch was needed. And it was electric. His body awakened and responded to her touch.

"You want to get out of here?" Brayden asked.

"Yeah."

Brayden stopped thinking, turned the logic button in his brain to the off position. Now was not the time for thinking. It was the time for feeling.

For feeling what he hadn't felt in a very long time.

Chapter 55

This is the first time I've gone outside since my baby died. Kara is forcing me out of the house for a spa day. I'm sitting in the spa's parking lot, not really wanting to go in. Not because I don't think I'll enjoy it. Who wouldn't want a full-body massage, facial, manicure, and pedicure? Who wouldn't want a full-body sugar scrub with honey? Who wouldn't want to sit submerged in a hot tub while all of the toxins exited their body?

I will enjoy it. But do I deserve to enjoy anything? My baby is gone from this earth. He'll never get to enjoy anything ever again.

I can't say how many times I've thought of ending it all since Quincy died. The hurting and then the nothingness—the endless cycle of sadness, anger, guilt, and then sadness again. It's too much.

I'm watching Brayden heal. He says he's with me, but he's not. He's moved past where I am. He's like a paralyzed person getting the feeling back in their legs. I'm not there yet. Don't know if I'll ever be there.

Part of me wants to tell him to go on and figure out how to live the rest of his life. The other part wants him with me, so that he can experience what I feel. The sadness. The anger. The guilt. Why should he get to be whole again?

I'm glad he's in Portland, though. Seeing him getting over the loss of our son is almost as hurtful as losing him. Because there's no getting over this for me.

There's a tap on the driver's-side window. Kara.

"Come on, girl. Don't stay out here in the car. Let's go."

I roll my eyes and swing the door open.

"You were thinking of going back home, weren't you?" Kara asks. "You need this, Chenille. Stop thinking you're not supposed to have any joy, ever again."

"Who said that?"

"It's not what you say. It's what you do. Or don't do. Today is about pampering."

I feel the tears well up in my eyes. I don't let them fall. She's right.

She puts her arm around me, and we go inside. The girl at the reception desk smiles and greets us. We're members here, although it's been a while since I've had treatments.

"Mrs. Carpenter," the receptionist says. "It's good to see you again."

I smile and nod at her. I'm afraid if I open my mouth to say something that I'm going to start sobbing. I don't want to embarrass myself in here.

"Come on," Kara says.

We go back into the locker room and change into our robes. I look at myself in the mirror. Shoulders slumped, eyes puffy and red. I look like hell. Ten years older. Grief ages a person. It's aged me.

"Yeah, girl. You look a mess. It's all good. You already got a man," Kara says.

"Do I?"

"Brayden ain't going nowhere."

I shrug. "Don't think I care either way."

"You do. Or you'd already be gone. You're just punishing him."

Now this pisses me off. She must be ready to fight up in here.

"He deserves to be punished. He killed my baby."

Kara sits down on the bench and looks me in the eye. "He pissed you off, being a jerk like he always does. But there was an accident. The baby's death was an accident."

I swallow hard. There *has* to be someone to blame. This can't just be a random choice of the universe, because then what?

"It's his fault, though."

"Why do you think you're still here?" Kara asks.

"What do you mean?"

"You survived the accident. Why?"

"I don't know. My injuries weren't as severe. I'm healthy. Lots of reasons."

Kara shakes her head. "Nope. You're here because God still wants you here. Every day that we're here is because we've got some purpose."

"And my baby had none?"

"I don't know. Maybe he was here to draw you and Brayden closer together."

"But we're farther apart than we've ever been. So that mission failed."

"God doesn't fail. But you're resisting. You won't talk to Brayden. You're pushing him away."

"You think I should forgive him."

"I think you need him, as much as he needs you. I'm not saying let him all the way back in yet. But maybe when he gets back from Portland, you could . . . you know . . ."

"Ugh. No."

"You need it, too. That's why you look like that. All humped over like an old lady. Gone head and get some of that elixir."

I want to yell at Kara, but she is hilarious. I can't help it. I'm laughing so hard that my legs are wobbling. I have to sit down.

"Gone head and get you some, girl."

She is stupid as hell. But maybe she's right.

Chapter 56

Brayden considered prefacing his confession with a gift of some sort. A piece of jewelry. Flowers. A pair of designer heels.

But none of these would help soften the blow of what Brayden was about to reveal.

Breakfast was the only atonement offering he had. It damn sure wasn't enough.

Chenille took her time walking to the table, using her cane, each footfall careful and measured. At least she no longer winced with each step. She'd be whole again soon.

"What's all this for?" She looked at the spread and chuckled. "What did you do?"

Brayden swallowed and reconsidered his revelation. Chenille's spirits were returning. She spoke to him every day now, and even, on occasion, accepted hugs and kisses. This would be a tremendous setback.

They might never come back from this.

But Brayden knew he didn't want a marriage of secrets. He didn't expect perfection from Chenille, but he did expect honesty. He couldn't ask of her what he wasn't willing to give.

"Let me get your chair."

Brayden jumped up from his seat to help Chenille into hers.

He took the cloth napkin and laid it across her lap like he was a waiter in a fine restaurant.

"All your favorites," Brayden said. "Bananas Foster French toast, quiche, shrimp and grits and fruit."

"I know you didn't cook this."

"You are correct. I had it delivered. It's way more delicious that way."

"Well, I'm glad about it. I'm starving. Do you want to bless the food?" she asked.

How was he supposed to send up a prayer for his wife when he was about to say what he was going to say?

"Um, okay. Lord, we thank you for this food. Please bless it and make it fit for nourishment. And Lord, we ask you to forgive us our sins. In Jesus' name, amen."

"Amen."

Brayden got up again to put food on Chenille's plate so that she didn't have to lunge across the table or stand up.

"Full service, huh? Do I have to leave a tip?"

She gave him a tentative smile, but he couldn't smile back. In an instant Chenille's smile faded.

Usually, in the time before he'd broken his vows, Brayden would've made a cute joke about her leaving him a tip in the bedroom. But his mood wasn't lighthearted. Outside of burying Quincy, this was the hardest thing he was ever going to do.

"Why are you so quiet?"

"Babe, I don't know how to tell you this."

"Tell me what?"

"Remember when I went to that counseling session?"

She nodded. "The one I didn't want to go to?"

"Yes, that one. At the session, there were other parents who'd lost their children. We talked. Shared our feelings. It was a very emotional session."

"Okay . . ."

Brayden cleared his throat and exhaled before he continued.

"While I was at the session, I met a young woman . . ."

Chenille scoffed and shook her head. She slammed her fork down on her plate.

"I can't believe this bullshit," Chenille said. "You cheated on me?"

He should've known Chenille wouldn't let him get the words out. She could damn near read his mind sometimes.

"It was one time, and I know this is a cliché, but it meant absolutely nothing. We were just in pain and turned to each other."

"You were supposed to turn to me."

"Was I? This is no excuse, but, Chenille, you just started talking to me a couple weeks ago."

"Oh, my bad. Sorry for trying to heal from a devastating injury and mourn my only son."

"We're both mourning. I miss him every day. I miss *you* every day."

Chenille rolled her eyes and her neck. "I sure can't tell."

"I never saw the girl again. She didn't come back to the next session. She didn't leave a number. I only know her first name."

"Why are you telling me?"

"Because I don't want any secrets between us. Because I love you, and I am not giving up on us or going anywhere."

"Really? Are you sure this isn't about to be front page news? I know how you like to live your life in the media."

"No. No one knows."

"How you know this chick isn't about to sell pictures of your penis to the blogs?"

"I don't think she knew who I was."

Chenille laughed. A loud, throaty sound that filled the room.

"You are so damn stupid and gullible."

"I really don't think she knew."

"Hoes always know, fool! Did you use protection?"

Brayden didn't want to answer this, although he had known she'd ask. Chenille thought of everything and pondered every possible solution.

"You're taking too long to answer. So, you met a ho, and screwed her raw, but you up here telling me you're not going anywhere? You're getting the hell up out of here, Brayden. Nasty ass. Bet you ain't even get tested for STDs."

Brayden took all of her verbal assault without a word. He deserved it. Every bit of it.

"I will get tested tomorrow. You're right."

"I don't care what you do."

"I love you with everything in me. That is the only reason I'm telling you this. I have made a mistake, but I'm going to fix it."

Chenille's nostrils flared and she rolled her eyes. She pushed the food away from her.

"You know what's funny? I don't even feel anything. I can't even cry about this. This is like the rotten cherry on top of a bullshit sundae."

"I swear it's gonna be the last time I hurt you."

She laughed again until tears filled her eyes.

Then, she finally said, "Whatever, Brayden. Leave or don't leave. Screw who you want. Just leave me alone."

She pushed herself up from the table. Brayden jumped up to help, and she shoved him away.

Brayden wanted to follow her out of the kitchen, and beg Chenille to forgive him. Their son had been gone for months, but it felt like there was a lifetime full of pain between them. Maybe she was numb and couldn't feel, but Brayden felt everything all at once: anger and grief at the loss of his son, and overwhelming love for the wife that he had probably just lost.

Their son's death was not supposed to separate them. That wasn't a part of the marriage vows. And although Brayden had no idea how he was going to fix this, he *was* going to fix it. Chenille was his everything. She and football were all he had left.

Chapter 57

I call Kara and tell her to come over, mostly to keep me from doing anything stupid like destroying all of the expensive stuff in this house. All of these things are mine, too, so tearing it up isn't worth it. At all.

But I still want to break things, if that makes any sense. I want Brayden to pay for this.

A damn groupie.

With no damn protection.

I don't even know why the hell he told me about it. Was I supposed to say "I forgive you"?

I let Kara in and take her straight to the bar.

"Oh, we need wine for this?"

I just give her the look. The one that communicates that shit is about to hit or has already hit the fan.

"Oh, snap," she says.

I pour two large glasses of Pinot Noir. This is not a fun, flirty Moscato tale. This needs a robust and full-bodied wine.

I take a long, satisfying gulp. "He cheated."

"Brayden . . . noooooo."

"Some chick in Portland."

"How you find out? Did you check his phone? His in box?

His DMs? She reached out to you, didn't she? Hoes don't never know how to stay in a ho's place."

"He told me."

"You didn't have any clues at all?"

"Not one."

Kara drinks her wine, probably trying to come up with a non-wretched strategy. I can't think of one, but then, I'm not opposed to doing something wretched, either.

"Is he leaving you for her?"

"I wish he would leave. He's apologizing and begging me to forgive him."

"Oh."

"Oh? I need you to get angrier than this."

"Did he give you an STD or something?"

"No. We haven't slept together since Quincy died."

Kara's eyes widen. "Since January?"

"Yeah, and?"

"That's a long time, girl."

I know she's not trying to imply that this might be my fault for not giving him some ass. I have called the wrong friend over. I wish I had another one, but she's it.

"How many times did they hook up?" Kara asks.

"He says once."

"Does he love the girl?"

"Why does any of this matter?"

"I'm just saying . . . he told you, and didn't get caught. It was one time . . . y'all going through . . ."

"So you think he should get a pass?"

"Not a pass. I . . . I just think you shouldn't throw him away. Brayden is a good man."

I pour the rest of the wine bottle in my glass and spy the bar for the next one. We're gonna need more wine.

"He threw our marriage away when he hooked up with a groupie."

"So the groupie wins?"

"What?"

"I'm sick of hoes winning. I respect marriages. I don't mess

THE OUTSIDE CHILD   269

with anyone's husband, because one day I want what you have. Brayden looks at you like you're oxygen."

Well, he can suffocate, then.

"I will not be cheated on, Kara. I don't want to live my life like that."

"Girl, Beyoncé out here getting cheated on."

"So, because Jay-Z cheated, I should just let Brayden stick his little pecker wherever it wants to peck?"

"No . . . I'm just saying, there are women getting cheated on by bus drivers, by janitors, by preachers, and by deadbeats. There are beautiful and flawless women getting cheated on by their rich husbands."

"Some of those women walk away."

"And some of them have situations that can't be fixed. I don't think that's y'all. You can't blame people for what they do when they grieve."

"I didn't cheat on him. Somehow I was able to not fall in the bed with someone."

"You didn't cheat, but you broke your vows, too. You disappeared on him."

"Get the hell out of here! And whose side are you on? Did Brayden cut you a check?"

"Girl, I'm on your side. I want you to save this marriage to this good man. That's what I want you to do."

"Well, I didn't disappear. I've been right here this whole time. Barely left the damn house."

Kara taps on the center of my chest. "Your heart has been closed off to him. You closed it the day y'all buried Quincy. Maybe before."

I let out a long sigh. Dammit, she's right.

"Admit it," Kara says, "you're angry about his cheating, but you're not really hurt by it."

"It hurts."

"You haven't shed one tear this whole time."

"Okay, shit. I'm mad."

"And you need to work on your anger, Chenille. You really do."

It was my anger that made me run out of the house that day

in a rage instead of standing my ground and talking to Brayden like I should've. My anger has kept my heart (and legs) closed to Brayden for seven months.

I sit my glass of wine down. "I don't know what to do. He can't just get away with this."

"He isn't, girl. He is broken right now thinking you aren't gonna take him back."

"Well, let him stay broken for a while."

"You know what I think we should do?"

"Oh, Lord. What?"

"We should take a he-cheated-on-me vacation. Let's just get on a plane and fly somewhere. On his dime, of course."

"Where you wanna go?"

Kara's eyes light up. "For real?"

"For real."

"St. Barts is nice this time of year."

"Go home and pack. Be ready to fly out this evening, or on the first flight out in the morning."

"Ooh, girl, let me go before you change your mind."

"Pack some party clothes. We're gonna get lit."

I swear I've never seen Kara scurry that fast. Girlfriend is out the door before I can say another word.

This trip will not be as fun for me as it will be for Kara. Yes, I'll spend time at the beach, at the spa, and at the nightclub. I'll eat, drink, and pretend to be merry. But the entire time, I'm going to be asking myself if Brayden should stay or go.

Chapter 58

Brayden refused to go to a hotel or even to his condo in Dallas. If he went to either of those, the paparazzi would report that he was staying away from home and wonder why. They already weren't being too kind to him, because he'd left for the Portland, Oregon, expansion team. The fans were angry that their hometown boy had left the Knights, even though he'd thanked the city of Dallas and promised to continue all of his charity work.

He wondered if they held a grudge like Chenille. If so, he should probably relocate to another city even during the off-season. It wasn't worth it.

At any rate, he was staying at his parents' house.

This was the second night in a row Marilyn was having his favorites for dinner. She didn't cook the favorites, she just had them prepared. Tonight was lasagna.

"This doesn't make sense that you can't even rest your head in your own home," Marilyn said. "You allow Chenille to have too much power."

As usual, Brayden ignored Marilyn's advice about his wife. They would never have an argument where Marilyn was on her side.

"Son," Joseph said, "why don't we have dinner in my game room?"

"I don't like you eating in there," Marilyn said.

"Well, I'm gonna take the advice you just gave my son, and take away some of your power. Let's go on downstairs to eat, son."

If Brayden wasn't feeling so dejected about being put out by Chenille, he would've found his parents' banter funny. He usually loved when his father put his mama in her place. She sometimes tried to be husband and wife.

As soon as Joseph closed the game room door, and locked it (presumably to keep Marilyn out), he poured them each a shot of whiskey.

"Here you go, son. You look like you need this."

Brayden swallowed the strong liquor and felt it burn his throat. "Thanks."

"So, what's going on with you and my daughter-in-law? Why did she put you out?"

Brayden didn't want to admit his shortcomings to his father, but he was the only one who might have advice that would work for him.

"Dad, I cheated on her."

Joseph blew a huge puff of air out of his lips. "Son. That girl has been through enough. Why'd you let her find out about it?"

"I told her, because I thought that's what you were supposed to do. I thought honesty was the best policy."

"Well, sometimes, you should let things get to a better place first. I wish you'd come to me before you did that."

"What now, though? She's kicked me out. How do I get back home?"

"You've got to show Chenille that she's the most important thing in your life."

"Dad, she knows I love her more than anything. I don't know what more to do to prove it to her."

Joseph shook his head and poured each of them another drink.

"You haven't shown her that you love her more than football."

"What do you mean? Football takes care of us."

"Until you put your wife before your career, she's never going to be happy again. She's lost her son, Brayden. You don't know what it's like for a woman to lose their baby. Shit, I don't know. But I remember watching my mother descend into dementia after my sister died."

"Every time I get on television or when I win an award, Chenille's name is the first name out of my mouth. God, and then my wife. What else do I need to do?"

"Talk to God about it. Ask Him what you should do."

How could Brayden prove to Chenille that she was the first thing in his life? She wouldn't move to Portland, and Dallas wouldn't have him back. He was already in a contract with Portland, anyway, so that wouldn't work. Maybe they could move to Atlanta and he could play there and she could relaunch her makeup business. Perhaps Chenille wanted to be at the table when he negotiated and be fully a part of the deal.

So many options to consider, but Brayden couldn't make a choice until he did what his father told him to do. He'd talk to God about it, and then the way would be made clear.

Chapter 59

The resort that I chose for our he-cheated-on-me getaway is a celebrity hangout spot. It costs ten thousand dollars a night for our suite. I booked it for ten days. Might extend it for another week.

Kara is going crazy seeing all these musicians and ball-players. She packed every single last one of her thong bikinis and a suitcase full of wigs. With her big sunglasses and perfect body she looks like a celebrity herself. If nothing else, it's entertaining watching her do what she normally does, and that was hunt for men.

She takes a selfie and posts it on some social media site. I have no idea which one, because she's on all of them.

I am not taking any photos myself. I'm just soaking up the sun, and these good margaritas.

"I can't understand why we haven't made it to the blogs yet," Kara says. "This place is crawling with paparazzi."

"Probably because they don't know who we are. You'd probably be better off trying to photobomb somebody. That'll get you on the internet."

"Funny. If I make it to straightfromthea.com I'm good. I want all the haters from back home to see me here in St. Barts."

"Girl, you are crazy. I thought they were already hating on you for being in Dallas."

"Yeah . . . they are . . . Oh, my goodness!"

I sit up in my beach chair and take a sip of my margarita. "What's wrong?"

"Did you know that Brayden was retiring?"

Now I take off my sunglasses and snatch her phone. "Brayden who?"

I look at the blog post that Kara has on her screen, and, sure enough, it says *Former Dallas Knights MVP Brayden Carpenter Retires.*

"How do I see the rest of the article?"

"Let me see. I think there's an interview."

Kara swipes a few times on her phone, and then hands it back to me.

"Press play," she says.

I press it, and it's an interview with Brayden and an ESPN reporter. He looks solemn sitting in the director's chair. Solemn, but peaceful.

"Tell me about this retirement," the reporter in the video says.

"As you know, my wife and I experienced a great loss when our son passed away after an accident. We've been grieving separately, and I want to be able to focus all of my time on her. I want us to grieve and heal together."

"What about the Portland Beachcombers?"

"They're a great organization with a strong foundation. I think they will be good after they put the rest of the pieces of that squad together."

"Why now? Why not before you accepted Portland's offer? Why not right after your son died? What changed in your life that made you want to retire right now?"

"Honestly, I made a horrible mistake. I cheated on my wife. The woman I love. I betrayed her trust, and I'm willing to do anything to regain that trust and her love."

"Even retiring from a lucrative NFL career?"

"Especially retiring from this career. It is all-consuming."

"I know a lot of NFL wives who wouldn't change that for the world.

What was your wife's reaction when she found out you were doing this?"

"She doesn't know. She's going to find out when your fans find out."

"Well, y'all heard that. This is an exclusive scoop from Brayden Carpenter. Brayden, we wish you all the best."

"Thank you, Jules."

I rewind the video and watch it again. Then again.

He's walked away from the NFL. For me. For our marriage.

"He retired? So y'all about to be broke, huh?" Kara says. "Do we need to downgrade our room? Check out early?"

"No. We've invested well."

If Brayden never plays another season, we will be good.

Wait.

I just thought of us as *we*. Just a few days ago, I was almost sure that I wanted this to be over. Even Kara's speech about Beyoncé and Jay-Z didn't completely change my mind.

But this.

He's walked away from the one thing I always believed he loved more than me. He chose me.

"And he just had to go on TV with it," Kara says, shaking her head. "Couldn't just call you up and say, 'babe, I retired'? Had to go on TV."

"You're just mad nobody wants to interview you." Brayden's voice surprises me.

Kara and I both break our necks to turn around, and there he is, standing right behind our beach chairs.

"Ew. You're a stalker," Kara says.

"I guess that was a prerecorded video," I say. "So, you think that's what it takes to get me to take you back?"

"Yes, I do think that's what it takes. I don't need football. I need you."

"We need to start off slowly. Starting with your clean bill of health."

Brayden hands me an envelope. I open it and see that he isn't infected with anything. That's a start.

"You got on a plane with your doctor's note?" Kara asks. "You must be trying to get some booty."

Brayden presses his lips into a tight line. "Kara, will you please excuse me while I talk to my wife?"

"Girl, are you okay? You want to talk to him?"

"Yes, I'm good. Thank you."

Brayden sits on Kara's beach chair.

"You're going to be covered in glitter and highlighter when you get up from there," I say. "She's sparkling all over the place."

"I can't believe Kara doesn't have my back."

"She does. She's been trying to convince me to forgive you since we got here."

"So . . ."

"Brayden, all I can say is that I'll try. You're clearly trying. You quit your job. I can't . . . won't make any promises, but I'll try."

"Babe, I love you. It's just going to be me and you right now. We can travel around the world if you want."

"What if I just want to sit in bed and watch Netflix?"

"Then I'm making the popcorn."

Brayden reaches over and takes one of my hands in his. When I don't pull it away, he covers it with his other hand and kisses the top.

My stomach flutters, and I realize that I've missed his hands on me. I've missed his warmth and his scent. I haven't wanted it until this moment.

"You want to go up to our room?" Brayden asks.

"Wait, what is Kara going to do?"

"I've already gotten her another room, and had her bags moved."

"She might be mad. This is supposed to be a girls' trip."

Brayden laughed. "Who do you think told me where you were?"

Normally, I'd be mad about them ganging up on me and tricking me, but this time I can't be mad. This is about restoring my marriage.

This is about taking my man back.

Wives one. Hoes zero.

Chapter 60

Brayden didn't know what was better—their first honeymoon after they got married, or the second honeymoon. He and Chenille stayed in St. Barts another fourteen days. They spent most of the time making out on their balcony and making love on the huge four-poster bed with the ocean air in their lungs and the ocean spray moistening their faces.

He worried that when they got home, the spell would be broken and Chenille would change her mind all over again. That she'd kick him out and finally be done with it.

But everything was going well so far.

Since the oppressive Texas heat had kicked in, Brayden went out to the extra freezer for his ice cream bar stash. He'd share his Dove bars with Chenille, although he usually didn't. They were on a second honeymoon, so snacks would be shared.

Brayden threw open the freezer and noticed that instead of his boxes of ice cream being on top, it was covered with frozen breast milk.

His first reaction was that the milk should just be thrown out. It must be old. Quincy had been gone for eight months. He didn't need it anymore.

Brayden grabbed the first few bags to take them over to the

sink, and was taken aback when one of the bags was warm. Brayden studied the date on the bag. It had today's date on it.

Why was Chenille still pumping and storing milk?

"Babe what's taking so long with the ice cream?" Chenille asked from the kitchen.

Brayden heard her footsteps coming into the freezer room and quickly deliberated. Should he ignore this while everything was going so well? Maybe it wasn't a big deal anyway.

"Brayden . . ."

He hadn't deliberated fast enough, because he forgot to put the milk back into the freezer. He was holding it in his hand when Chenille opened the door to the freezer room.

"Are you still pumping your milk?"

The obvious answer to that question was yes, but Chenille just stared at the little bag without responding.

"Babe, you can talk to me about this. Do you want me to go to the doctor with you to get medicine? Do they have something to stop the milk from coming?"

Chenille shook her head. "I don't want the medicine. I don't want to stop pumping Quincy's milk."

"But . . . Quincy doesn't need it anymore."

Brayden's voice was gentle and kind, but Chenille burst into tears anyway. Brayden pulled her into an embrace.

"Don't cry, love. It's okay. If you want to fill up all of our freezers with breast milk, I don't care. No one has to know but us. It's your body."

"And Quincy's milk," Chenille whispered.

"And Quincy's milk."

Brayden rocked Chenille back and forth in his arms. He kissed the top of her head and inhaled her coconut oil and shea butter scent.

Brayden was glad he retired from football. If he hadn't done it, hadn't been home spending time with Chenille, he wouldn't have known that she was beyond broken.

She was unraveling.

Chapter 61

It's weird that it's October, and football is not the main theme of our house. Brayden has decided to learn how to make apple cider. The entire house smells like apples and cinnamon. I don't know how much apple cider we can drink, though.

"Are you giving some of these jugs away?" I ask, as I watch Brayden line up five gallon jugs of cider on the counter.

"I'm about to take these down to the City Mission. They've got a fall buffet tonight, and would love to have some."

"Well, good. That's five less jugs to have in our house."

"You don't like it?"

"Yes, but, Brayden, I am gonna get diarrhea if I drink another glass of apple anything."

He laughs. "You need to just shore up your colon a little bit. It's good for you."

"You sound like somebody's grandpa."

Silence falls between us. We have these awkward moments where we both end up thinking about Quincy. Of course we're never going to be grandparents. Quincy's gone, and my shattered pelvis can't support a pregnancy.

Luckily, the awkward moments are fewer and fewer.

He even stopped mentioning the breast milk when I found

an organization to donate it to. There is a huge need for breast milk for moms who can't produce milk and want their babies to have the best nutrition.

I hear Brayden's car pull out of the garage and feel myself relax. I love him being here, but I have to get used to him *always* being here.

I heat up yet another mug of apple cider and curl into a ball on the couch in our TV room. This is the most comfortable sectional ever. Makes me want to fall right asleep, every time I sit on it.

Kara has got me using social media and following celebrity pages. They actually are kind of entertaining. I can see why she is so obsessed with it. I don't mind looking at other people's pages. As long as the bloggers aren't posting pictures of me and Brayden on Facebook.

I see a little number in the upper right corner of my screen. It says "2.' I guess that means I have two notifications.

I click on the little red button to see what comes up, and there are two messages. One is from an African man that starts, "Hello beautiful lady."

Delete.

Then I open the second one, and on first glance, I think it's a chain message, because it's so long. I get ready to delete it, because I'm not going to forward any messages to seven people including the one who sent it to me.

But right before I delete, I see Brayden's name in the message.

So I start from the beginning and read.

Hello, Chenille,

My best friend, Tia Somerfield, an inmate at the Northfield prison in Washington, wanted me to reach out to you. She was briefly an associate of your husband, Brayden Carpenter. She saw the news of him retiring from the NFL on television, and she would like to have you meet her in person about an urgent matter regarding your husband.

Please call me at 804-778-9879 for more details and instruc-
tions.
Regards,
Nicole R.

I scroll over to Nicole's profile to see if I can make her picture bigger. She looks like a regular girl, nothing strange about
her. She's got a picture up where she's posing with what look
like her two children.

I slide off the couch and into the downstairs office, where I
boot up the computer. After I log in, I open up Google search
and type "Tia Somerfield" in quotes. A social media page pops
up, but when I click on it, there's no profile picture.

The second is the link to a registered inmate directory.
Maybe the girl really is in prison. I click on it.

A website with an olive green background opens, and right
in the middle of the page is the picture, name, and inmate
number of Tia Somerfield. She's got chunky box braids in her
hair and she's extremely pretty. Like model pretty. Perfect facial bone structure. Smooth skin. Beautiful eyes.

Why in the world is this girl in prison? The charges on the
page say "Manslaughter, and Endangering of a Minor," but she
looks like she could be any college freshman on the campus of
a historically black college.

Now I'm curious. So I call the number.

"Hello?" says a raspy voice on the other side of the call.

"Hello, may I speak to Nicole?"

"This is Nicole."

"This is Chenille Carpenter. You messaged me about your
friend Tia."

There is a long pause on the other end.

"Hello?" I ask. "Are you there?"

"Yes. I didn't think you would call. I told Tia you wouldn't answer."

"Well, you were wrong. What is all this about?"

"Tia wanted to meet you at the prison."

"Do you really think that I'm going to get on a plane and fly to Washington, to a prison, to see a stranger?"

"It's safe."

"Tell me what this is about, and maybe I'll be open to meeting her."

"I will say this part. She slept with your husband one time in Portland. She met him in a support group, never saw him after that first time."

Okay, this corresponds with Brayden's recollection of events.

"So, I already knew that she had sex with him. What is it that she wants to see me face-to-face about?"

"That part I can't say," Nicole replies. "You'll have to go and see for yourself."

"And if I don't?"

"Then it won't matter. Like I said, I never expected you to call. I didn't think that you would."

"Well, thank you for the information."

"You're welcome."

Calling Nicole just made me even more confused. She was too secretive, so now I'm worried about what Tia might have to say to me. Did something bad happen to her while she was with Brayden? Did he hurt her?

Awww . . . what the hell? I type in the website for plane tickets and start searching for flights to the Portland area.

I need to see what this girl is talking about. Although I believe that finding out whatever I find out about Tia will probably be shocking, I'd rather know than not know.

Guess I'm flying to Washington.

Chapter 62

The visiting room at the Northside Prison is cold and dreary. The walls look like they used to be yellow, but now they're a pale color between yellow and off-white. The linoleum on the floor also used to be some color other than the greenish-gray that is under my feet.

I didn't tell anyone I was coming here. Not Kara, not Brayden. I left him a note saying that I was going to Atlanta for a couple of days to transition my remaining clients over to a new Atlanta makeup artist.

I'm sitting at a round table in a room full of round tables. About half of the tables have a person also sitting there. Visiting day at Northside doesn't seem to be well attended.

The inmates were brought out one by one. I don't know why I thought they'd be wearing orange. They all have on gray sweat suits. Maybe they want the girls to feel like they live at the gym and not in a minimum-security prison.

I gasp when they bring Tia out. She has the same box braids and the same pretty face as from the photo on the internet, but she has an additional accessory that I'm sure is the reason why she called me here.

Her stomach is huge with pregnancy. I don't have to guess hard to figure out who the father must be.

She eases down in the seat in front of me and lets out a huge breath. "Hi."

"Hi."

"I'm Tia."

"Tia, I'm Chenille. Let's dispense with the pleasantries. You wanted me to know that you're pregnant with Brayden's baby? Is that what you want? We could've done that over the phone."

"Yes, that's part of why I asked you to come here."

"So, do you want me to write a check or something? You want money to keep quiet about this? Why didn't you just reach out to Brayden? He's the one you slept with. I bet you planned this from the start, and his stupid ass just fell right into your trap. I told him NFL players are targets."

"Wait. I didn't know he was an NFL player. I met him in the support group for losing children."

"So, that's where you find your marks? Grieving men?"

"Brayden wasn't a mark. He was just a nice guy that I met, who was sad about losing his son. We connected that day, but I never talked to him again."

"Now all of a sudden you're reaching out to his wife on social media. Wonder how that works. How. Much. Do. You. Want?"

"I don't want money. That's not what I need."

"Well, what, then?"

"I wanted to ask you to take my baby and raise it. Closed adoption. You'll never see me again."

"What? Again, why didn't you ask Brayden?"

"Don't you understand? I could contact Brayden and let him know about this, and he would take our child, no questions asked. But you. You don't have to be a part of it. You can say no. You can walk away from him and the baby. I'm asking you to say yes."

"Why? Why do you want me to raise your baby?"

"Because you lost a child, just like I did. And I know you will love and care for her like she's your own. I'm not a mistress. I'm not someone who was in a relationship with Brayden. There are no feelings. But there is this baby."

I look down at her swelling belly, wondering how many months I have to make this choice. And I am considering it already. The idea of holding and nursing a fat infant in my lap fills me with a desire I didn't think I still had inside.

But what if she's some kind of crazy murderer? I don't want to raise a child with mental illness.

"Why are you here?"

Tia looks down at the table. "It's because of what happened to my first baby."

"You hurt your baby?"

She looks up with tears in her eyes. "Yes, but not on purpose. I was an alcoholic. I got wasted one night. Pills, alcohol, and who knows what else. The next morning, I was still drunk. I got myself dressed, and the baby dressed. Drove to the day care, and passed right out in the parking lot. It was hot that day, record high temperatures. All of the windows were shut and the doors closed. Bella was too little to let herself out of the car."

"Why didn't someone from the day care come out and help?"

"It was Sunday. I didn't even know what day it was. When the police found my car, I was severely dehydrated and on the verge of heat stroke. I had to be hospitalized. When I woke up, I was in handcuffs. My Bella was dead."

Damn. I don't even know how to react to this story. I don't know how she continues to put one foot in front of the other every day. I couldn't.

"How long are you in here for?"

"I got fifteen years for manslaughter and endangering a child. I don't feel like the sentence is long enough. It should be longer."

She's got a life sentence in her mind and heart, though. No matter how much she tries to forget, it will always be there.

"God blessed me to get pregnant again. I don't know why He did that. I don't deserve the blessing. Then, when I saw Brayden on TV and realized he was a football player, I looked him up online."

"Y'all got internet access in here?"

"It's restricted. Can't do much."

"Oh."

"Anyway, I researched and saw all the news clippings about what happened with your son. His heart condition. The accident. Then I knew why I got pregnant with this baby. The baby is God's gift to you."

"I'll raise your baby. But it doesn't need to be a closed adoption. You can see the baby when you get out. Do you know the sex?"

I hear the words rushing from my mouth, and I can't believe I'm saying them. It's like my heart is blurting before my logic has the chance to catch up.

"I don't know, but I feel like it's a girl. Would you like a daughter?"

I don't even need to deliberate on this. The answer is yes and was yes from the moment she started telling her story. I'm surprised with my lack of animosity and anger. I have none. I don't search myself trying to find it, either. There's a reason it's not there.

"So the answer is yes?"

"I mean, I have to ask Brayden, but I don't see how he could say no."

"I don't want to see or talk to him. I'd like you to handle it all. This is not about me and him. There is no me and him. This is about my baby's new mother."

"Can I give you a hug?"

"Yes."

I walk around to her side of the table as she struggles to stand. I wrap both my arms around her and kiss her cheeks.

The baby kicks up a storm.

"The baby already knows you."

Then Tia touches her belly.

"Your new mommy is here. Say hi, mommy."

The baby kicks again, and I burst into tears.

"Hi, baby. I can't wait to meet you."

And I can't.

Chapter 63

Brayden cautiously sat down at the dinner table. Chenille had cooked a huge feast: smothered chicken, macaroni and cheese, deviled eggs, collard greens, rice and gravy. Lots of southern comfort food.

But why? It was September and no holidays were in sight. So why was she cooking? Was something wrong?

He didn't know if he could take another bomb dropping. Their marriage couldn't survive another one.

"This looks good," Brayden said as Chenille heaped food on the table. "Are we having company?"

"No. Not company. I don't know why I made all of this. We'll freeze some."

"Maybe we can make boxes and take them downtown to feed homeless people."

Chenille stared at Brayden for a moment.

"No cameras," he said, reading her mind. "I don't need any more media attention."

"I'm so glad to hear you say that, and yes, I would love to go and feed homeless people today. Or any day."

"Good."

Brayden tried to read Chenille's mood. She seemed nervous,

but not. There was something joyful right under the surface.
He could almost catch onto it, but it was right out of his reach.

"I have something to tell you," she said.

"Oh?"

"It's good news, so you can relax."

He *did* relax, but not completely. He was the one who liked
giving surprises, but he didn't necessarily like receiving them.

"Do you remember Tia? The girl you met in Portland?"

Brayden's stomach dropped. Appetite disappeared. He knew
he could trust his gut about bombs dropping. He wished he
could run for cover.

"What about her?"

"I met her a couple weeks ago. She's pregnant with your
baby."

Brayden froze.

"That's not possi . . ."

"How isn't it possible, Brayden? Didn't you say you had un-
protected sex with her?"

"I did."

"So it's possible."

Brayden felt like saying all the excuses a teenage boy would
give for a baby not being his baby. It was only one time. He
pulled out. All of the excuses expressed by boys who end up
with a responsibility that they never intended on having.

"So, she wants child support. What else? Is she going to the
blogs?"

"You don't know what happened to her other baby, do you? I
don't know why I assumed that you knew."

"We didn't talk all that much."

This struck Chenille as funny for some reason. She chuckled
and then gave a full-bodied laugh.

"Well, babe, she's in prison. She killed her other baby acci-
dentally. She was drunk and left the baby in a hot car."

"She's in prison?"

"Yes, she asked me to raise her child. Your child."

"Of course, I want custody *if* it's mine."

"You know, I thought about the possibility that the baby isn't yours. I don't think the girl is lying, but she could be. There is a slim chance that she is."

"Yeah, I don't know how many other men she was seeing at the time."

Chenille lifted an eyebrow. There was a response on the tip of her tongue, he could tell. She held it back.

"Well, I've decided I will raise her baby even if it's not yours. Either way, that child will not go into the system. She wants to do a closed adoption. No contact with us after the baby is born."

"She's gonna flip the script. Watch. She'll get money hungry and she'll change."

"Brayden, she didn't even know you were a ballplayer. She just happened to see your media moment when you retired on TV. The fact that she didn't reach out to you speaks volumes. She took the most difficult path. She asked me—the wife—to raise her baby."

"And you said yes."

"Without hesitation."

Brayden was nothing short of stunned. She had said yes to raising a baby that could be his, but with his one-night stand.

"I'll call my lawyer to draw up the paperwork, then. I want us to be protected."

Chenille beamed a smile at Brayden, and he didn't know if his wife was going crazy or finally finding herself and her purpose. He hoped it was the latter, because he was in it for the long haul.

He wondered what Marilyn would think about her new grandbaby.

Chapter 64

I can't tell if Tia's labor pains are bad, because she doesn't cry out or even flinch when she has a contraction. The only reason I know she's having contractions is because I see the little squiggles on the monitor rise every few minutes.

"You just talked through your whole contraction," I say.

"I did?"

"Yeah, you did. I feel useless as a coach. Do you need ice chips or anything?"

Tia pokes out her bottom lip and shakes her head. "I don't think so. Not yet."

"Well, I have a whole list of what I'm supposed to be doing, and you haven't needed any of it."

"It does hurt, but I've been practicing my concentration techniques. When they start, I just picture myself on the beach."

"Which beach? I hope not Galveston."

Tia laughs. "Nah, girl. Miami Beach is my favorite. Have you been there?"

"Yes, but I don't know how much I remember. I was a tad bit inebriated every time I went."

"Inebriated? You mean drunk as hell."

We both bust out laughing. This would almost feel normal, like one friend coaching another friend through labor and delivery if there wasn't a prison guard standing in the corner of the room. Oh, and if this wasn't Brayden's one-night stand giving birth to his baby.

I notice Tia's lips make the shape of a tiny circle as she exhales slowly. I glance at the monitor again. Another contraction.

"That was about two and a half minutes since the last one."

"Okay, good. That means I'm getting close to being fully dilated," Tia says. "Your baby will be here soon."

"Our baby."

Tia closes her eyes and exhales through the rest of her contraction.

"You don't have to sign away your rights," I say. "I can bring her to visit you, and you can be as much a part of her life as me and Brayden."

"No. I don't want her growing up knowing her mother is in prison."

"We can help her understand."

"And then what are you going to tell her when she asks why I'm here? You're going to tell her what happened to the older sister she never got to meet?"

"Okay, I understand. Let's just focus on getting her here."

"Okay."

The nurse midwife, Janice, comes into the room.

"It's time to check your dilation," she says.

Tia nods and spreads her legs. I remember how annoyed I was when I was pregnant with Quincy. I hated being touched, but more than anything I hated vaginal exams. Tia doesn't seem to have the same hang-ups.

"Whoa, you're at about nine centimeters. You dilated quickly," the nurse says. "It's going to be time to push in a little bit."

"Good," Tia says.

"Do you need anything for the pain?" Janice asks.

"No. No drugs. I'm fine."

"I've got another mother in labor on this floor. I'm going to check on her, and then I'll be back in a little bit."

"Okay."

"When I get back, you're going to push that baby out," Janice says. "Do you want the father to come in?"

"Absolutely not," Tia says. "He can see the baby in the nursery after she's born."

I know she's doing this for me, to make sure that I am okay. She cares more about my feelings than she cares about Brayden's.

"I don't mind if Brayden comes in," I say. "I have forgiven him . . . and you for that one time. I wouldn't have agreed to any of this if I hadn't."

"I know you forgive me," Tia says. "I just don't want any image in your mind of the two of us together, because what if my baby girl looks like me? I don't want you to have that picture in your mind while you're raising her."

I want to tell Tia that I'm not that kind of woman, and forgiveness for me truly means forgiveness. But I don't. She needs for Brayden not to be here. She needs assurance that her baby will be safe and nurtured. Asking me to be the one to raise her was a risk, but the right choice. I'm going to love that baby with everything in me.

The monitor indicates that Tia is having another contraction. This one must be stronger than the others, because her breathing changes, and she grips the bed rails.

"Do you want me to get the nurse?"

"She said she would be back. I just . . . feel like I need to push."

"Don't, girl! Hold on a second. Don't push until I come back!"

I run out the room to find the nurse midwife. Brayden, who is sitting near the delivery room, stands.

"Is everything okay?" he asks.

I nod. "She's about to give birth."

"I want to be in the room."

"She told the hospital staff no. She doesn't want to see you. You can see the baby when she's in the nursery."

"I don't want to see her, either. I just want to witness the birth of my child."

"Sorry . . ."

I see Janice and grab her arm. "Tia is ready to push now."

"Let's get this show on the road, then."

Brayden tries to follow us into the room. The nurse stops him.

"Mr. Carpenter, don't make me call hospital security on you."

Brayden looks at the petite nurse, like he's sizing her up. She stands as tall as she can, and gives him a look that's a threat and a promise. Brayden scoffs and goes back to his seat across from the room.

"He's a stubborn one, isn't he?" Janice says.

All thoughts of Brayden's defiance are forgotten, when we both hear Tia's prison guard's scream. We rush into the room and see Tia gripping both of the bed rails with her legs pulled back.

"Tia, wait," Nurse Janice says as she pulls a stool up to the end of the bed.

"I have to push," Tia says. "I can't help it."

I grab Tia's hand and let her squeeze. "Okay, honey," I say. "It's almost over."

"All right. With the next contraction, give me one good push. The head is crowning."

Tia squeezes the hell out of my hand and lets out a low groan as she closes her eyes and pushes.

"Almost there," the nurse says. "Just a little bit more."

Tia keeps pushing for a few more seconds, and then she relaxes.

"Your baby girl is here!" Janice says.

"Hand her to Chenille," Tia says. "I don't want to hold her first."

"The baby needs skin-to-skin contact. Take off your shirt."

As Janice takes care of cutting the umbilical cord, I peel off my t-shirt and strip down to my bra. Janice cleans the baby a little bit, then puts her in my arms.

She's red, angry, and beautiful. She opens her mouth and screams with her tiny fists balled. Then I feel that unmistakable tingling in my breasts. The feeling of my milk—Quincy's milk—letting down.

"I think . . . I think I can nurse her," I say. "Should I?"

Janice looks at Tia, and Tia nods. "Yes, please do."

I pull down my bra and offer my nipple to the newborn. Instinctively, she latches on and greedily sucks. She stares at my face, probably trying to focus, as she swallows the milk.

After her little head rolls to one side, the nurse takes the baby from my arms.

"Did you know you were still able to produce milk?" Tia asks.

"I was still nursing my son when he died, and I've been donating my milk ever since. Maybe this is why."

"Do you want to name her?" Tia asks.

"Why don't you?"

Nurse Janice places the baby in Tia's arms. She's drifting off to sleep now, but Tia stares at her and kisses the top of her head.

"I think she looks like Brayden," Tia says. "That's good. I don't want her looking in the mirror and wondering why she doesn't look like anyone she knows."

I refrain from commenting. I know she's trying to convince herself she's okay with this, and it makes sense.

"How about Anastasia?" Tia says.

"That's beautiful, Tia. Simply beautiful," I say. "What about a middle name?"

"Anastasia Christina Carpenter."

"That is a pretty name," Janice says. "Does it mean anything?"

"No. I just like the way it sounds. Take the baby now. I don't want to get too attached to her."

Again, I don't say anything, because I don't want to make Tia's grief in giving up her baby any more difficult than it has to be, but she's always going to be attached to Anastasia. There's no way around that. You can't carry a tiny human for nine months and not be attached to her.

"We have counselors here who can help you through this process," Janice says. "Would you like me to have someone come talk to you?"

Tia shakes her head. "Oh, no. This is the best decision I've ever made. She's going to be with her daddy and an awesome mother."

My heart seizes with guilt at what happened to my baby. I wasn't an awesome mother that day.

"I will be as good of a mother as I can be. I will treat her like she came from my own womb."

"I know you will," Tia says. "And what happened with your son was an accident. You *are* an awesome mother."

Tears spring to my eyes, and I am not sure if they're tears of joy at my new charge or sadness at the loss of Quincy's life. I don't think I will ever stop crying over my baby, but I sure can love Anastasia with all the love I can't give to Quincy.

"Since she's in a milk coma," Janice says, "we're going to give Anastasia a warm sponge bath and swaddle her. Do you want her in the nursery or to stay in the room?"

"The nursery."

Janice was looking at me, but Tia is the one who answered the question.

"It's fine if she stays in here," I say.

Tia shakes her head. "No. She needs to bond with you and Brayden."

"Okay."

I don't know what's left. It feels like this is goodbye, but that it shouldn't be. I walk over to Tia and kiss her forehead.

"You're going to be fine. I'm gonna put money on your books."

Tia laughs. "Now, I'm definitely not turning that down. Thank you. Thank you so much for this. I can finish my time now. I didn't think I would make it, but now I know I can."

"You're welcome."

The nurses start to clean Tia, and the prison guard closes in as if to let me know my time is up. It breaks my heart to see them putting the handcuffs back on her wrists, when she's not a flight risk. She has nowhere to run.

But at least she knows her baby is safe.

And loved.

Epilogue

"Hold still, Anastasia. I'm trying to tie this bow."

I swear, this girl squirms at the very sight of a dress. She is a ball of energy and hates all of the lace, crinkles, and folds of the Easter monstrosities Marilyn buys for her. Honestly, I don't blame her for wanting to get free.

"Mommy, it itches."

She fusses and wiggles in front of the full-length mirror in her room. She is Brayden's twin, except for her eyes. She gets those from her mother.

"Where does it itch? Your back? Let me scratch it for you."

I scratch all over Anastasia's back, and she giggles while she squirms even more.

"It still itches!"

"Where?"

"All over. Can I wear my purple overalls?"

"No, silly. You have to give your Easter speech."

"Grandma wants me to do the speech. Do you?"

She's so smart and strategic. I can tell she's about to launch into an argument that she thinks will release her from having to do the speech. Unfortunately for Ms. Anastasia, I see right through her.

"I want to help you make Grandma happy," I say. "A happy grandma is a friendly grandma."

As much grief as Marilyn gave me for being too ghetto for Brayden, I just knew she wouldn't find herself close to the outside baby with a woman locked up in prison. I was wrong. Marilyn makes Anastasia the daughter she never had. She spoils her rotten in exchange for Grandma moments like this—an Easter speech at Marilyn's church.

"You look perfectly perfect, honey," I say as Anastasia's squirming ceases.

"Thank you, Mommy."

Every time she says "Mommy," my heart swells with all the love I have for her. I lavish her with everything that was left over from Quincy, and every day she finds a way to put a new lasso around my heart. I've never known a love like this.

Brayden steps into the room. "We're running late, beauty queens."

"There's only one beauty queen in here!" I say. "What do you think? Do a spin, Ana."

She spins and curtsies for her daddy, and he scoops her up into his arms. He covers her in kisses, and she giggles because of his beard. This girl will be loved. She'll never go without it.

I imagine Quincy looking down from heaven and smiling at his sister.

I imagine Bella looking down from heaven and smiling at her sister.

And I imagine God, smiling down at our family, sending healing light and love.